CHRISTMAS
Comes to
Bethlehem,
Maine

The Annual Live Nativity Event
Becomes a Backdrop for
Four Modern Romances

Lorraine Beatty, Elizabeth Ludwig,
Sandra Robbins & Virginia Vaughan

BARBOUR
PUBLISHING

THE CHRISTMAS GIFT

By Virginia Vaughan

Chapter 1

This December, journey to Bethlehem to experience for yourself the true meaning of Christmas. Think the trip's too far? Not so. The city of Bethlehem, Maine, presents its first annual live nativity. Join Mary, Joseph, and a host of other biblical figures as they reenact the events leading up to the birth of Christ. This event takes place from six thirty to nine o'clock every Friday and Saturday night from Thanksgiving until Christmas. Bethlehem—it's closer than you think."

Kate Walters caught her breath as the commercial announcing the town's live nativity played for the first time on the radio. A thrill rushed through her. The live nativity had been her idea, and she'd been the one to push the project through. Now, it was Thanksgiving week and the premiere was only days away. Her hands shook with a mixture of excitement and nervousness. This project would likely be the defining mark of her first term as town manager of Bethlehem.

Her office door opened, and Lisa, her assistant, burst in, clapping and smiling. "I heard it! I heard the commercial!"

Kate pushed back from her desk. "I heard it, too. Isn't it exciting?"

The phone on her desk rang at the same moment her cell phone buzzed. Lisa answered the office phone while Kate checked her cell. It was her husband. She considered letting it go to voice mail as Lisa accepted congratulations and people began to meander in to comment on the commercial, but she couldn't ignore the nagging feeling that she would be doing something wrong. She stepped away from the emerging group and answered her phone.

"I just heard the spot on the radio." David's voice was upbeat, full of encouragement and support. "I wanted to be the first one to congratulate you."

Kate turned to look at the crowd gathering in her doorway. "It's amazing. I can't believe this is really going to happen."

"Of course it's going to happen, and it's going to be great. You've poured your heart and soul into this project, and we both know that when you give something one hundred percent, it can't fail."

Despite the excitement buzzing in the room, Kate felt a sting at David's comment. What did he mean by that one hundred percent remark? Did he think she'd neglected her family?

She shook her head. She was overreacting. David was only trying to pay her a compliment. She had a crowd gathering and she needed to get off the phone and back to business. "Well, there's still so much left to do, and we only have three days left to do it. I have a group in my office waiting to see me, so I'd better let you go."

His resigned sigh spoke volumes that his words didn't. "I'll see you at home later. I love you, Kate."

"Bye, David." Kate ended the call and joined the others in celebrating this exciting milestone of her first major event in office.

꩜

David Walters snapped his phone shut, resisting the urge to toss it across the car. He wouldn't take out his frustrations on an innocent cell phone, especially one that he paid for. He'd heard the radio spot and felt compelled to call to congratulate Kate. The live nativity was a big event for the city, and she was getting the credit she deserved for its conception. His wife had vision and the determination to make her visions reality. It was one of the things he loved about her. Plus, she'd answered his call. He supposed that was a good sign, but he couldn't shake the feeling that even while she was speaking to him, she'd been itching to get him off the phone.

He drove past her office but couldn't catch a glimpse of her through her office window. Across the street, Bethlehem Green was being transformed for the nativity.

David parked the car, hiked up his coat collar, and went to check out the progress on the construction. The area was blocked off with city barriers to keep unauthorized people out, but he had signed up as a volunteer on the set-building committee. They left the big work, the set design and construction, to the professionals, but David was handy with a hammer and nails.

His and Kate's sons, twenty-one-year-old John and eighteen-year-old Keith, were also signed up to help with the set. David had urged the boys to volunteer, although he hadn't had to do much arm twisting. John had worried that he wouldn't be available enough while he was away at college, but David had signed him up to work during his vacation breaks.

It was important to him that they all participated in this project. . .and not just because it was their mother's brainchild. The nativity was good for the city and good for Christmas. It celebrated the true reason for the season—the birth of Christ—while also promoting the city of Bethlehem. It was a good idea all around, and as he watched it come to life around him, he could hardly believe that no one had thought of it before his wife came to office.

"Hey, David, are you here to work or just to stand around and look pretty?"

David glanced up to find Bill Mitchell, the head of the set-building committee, staring down from the roof of the structure that was to be the inn from which Joseph and Mary were turned away. "I was looking at the progress."

"Well, grab a hammer and join in."

David had only left the office for lunch, but he was in no rush to get back. He stared down at his clothes. He wasn't exactly dressed to work, but his khakis and polo shirt could be cleaned. He wanted to do his part, and he had signed up to work.

Besides, it might feel good to work out his frustrations for a while.

In the months leading up to the nativity, Kate had had weekly meetings with the different committee chairs for status reports and updates. Now, with three days left until opening night, she'd scheduled a meeting for them all to meet together to make certain everything was covered.

She started the meeting by thanking those in attendance for helping her bring the project to life. "As most of you know, this project has been my dream for a long while. Now it's come to fruition. I'm anxious and excited all at once. As town manager of Bethlehem, I'm proud that our community has the courage to step out and make such a bold statement of faith. I'm also very proud of the way this town has rallied to put this event together. There are so many jobs to do, and there has been no lack of willingness to do them. Such unity makes me very proud to be a part of Bethlehem."

She slipped on her reading glasses and turned to page one of her agenda worksheet. "Now then, let's get down to the business of this meeting. The first performance is three nights away. We need to go over the status of all areas. Let's start with costumes." She turned to Janet Burgess, who headed up the sewing committee.

After hearing from Mrs. Burgess, Kate listened to updates about maintenance and parking issues, care and feeding of the live animals, and the response so far to the promotions the city had been producing.

After the meeting was adjourned, Kate returned to her office and fell into her chair. The meeting had taken more out of her than she'd expected.

Lisa brought her a glass of water and a bottle of aspirin. "You look like you could use this," she said at Kate's questioning look.

"Do I look *that* bad?"

"Of course not. You just look tired. It seems like you've been extra tired recently."

"Well, this project has taken a lot out of me. Plus, with the holidays. . ."

"Are you sure that's all it is? You've seemed out of sorts the last few weeks—moody, irritable, unusually tired. Plus, you've stopped downing coffee, your all-time favorite drink."

Kate realized Lisa was right. Recently, the smell of coffee made her stomach turn.

"Please don't fire me." Kate noticed the mischievous grin on Lisa's face as she handed Kate a paper bag.

"What's this?" Kate took it and pulled out a pregnancy test. This was what Lisa thought was wrong with her? "No," she said, pushing it back into the bag. "I am not pregnant."

"Are you sure?"

"Of course I'm sure." She jumped from her chair and stacked her papers nervously. The idea that Lisa thought she was pregnant was outrageous. "Obviously I'm too old to be pregnant."

"My mother was forty-six years old when she had me."

A nervous twitter lit through Kate as she thought back on the past few weeks. She had felt out of sorts recently. No! She stopped herself before she allowed her thoughts to go down that road. She was already the mother of two nearly grown boys. She was not pregnant. She couldn't be. While she appreciated Lisa's concern for her, it was a ridiculous notion to even consider. God would never do that to her. She was just too busy to be pregnant.

But, as Lisa left the office, that plain brown bag on her desk began to mock her. She picked it up and stuffed it into her briefcase.

Chapter 2

The morning alarm sounded.

Kate reached to turn it off but didn't get out of bed right away. She considered staying put and taking a sick day, but that thought came and went in a flash.

She pushed back the covers and willed her feet to the floor. Mothers didn't get a sick day and neither did town managers, especially now that Thanksgiving had come and gone and the nativity premiere was only hours away. There was still much to do. Kate had status meetings planned for the morning and a television interview to promote the project on the noon report. As she stumbled toward the bathroom, she faced the facts—if she wanted a sick day, she would have to cough up a lung or something major like that.

She stared at her reflection in the mirror, noticing the bags beneath her eyes, and realized she probably could pull off being sick. She looked as tired as she felt. Sure, it was the busy time of year. Sure, she was overworked and overstressed. But all that was nothing new to her. Overworked and overstressed was her life. She usually thrived on it.

Kate remembered Lisa's comments earlier that week. Had she been so cranky that everyone around her had noticed? Had David noticed? She certainly didn't need him to know how worn out she was. He already believed she took on more responsibility than she could handle.

What would she do if she had to take on the responsibility of a baby as well?

The pregnancy test was right where she'd tossed it, hidden beneath the sink under a stack of towels in the very back of the cabinet, sure to never be found. Kate had not been able to bring herself to throw the thing in the trash once and for all. And as the days had passed and she'd had more and more time to dwell on the notion, she decided the idea might not be as impossible as she'd first decided.

She fell to her hands and knees and dug through the contents of the cabinet until she found it. She held it in her hands, fearful of the results this test might hold and the changes those results might have for her life. How would a baby affect her career? Could she manage being the town manager and the mother of an infant? Her boys had been teenagers by the time she'd reentered the workforce.

And what about David? Could their marriage survive another baby? Kate knew how much he loved their boys, but she also knew he was looking forward to the day when they were both out of the house. David wanted to have the freedom to travel, and he was already making plans for the day when Keith left for college. Kate had yet to ask him how her job would fit into those plans, but a baby would definitely ruin them.

She decided to take the test and stop worrying about things she couldn't control. Good or bad, it was done now. Either she was or she wasn't pregnant.

After the appropriate time, she checked the test. Hot tears burned her eyes when she saw the results.

∞

The music playing on David's headphones matched the thump of his feet against the pavement as he finished his morning run. He slowed to a walk a few houses down from his own in order to cool down. He admired the houses as he walked.

This was a nice family neighborhood, but he and Kate were about to be without a family to inhabit it. Keith had received his college acceptance letter only this week. His future was planned, and he was ready to get started on it. John was already away at college, and it was like pulling teeth most times to even get him to come home. Not that David was complaining. He was glad his boys were independent enough to want to live their own lives. It meant that he and Kate could soon have the freedom they had earned without so many restrictions. He could sell his business and Kate could step down from her job as town manager. They would finally be able to get away together and reconnect.

As he reached his yard, he stopped to pick up trash that had somehow been tossed on the lawn. He stopped and took a good long look at the house, wondering if they shouldn't think about selling it. It would soon need a paint job, and this would be the last spring he would have Keith around to help with the yard upkeep. They would have little need for so much space once both boys were out of the house. And since he and Kate hoped to travel, they didn't need a big yard and a lot of maintenance issues to tie them down. He would call and talk to a Realtor about their options after the holidays.

He entered the house through the patio off the master bedroom. The bed was empty and the bathroom door closed, indicating that Kate was already up. This was her big day, and he imagined she was anxious to make an early start. He grabbed his clothes and decided to shower and change in the hall bathroom.

By the time David finished dressing, the boys were up and making breakfast. When he entered the kitchen, he saw John, who was home for the Thanksgiving break, digging into a plate of toasted waffles while Keith poured himself a bowl of cold cereal. "What are you boys doing up so early?"

"We promised to help Mr. Mitchell finish up the set construction," John said.

"Yeah, everything has to be perfect," Keith chimed in. "This is Mom's big day. We want everything to go off without a hitch."

John smacked his brother on the shoulder. "This isn't just about Mom, you dope. This nativity reflects on the whole town of Bethlehem."

"Maybe so, but who gets the blame if it doesn't go well? Mom."

"That's enough, both of you," David said, putting an end to the bickering.

They were both right, but their argument was moot. The nativity would do well. Everything Kate touched succeeded. She was a winner. She always had been. Plus, this time she had the entire backing of the community behind her. This project didn't belong to only her anymore. Though Keith was right—if it didn't go well, she would be the one to bear the blame.

As his boys often did, they quickly moved on to another subject. Keith unfolded a piece of paper and mounted it to the freezer door with magnets like a child displaying art he made at school.

"What's that?" David asked.

"He's been mooning over that thing for two days," John said.

Keith grinned from ear to ear. "It's my letter from UMF. I thought I'd showcase it here for everyone to see."

David patted his shoulder, as proud of Keith for his acceptance into the University of Maine at Farmington as Keith was. "I think that's a good idea, Son. Now why don't you two finish up your breakfast? You don't want to keep Mr. Mitchell waiting."

John turned back to his waffles, but Keith took a moment to straighten his letter before returning to the table.

David poured himself a cup of coffee then opened the morning paper. It was full of listings, but he wasn't interested in buying more things to fill up the house. In fact, his mind was already on the idea of downsizing. He turned to the real estate section and began looking through the ads for condominiums for sale. He wanted to have a good idea of what they were looking at before he presented the topic to Kate.

"Mom, have you been crying?"

Keith's question brought David's attention back to his current home. Kate was standing in the doorway of the kitchen. Her eyes were swollen and her face held an ashen look to it like she had, indeed, been crying, despite her obvious attempts to hide it with makeup.

"No, I'm fine," she said. Her assurances, however, did not prevent any of them from getting to their feet to make certain.

David touched her arm. "Kate, are you sure you're all right?"

"Yes, I'm fine." She opened the refrigerator, an obvious attempt to escape their gawking stares.

"This is because of my letter, isn't it?" Keith was now standing on the other side of the opened refrigerator door, eye to eye with the UMF acceptance letter he'd mounted only minutes before.

Kate closed the refrigerator. "What?"

"Of course this is because of your letter," John told him. "You're the baby, Keith. Once you're gone, what will she have left?"

John had a way of speaking as if he knew the answer to every question in the world, and for some reason that David had yet to figure out, Keith believed every word he said.

"I'll only be two hours away." Keith looked back at his mother. "Don't you want me to go away to college?"

Kate had that deer-in-the-headlights look in her eyes. It was obvious Keith was about to pull her into a conversation she was unprepared to discuss. He had to intercede.

"Whoa, hold on there now," David said. He put his arm around Kate's shoulders in order to present a united front in this matter. "Keith, your mother and I are both thrilled that you got into the school you wanted. Honestly, we couldn't be happier for you."

"Then why is Mom so upset?"

David pulled her tighter against him, a little curious that she was allowing it. Where was her spitfire? Where was her grit? Something must have her really rattled this morning. "Cut your mother some slack. She's under a lot of stress with this nativity project plus the pressure of running an entire city and this household. Weren't we just talking about how important today was? Sometimes people just need to let off a little stress. Okay?"

John nodded. "Sure. We're sorry, Mom. Everything's going to be great today."

Keith was a little more hesitant, but he finally came around. He gave her a hug. "Tonight's going to be awesome, Mom. Don't worry."

Once both boys had returned to their breakfasts, David turned to Kate. Was that gratitude he saw in those red, puffy eyes? How long had it been since she'd been grateful to him for anything? "You want some coffee?" he asked her.

"No, just juice." She poured herself a glass from the carton she'd taken from the refrigerator.

Since when did she not drink coffee in the morning? "Are you sure you're okay?"

"Yes, David, I'm fine. Just butterflies, I think. Like you said, it's a big day."

Spurred on by the gratitude he'd seen in her eyes, he decided to take a leap. "Why don't we have lunch today?"

The way she almost choked on her juice at his invitation spoke a thousand things she never would. "I have project meetings most of the day and a television interview at noon to promote the nativity."

"You have to eat."

"I'll probably just send out for something and eat at my desk. Once the nativity begins—"

"You'll be knee-deep in issues stemming from it. Face it, Kate, after today, I probably won't see you again until New Year's."

Her phone on the counter buzzed. David dared her with his eyes to pick it up. She must have seen his challenge, because she let it go unanswered.

"What do you want me to say, David? This project was my idea. I put it together. I know it's a lot of work and sacrifice, but it is important to me."

"Tell me something, Kate." He leaned across the counter toward her so they were almost eye to eye and lowered his voice so the boys couldn't overhear. "When exactly did I stop being important to you?" He picked up his briefcase and keys, waiting for her to respond.

She didn't.

The phone buzzed again as David turned to leave. "You'd better get that," he told her. "It might be someone important."

He walked out the door leading into the garage and leaned against it as it closed behind him.

Lord, when did I stop being important to her, and how can I get it back?

⤜⤝

Kate watched the door close.

That wasn't fair. David had to know he was important to her. But his request for lunch caught her off guard and she'd had to scramble to come up with a quick excuse. It's not like she could tell him she was going to the doctor during lunch to confirm the pregnancy of their midlife child. No, she wouldn't tell him about being pregnant until a doctor confirmed it.

Her phoned buzzed again. Kate checked the caller ID then groaned. "Myles."

She'd tasked Myles Sandford from her staff to handle the production part of the nativity, and while she thought he was doing a great job, he was also driving her crazy with every little detail.

"What does he want this early?"

Keith pushed back from the table. "He probably wants to give you a heads-up about Kaylee Martin. She broke her arm skiing yesterday."

"How do you know that?"

"She posted it last night."

The phoned stopped buzzing then immediately began again.

"Why would he be calling me about a teenager with a broken arm?"

"Kaylee was supposed to be Mary in the nativity tonight. Remember?"

Of course she should have remembered that. Kate's heart leaped at this first snag in their production schedule. Thank goodness they had backups. She picked up her phone and greeted Myles as she moved into the living room.

"I have bad news about Kaylee Martin," he said.

"I've already heard. Who do we have to replace her?"

"Well, that's what I need to talk with you about. I need you to do it."

"Me? Don't be ridiculous."

"I'm not, Kate. I've already started phoning our backups and, well, with the holiday weekend, there's no one else who can do it."

"Myles, I'm too old to play that part."

"Ah, but you look so young, Kate."

She groaned at his flattery. She knew better. Mary had been a teenager of fourteen or fifteen when she gave birth to Jesus. The role was traditionally played by a teenaged girl. There was no way Kate looked young enough to play that part.

Her hesitation must have gone on for long enough to convince Myles that his flattery wasn't working, because he changed his tactic. "Kate, this project is your baby. The town needs you."

She groaned again, this time because Myles knew how to push just the right buttons to get her to agree. "Fine, I'll do it."

Kate closed her phone and turned to her sons. "Do you believe this? He expects me to be Mary."

"Mom, you can't be Mary. You're too old."

John punched his brother in the arm. "Way to go, Keith. If she wasn't crying before, she will be now that you've called her an old woman."

Although Keith's comment echoed her own, hearing it aloud did sting. "I'm only forty-four."

"Sorry, Mom. I didn't mean *you* were old. I only meant. . .well, Mary was a teenager and. . .well, you're not." His voice trailed off as if he realized his words were not helping. He looked to his brother for affirmation, but John shook his head and rolled his eyes.

"How do you survive here without me?" he asked.

"It's not easy."

The boys put their dishes in the sink then gathered their coats and headed out the door.

Kate retouched her makeup to make certain no one else would know she had been crying. She didn't want a scene at work like the one she'd had at home. . .especially since she didn't have David there to lean on.

She remembered the hurt expression on his face when he'd left. Was a simple lunch with his wife really too much to ask? She pulled out her day planner, scanned the scheduled project meetings, and suddenly felt overwhelmed by the sheer enormity of her day. Meetings with the maintenance staff, costumers, food service providers, budget planners, the sheriff, and the police chief. Plus the television interview. Kate closed her day planner. She was already exhausted and her day had hardly begun.

As she left the house, she made a decision—the idea of her playing Mary was utterly ridiculous. She didn't have the time to devote to one more thing. Young girls played the role of Mary because young girls had babies. She was an old married woman with one son in college and another son about to graduate from high school.

Once she reached her office, she would put any and all available personnel on finding someone else to fill that role. No one in their right minds would believe she was young enough to have a baby.

Chapter 3

David spread travel brochures across his desk. He had the world at his fingertips. He had only to choose the destination.

In August, Keith would leave for college. However, he planned on working as a counselor at a sports camp for the summer, so he would essentially be gone from the house once he graduated in May. For David and Kate, that opened up a world of opportunities, and David was looking forward to enjoying the freedom that came from being empty nesters.

The back door opened and shut. He gathered the brochures and put them away as his friend and business partner, Mike Purvis, entered. He and Mike had started in the insurance business together and had opened their own agency nearly eighteen years ago. "How did it look?" David asked.

The office was usually closed the day after Thanksgiving in order for the staff to spend time with their families, but Mike had taken a call from a policyholder who had experienced a kitchen fire while cooking her Thanksgiving meal. "It looks like the Martin family ate their Thanksgiving dinner out this year."

Mike grinned as he deposited a file on David's desk then planted himself on the sofa. "I cut Mrs. Martin a check. She's probably out purchasing a new stove as we speak."

David scanned the paperwork then pushed it away. He had another matter he wanted to discuss. "Look, Mike, since we've got the office to ourselves, I thought this might be a good time to mention something to you."

"Sounds serious."

"It is. I was thinking of letting you buy me out of my share of the agency."

"You're kidding."

"No, I'm serious. Keith is graduating in a few months, and Kate and I want to do some traveling once he's gone. I won't be around as much." When Mike didn't respond right away, David urged him on. "Well? What do you think?"

Mike shook his head. "I don't think I can do that, David."

"What? Why not?"

"Tina's pregnant." He stared up at David. "We're going to have another baby. We got the news on Monday."

David leaned back in his seat as the weight of his friend's news hit him. Mike and Tina were younger than he and Kate, but they already had three school-aged children. "I don't know what to say."

"Well, you can at least pretend to be happy for me."

"Do you mean to say that you're happy about this?"

"Yes, I'm thrilled that I'm going to be a father again. Tina and I are both thrilled that God has chosen to bless us this way."

"What about your plans to retire early? With a new baby, that won't be possible."

"I guess that's true, but it's a small price to pay."

"You say that now, but you'll be wishing you'd done things differently when you're my age and retirement seems a lifetime away."

"Maybe you're right. It will be a struggle financially—that's nothing new for us—but it does mean I won't have the money to buy you out of your share of the business. Even if I did, with a new baby coming, I can't operate this place by myself and still give my family the attention they deserve." He stood to leave but stopped at the doorway and turned back. "Maybe this isn't what we had planned for our lives, David, but I suppose God had other plans, and I know His plans are always good."

David watched his friend leave. He hated the way that conversation had gone. He didn't want Mike thinking he didn't love being a father. He loved John and Keith and had a thousand memories of their childhood that he would cherish. And he wasn't naïve enough to believe that because the boys were away at college that his responsibility as a parent had ended. But his role in their lives had changed, and that could not be denied or ignored.

Some parents couldn't handle that change. Some had nothing in their lives except their children, and when that role change occurred, they were left with nothing but empty shells as lives. Not he and Kate. They had plans. They saw this time in their lives for what it was—an opportunity.

Or at least it was supposed to be. After this morning's break-down, it was obvious to David that Kate was not going to han-dle Keith's impending departure well. He couldn't understand it. She wasn't usually so emotional. If she was already crying in December, what would she be like come May? It wasn't like her. It wasn't his Kate.

He searched through the brochures again and pulled out one for a tropical destination that he'd had his eye on. White beaches, blue sky, and two weeks of soaking up the rays—enough fun in the sun to put a smile on anyone's face.

He put away the rest of the brochures. He'd made his choice. And he couldn't help but be thankful that God had chosen to bless Mike and Tina instead of him and Kate.

∽

Bethlehem Green had indeed been transformed into the ancient marketplace through which Joseph and Mary would have trav-eled. Kate felt the excitement in the air at the anticipation of the premiere as volunteers rushed to complete final preparations. Beginning tonight, visitors would travel through the streets of the ancient city and get a firsthand view of what the young cou-ple saw on their journey, all the while listening to the Christmas story over the mounted speakers.

She approached the pavilion, now transformed into a barn. Hay was scattered across the floor, and the cradle for the baby Jesus was already positioned. Above her, on the roof, an electri-cian worked, no doubt running electricity to the star that pointed the way to the Christ child.

Kate sat on Mary's stool and examined the scene. This was the place where she used to bring her boys to play when they were little. Her mind drifted back to the days when they ran and romped and tackled one another. She touched the cradle where the baby Jesus would be placed and thought back on the days when her own children were small enough to fit in such a space. Her eyes welled up. That seemed so long ago.

"Kate!"

She looked up to see Myles heading toward her.

"I'm glad I found you. We need to have your final fitting for your costume."

She wiped away a trickle of a tear on her cheek, kicking herself for getting overly emotional in public. What if Myles saw her crying?

She got up as he approached. She was always more commanding when she stood. "Myles, I need to speak to you about that. I don't think I'm a good choice to fill this role. Surely there's someone else who can—"

"Kate, there is no one else. The nativity is in nine hours. You're the only one who's been to all the rehearsals. You're the only one who knows what to do on such late notice."

"I'm too old to play Mary. Mary was a child. I mean, Matt Parker is playing Joseph, and he's only twenty-three. I'm old enough to be his mother."

"I've already taken care of that. Matt is going to switch roles with David. Matt will be a shepherd and David will play Joseph. Problem solved."

Kate sank back onto the stool. "I don't think I'm up for this."

"Playing sick won't help you. Face it, Kate, you're out of excuses. This town needs you. This production needs you."

Kate leaned into her elbows as her head began to spin.

Myles bent down beside her, concern suddenly touching his voice. "On second thought, you do look pale. Maybe you should go to your office and lie down for a while."

"I can't. I have an interview at Channel Four in a half hour."

"You'd better let me handle that."

Normally, Kate would never agree to hand off her responsibilities, but this was not a normal moment. If she looked as poorly as she felt, she wouldn't represent the project well. Letting Myles step in and do the interview was the better alternative. "I think that would be best." She allowed Myles to help her to her feet.

"I'll walk you to your office." His phone buzzed at his hip. He glanced at the message then at Kate.

"I'm fine, Myles. You go ahead."

He looked around. "I'll get someone to walk with you."

"I said I'm fine." She stood straight and tall just to prove her point.

Myles's phone buzzed again. He glanced at the message on the screen. "There's a problem at the shepherd's pen. Excuse me, Kate. I have to go." He headed off.

Kate fell to the stool again. Putting on an act for Myles's sake had taken all the energy she had. But she couldn't sit here all day, either. What would the selectmen think if they saw the town manager just sitting around? Besides, how long could she sit looking sick and pale before it got around to her husband and sons and they came asking questions of her? She didn't want that.

She pulled herself up and headed toward her office. This pregnancy was going to be harder on her than the others had been. She was already feeling more physical effects than she had with either John or Keith.

As she reached her office, she realized she was already accepting this pregnancy as if it were fact even though she hadn't yet had the blood test. She also realized the blood test didn't matter. She knew the results. She felt it in her soul.

She closed her door, shutting herself away from the prying eyes and questions of her staff. She couldn't deal with them right now. She fell onto the couch and stared at the photograph of David on her desk. What would she tell him? He'd started making plans for the day when the boys were out of the house. A baby would obliterate those plans. This news would crush him.

So many questions poured through her, but one pressed its way to the forefront—why now? Why had God chosen this time in her life to give her another child? Why not ten years ago when her boys were younger, when she was younger and less established in her career? How on earth would she handle dealing with a teenager when she was in her sixties? And what if the child had problems? She was over forty, and that automatically put the baby at risk for complications.

She hadn't asked for this. She'd always been content with

what God had given her. Sure, at one time she'd thought she'd wanted a daughter, but she'd given up on that dream long ago.

How could God do this to her? What about her plans? She had a life, a career. Who would possibly take her seriously now?

She was too old to be a mother again. Her boys were grown. She had friends who were becoming grandparents, and she was about to become a parent again? It was outrageous.

Kate closed her eyes and tried to breathe as the reality of her situation sank in.

Chapter 4

Is this a surprise for your wife?" The travel agent, named Marcia, according to the plaque on her desk, had a glint in her eye as she took the information about the trip David wanted to book for him and Kate.

"Yes, it's a Christmas present."

"Oh, isn't that romantic. I know you two will have a wonderful time." She turned to her computer and began typing in the information from the questionnaire he'd completed. She stopped typing after a moment. "Kate Walters? Is this Kate Walters, the town manager from Bethlehem?"

"That's right. We don't have a travel agency in Bethlehem."

"Why, you're the ones putting on that live nativity tonight. I saw your wife on Channel Six just the other night talking about it."

"Yes, that was her. In fact, she'll be on Channel Four today at noon."

Marcia looked at the clock then leaped to her feet. "Allison, Allison, turn the TV to Channel Four. That lady from Bethlehem we like is going to be on again promoting the nativity."

David followed Marcia toward the sound of a TV changing channels.

"How do you know?" called Allison.

"That's her husband," Marcia stated as they entered the room, pointing to David.

Allison glanced at him then shook her head. "It's not fair. She gets the great hair *and* the good-looking husband."

"Mm-hm. And he's surprising her with a cruise, too."

"Some girls get all the luck."

David pretended to ignore their exchange, but he couldn't deny it bolstered his ego. Maybe he should let these women explain to Kate just how lucky she was to be married to him.

The news came back on and the anchor began to discuss the nativity. However, it wasn't Kate sitting across from him promoting the project. It was Myles.

"Hey, that's not your wife," Marcia stated.

As if he didn't know. David pulled out his cell phone. He'd turned it off earlier when he decided to come to the travel agency. He hadn't wanted anyone deterring him from his mission of booking this trip, but apparently he'd missed quite a bit. Something serious must have happened for Kate to step aside and allow Myles to take a television interview.

He turned on his phone. He had six missed calls and three voice mail messages. "Can we finish booking the trip another time? Apparently I'm needed at home."

Marcia rushed back toward her desk. "Sure. I'll go ahead and make all the arrangements then call you when they're done."

"That sounds fine. I wrote down my cell phone number."

She gave him a reassuring nod. "I'll take care of everything, Mr. Walters. Don't worry. And hey, maybe we'll see you tonight. I told my husband we should go."

"I'm sure you'll enjoy it. Thanks for your help."

David hit his voice mail key as he walked to his car. The first was from Myles, letting him know that there had been changes made to the program. Kate was now playing the role of Mary, and because of that, David had been changed to the role of Joseph. A second message from Myles asked David to meet him an hour earlier than planned to make certain both he and Kate knew their roles. The third call was a hang up.

David got in and started the car. His sense of urgency had been tickled. He needed to get back to Bethlehem. Something was going on. Kate would never voluntarily hand over a TV spot to Myles. And how had he talked her into taking on the role of Mary? Something was going on with her, and he was pretty sure he knew what it was.

He faced the facts. This thing with Keith was hitting her harder than she wanted to admit. It was the only explanation. She was having trouble dealing with him leaving home. And the fact that Myles could convince her to play the role of Mary was enough to assure David that she shouldn't take on the role.

Playing Mary would require her to hold a baby. In her already emotional state, how would that affect her? David worried it might only upset her more, causing her to dwell on the days when John and Keith were babies.

He dialed her cell, but the call went to her voice mail, so he hung up. He was suddenly glad Myles had changed his part, too. He needed to be Joseph so he could be there with Kate, beside her, to keep her from falling apart when nostalgia overwhelmed her.

He had to keep her eyes on the future and not on the past. Otherwise, all the plans he'd made for them were for nothing.

∼∞∼

"Where have you been? I've been trying to reach you all afternoon." David's accusing glare matched his tone when he cornered Kate in the fellowship hall of the Bethlehem Community Church, where the nativity crew and players were meeting to eat before the production. "You didn't answer your cell, and that assistant of yours kept giving me the brush-off."

"I was busy with last-minute project details."

"Did she tell you I called?"

Lisa had left Kate a note taped to her door letting her know that David had been phoning all afternoon. Kate had found it a half hour ago. Until then, she'd been locked up in her office staring at photos of her boys and wondering why God would choose now to ruin her life.

"I got your messages," Kate assured him. She wouldn't let Lisa take responsibility for her not getting them. Too late, she realized that admitting she received them also meant admitting she hadn't bothered returning them.

The stab of hurt in David's eye was quickly replaced with a glint of anger. "I understand I'm now playing the part of Joseph because Myles somehow talked *you* into playing Mary. I guess I didn't get my memo on that change."

"David, please, I'm not in the mood to argue." Her phone buzzed. She hated to check it in front of him, but she had no choice. It was a message from Myles. "They want us to pose for photographs."

"Fine."

Kate's costume included pregnancy padding. She changed in the women's restroom and found herself rubbing the bump of her stomach as she stared at herself in the mirror. In a few months, she wouldn't need the cushioning to appear pregnant. Her own child was already growing inside of her. She leaned into the mirror and took a deep breath. She couldn't have those kinds of thoughts. She couldn't go there tonight. It would only lead her down a slippery emotional slope. Somehow, she had to pull herself together and get through this evening.

David had changed and was waiting for her when she came out of the restroom. She should tell him about the baby. She really knew she should. He had a right to know, and keeping it from him wasn't going to change anything. But this wasn't the right time or the right place. Tonight, they couldn't afford to be David and Kate Walters. They had to be Joseph and Mary for the sake of the town and the production.

They took pictures and then Kate removed the pregnancy padding and they posed for more photos, this time with the baby. Kate was shaking as the child's mother handed him over. How long had it been since she'd held a baby? She stole a fervent glance up at David. His hands felt like weights on her shoulders. The tension between them was so thick and heavy that others had to notice.

"Try to smile," Myles suggested to them. "Joseph and Mary were happy when Jesus was born, remember?"

Kate choked back tears. Everything about the moment was wrong. Having a baby in her arms felt awkward and uncomfortable, and David's strained countenance shouted volumes—he was not interested in babies, even when they weren't his.

Kate was glad when the photo session ended and the baby's mother took him back. She felt ill-equipped to deal with him. How would she ever deal with a baby of her own? It was obvious to her that her motherly instincts had expired. Whatever skills she'd had to care for John and Keith were gone. Would they return when the new baby came?

As the nativity began, Kate tried to train her focus on the presentation. She could not think about the pregnancy or David's reaction. She had to be Mary. She had to get through this night.

Lord, please give me strength.

Kate moved closer to David, suddenly glad Myles had changed the roles so that he would be her Joseph. She trusted him to meet his marks and to lead her to where she needed to be. He always seemed to know when she needed him to be the strong one—like this morning when she'd needed him to step in for her with the boys. Why didn't he do that more often?

She sighed. She knew the answer to her question. She didn't often give him an opportunity.

"You okay?" David whispered to her, obviously hearing her sigh.

"I'm okay," she replied. But she wasn't. Maybe it was her hormones going crazy from this pregnancy, but she was beginning to feel very vulnerable when it came to David. He was a good husband and had been a good father to their boys.

Oh, God, I can't do this without him!

Why had she treated David so poorly? Why hadn't she appreciated what she had in him? Sure, he had his faults. Sure, he was wrapped up in this traveling thing. But what was so wrong with that? And why had she never told him she didn't want to leave her career and go with him? They should have discussed all of this long before now.

They reached the scene where the innkeeper offered them the manger. David followed him to the inn while Kate followed the innkeeper's wife off the set.

The scene transferred to the shepherds. Kate reconnected with David and they walked to the stable, where their next scene was to take place. Kate spotted the mother with the baby who was playing the role of Jesus.

"He just had a bottle, so he shouldn't be fussy. He'll probably go right to sleep. But if he doesn't, try humming to him."

The man beside her seemed irritated. "Pamela, the woman runs the entire town. I think she can take care of a baby for a few minutes."

Pamela handed the baby over. "Of course you can. I didn't mean to doubt you. After all, you're a mom, too. You raised two boys and they've turned out fine."

"We'll take good care of him. He'll be fine."

When they entered the stable, Kate saw the manger and felt relief flood her. At least she wouldn't have to hold the baby the entire time.

She placed him in the manger and made certain he was covered. She stroked his cheek and was amazed—she'd forgotten how soft a baby's skin could be. His lips were soft, too, and pink. He smiled up at her, and she noticed how his eyes held such innocence and trust. There was no fear or question in those eyes, only a certainty that he would be taken care of. She wondered if all babies were born with such trust.

Certainly the baby Jesus had had that trust. He had known with certainty that He would be cared for, because His earthly parents had been chosen for Him before He was born. God had handpicked Mary and Joseph to be Jesus' earthly parents—to care for Him and raise Him, until He was ready to start His ministry.

Then it struck her. Weren't all parents chosen? Children were not merely accidents of nature. Hadn't God chosen her and David to be John and Keith's parents just as He'd chosen Mary and Joseph?

And that woman had been right when she said John and Keith had turned out well. Maybe they weren't perfect, but they were good boys who both loved the Lord. She and David had done a fine job of raising them.

She touched the baby in the manger and felt a connection

to the child growing in her womb. She now shared a truth with Mary—that the child inside of her was a gift from God to be nurtured and cherished. God was not trying to ruin her life. God had a plan, and He was making her a part of it.

Relief and love swept through Kate as she let go of the burden she'd been carrying. God had given her this gift, and she knew He would give her the strength she needed when she needed it. He would help her become the mother she had been to John and Keith. He would help her regain her maternal instincts.

David nudged her, and Kate turned to look at him. She had something else in common with Mary—telling her husband about a baby he didn't plan for and obviously didn't want.

❧

David was glad to be able to shed his costume and put on some work clothes instead. Everyone seemed pleased with the production, and as the crowd began to dissipate, the townspeople were getting geared up.

David helped make certain lights and heaters were off and unplugged. He smiled, listening to the murmur of the volunteers as they went about their designated tasks. Some helped load the animals used in the production while others handed out coffee and hot chocolate. David asked for a cup of coffee and dropped a donation into the box.

"Mr. Walters! It's Marcia from the travel agency."

He turned to find a young woman heading toward him. "Hi, Marcia, yes I remember. I'm glad you came."

"It was wonderful, very authentic. I might see if I can

convince my husband to come back again next week. Was that your wife playing the role of Mary?"

"Yes, that was Kate."

"I know you two are going to have a great time on your trip."

He placed a finger to his lips. "It's a Christmas present, remember."

"Oh, of course. I'll let you know when the tickets arrive."

He waved good-bye to her then went looking for his wife. Tomorrow, they would do it all over again.

He found Kate accepting congratulations for her idea and the way the nativity went. Even Alex Littlejohn and Victor Patterson, two of the three selectmen who'd appointed Kate town manager, made an appearance and told her how pleased they were with the turnout.

David was tired and ready to get home, but he didn't rush her. She'd earned this praise. She didn't take the credit, though. She gave it back to the town and glorified God for their success.

That was his Kate, unselfish to the core. She gave everything of herself to whatever project she was involved in, and Bethlehem was lucky to have her nurturing their little town. He was proud of her, but he was also envious that others were receiving her attention instead of him. Why did this job, this project, have to pull her so far away from him?

He thought of the cruise he'd booked. Maybe with this trip, they could find their way back to the close relationship they once shared.

As they headed for the car, Kate seemed preoccupied.

"Who was that woman I saw you speaking to?"

"Which woman?"

"Just before we left. The pretty blonde."

He smiled, remembering his secret. "Marcia. She's actually a big fan of yours."

"How do you know her?"

"I don't. She came for the nativity and stopped to tell me how much she enjoyed it."

He opened the car door for Kate and she slid inside. He hated being coy, but he didn't want to ruin the surprise.

Chapter 5

David drove out to the marina to review a claim submitted by one of his policyholders for damage done to his sailboat.

Paul Matthews lived on his boat all year, often sailing down the eastern coastline for warmer weather. However, he was docked for a while after running into a rock bed in the bay. David surveyed the damage, took photographs, then assisted Paul in submitting a claim.

As Paul signed the forms, David admired the lines of the boat.

"Do you sail?" Paul asked, handing David back his iPad.

"Not for a long while. My wife and I used to dream about buying a boat and sailing down the coast. That was a long time ago." Before kids and jobs and responsibilities became their life. Suddenly, David envied Paul his freedom.

"You should do it," Paul told him. "There's nothing like having the ability to drop and go whenever you like. The weather is the only thing that determines the timing and the direction."

David smiled at the idea of him and Kate alone on the water. He'd been considering purchasing a condo. Why shouldn't he consider a boat instead? They could live on it and sail away on a whim. "Maybe I'll look into that."

"I have a friend down near Portland who is looking to sell his boat. I'll give you his number, if you're interested."

David took down the information. He was definitely interested.

❧

Kate's phone beeped again. Lisa had been texting numbers all morning. Indications were that the nativity was a success on all fronts. They'd dealt with a few hiccups, but nothing that couldn't be addressed for the upcoming performances.

Kate nibbled on a piece of dry toast as she thought about who she needed to schedule meetings with.

The door opened and David entered, dressed in his running clothes. He dropped his iPod and earbuds onto the counter and frowned at her. "What are you doing home?"

She still hadn't gotten up the nerve to break the news to him about the baby, so she couldn't tell him the truth—that morning sickness was kicking in strong and hard.

"I'm getting a late start."

"I'll say. You're usually at the office an hour ago, but since you're here, I'd like to take your car by the dealership and have your brakes checked. I'll leave you my truck if you need it."

"Is something wrong?"

"No. It's just a precaution. We're forecasted to get some ice over the next few weeks, and I want to make sure you're good to go."

She smiled at the way he thought of such things. She never had to worry about car maintenance or house repairs. He handled those things without complaining or making a big deal out of them. She also realized, a little ashamedly, that she was more likely to complain about being without her vehicle than to acknowledge his good intentions. "Thank you, David. You always take such good care of me."

He smiled. "I'm your husband. It's my job to take care of you." He started down the hall. "I'm just going to jump in the shower."

Guilt flooded through her. It had been four days since the nativity, and she still hadn't managed to find a good time to tell him about the baby.

She had to just do it. It would be a shock, but this was David, her David. He'd been a good husband and a good father. He was always looking out for her and the boys. And she knew he would be there for this baby, too. After the initial shock, he would probably even be happy about having another child.

She hoped.

∽∞∾

While David was in the shower, Myles phoned with an updated agenda for the meeting with the selectmen. While Kate was going over several details with him, her phone beeped then dropped the call. She glanced at the screen and saw her battery had died.

She rummaged through the kitchen drawer for her phone charger. Not finding it, she picked up David's phone and was dialing Myles's number when a text message popped up on the screen. The text was from "Marcia," and the message stopped Kate cold.

READY FOR A TROPICAL PARADISE? THE TICKETS ARE READY.

Who was this Marcia? And where and why was David taking a trip with her to some tropical paradise?

Was it possible she didn't know her husband as well as she thought she did? Was David having an affair with this Marcia?

Kate rubbed her stomach, but this time she couldn't blame her ill feeling on morning sickness. This was a different kind of illness, a my-near-perfect-life-is-falling-apart kind of illness. Her mind refused to comprehend that David was being unfaithful. Other men cheated on their wives, but not David.

But why shouldn't he cheat on her? She shuddered, remembering all the times she'd chosen work over him and all the times he'd openly expressed his agitation about it.

Panic gripped her. A few days ago, she'd been worried about his reaction to a baby. Now she was worrying about the future of her marriage.

God, this can't be happening.

He emerged from the bedroom, clean-shaven and his hair still wet. He smelled like aftershave, and Kate inhaled the masculine scent of him. Suddenly, the thought of losing this man, her rock for so many years, was more than she could bear. Tears pooled in her eyes, but instead of crying, she got angry.

"Who is Marcia?" she demanded.

He shot her a guilty look, and she waved the phone at him.

"Marcia. . .who is she? And why is she texting you about tickets to a tropical paradise?"

He grabbed his phone from her, a flush in his cheeks. "Kate, you weren't supposed to see that."

"David, I would like an answer."

He gave her a wry smile. "Okay, I confess. It was supposed to be a Christmas present, but now I guess the surprise is ruined."

"A present?"

"Marcia works at a travel agency."

She felt the heat of embarrassment warm her face. How silly it was to even think for a moment that David would be unfaithful.

"It's a little close to Christmas to be snooping, Kate."

Relief flooded her. Of course David wasn't cheating. But the incident had opened her eyes. David was a good man, decent and caring, and she too often took him for granted. What would she do without him if he ever chose to leave her?

She rubbed her stomach again, realizing that David would remain a good and faithful husband even if he was desperately unhappy with their marriage. She was suddenly overwhelmed with the desire that he stay because he was happy, not out of a sense of obligation.

But how could she convince him to be happy about a baby he knew nothing about?

⤨

Kate zippered her coat and walked downtown toward Bethlehem Café for a cup of hot chocolate. She enjoyed the ambience of their historic downtown. Their little community used to be flooded during the summer months with tourists enjoying the coastline and beaches, but in the last few years business had been slowing down. They needed a revival. Bethlehem was an undiscovered treasure for the state of Maine, and Kate was confident that its charm and quaintness could attract tourists to the area if they could only get the word out. They had a small but naturally made harbor and plenty of activities. If Bethlehem was to grow and prosper, they would need the exposure this live nativity could bring.

The aroma of fresh pastries met her as she turned on the block where the café was located beside a small cove. Kate opened the door and stepped inside, swept into the wave of warmth and pastries that greeted her.

"Good morning, Kate." Melissa Harris and her husband, Doug, had started this café six years ago, and Kate knew they were struggling to keep it afloat.

"Good morning." She placed her order then asked Melissa about the preparations they were making for the weekend, hoping this nativity would help bring in some much-needed income for all the town's businesses.

"We'll be staying open later the nights of the nativity and offering hot beverages. We even had a call from the *Bangor Daily News* wanting to do a story on the businesses in Bethlehem. It's exciting to see the publicity we're receiving because of this nativity. It's wonderful."

Kate smiled and wished Melissa well as she walked out of the shop. It was encouraging to hear such feedback from a business that was being affected by the nativity. These small businesses were the heart and soul of the town. She texted Lisa to find out more about this newspaper article and to offer any assistance they might need.

She rounded the corner, her mind still focused on her phone, and bumped into Murray Samuels, one of the selectmen who had appointed her. Mr. Samuels was a buttoned-up, old-fashioned man with old-fashioned ideas, who'd at first been concerned about a woman as town manager. Kate wished she felt more put together this morning if she were going to have to confront Mr. Samuels. She was sure she looked as weary as she felt.

"Good morning, Mr. Samuels."

"Good morning, Mrs. Walters." He pulled a newspaper from his coat. "Did you see we made the front page of the *Augusta Journal*?"

"Yes, I saw that. It's wonderful." She gave Mr. Samuels a recap of the discussion she'd had at the café and about the article being written for the *Bangor Daily News*.

Mr. Samuels eyed her then did something Kate had rarely seen him do. . .he smiled. "We've been pleased with your work, Mrs. Walters. Some in the community were hesitant when we appointed you, given your lack of work experience. I realize your years away from the work force gave you a disadvantage, but you've proven yourself a capable town manager. I see big things in your future. Big things. Perhaps even a state appointment."

Kate remained calm outwardly, but inside she was screaming

with excitement. Mr. Samuels was the selectman she'd been most concerned about when she accepted this position. He was from the old school and believed women weren't cut out for jobs in politics. To hear such praise from him was a boost to her ego. . . and to her career.

Yet as she walked toward her office, she wondered what his opinion would be when he discovered she was going to have another child. He'd made no bones about the fact that it was only because her boys were older that he'd even given consideration to a working mother. Would he now expect her to step down because of this baby?

Worry suddenly flooded her as she realized even her career might be in jeopardy.

~∞~

"Kate?"

She opened her eyes and saw David hovering over her as she lay on the sofa in her office. His worried expression spoke volumes. "Kate, are you okay?"

She sat up and he sat down beside her. "I'm not feeling well today."

He took her hand and squeezed it. "I think you should see a doctor."

She pushed his hand away and stood. "I'm fine. I'm tired, that's all." She got up and moved to her desk, but her hands were shaking as she slipped on her glasses and tried to concentrate on the papers in front of her.

David leaned over the desk. "I have a difficult time believing that. You've been working too hard on this live nativity. You're worn out."

She smiled. "You're right. I have been working too hard. That's why I've been trying to delegate to Myles and others. I suppose I'm finally beginning to believe I can't do it all."

He gave her a wry grin. "That's not the Kate Walters I know. She would never admit such defeat."

"I'm trying to think of it more as macro-management." The phone on her desk rang, and she reached to answer it then stopped and looked at David. "I should probably get this."

"Delegate it."

"It might be important."

"Kate, you just said that you need to delegate more. You don't have to handle everything yourself." He went to the closet and retrieved her coat. "Come on, I'm taking you home. You're taking the rest of the day off."

She hesitated, thinking of all the things she needed to handle. . .important things. But when she glanced up at the determination on her husband's face, she relented. It felt good to let him take charge, and she realized she'd missed letting him take the lead. Why did she always have to be such a control freak? She grinned, wondering what kind of politician she'd be if she weren't a control freak. What kind of wife or mom?

"What's so funny?" David asked, noticing her smile.

"I was thinking of arguing with you, then I realized how silly it would be to resist."

"I only want what's best for you, Kate."

"I know that, David. You've always taken good care of me. Sometimes I forget to be appreciative of how well you look after me and our boys."

His face lit up at her praise; then a bewildered look crossed his face and he laughed. "Who are you? And what have you done with my wife?"

Truly, what she wanted to do was fall into his arms and allow him to smother her with his warmth and kindness.

"I'll go get the car. Meet me downstairs in five minutes."

She nodded her agreement and watched him walk out.

She touched her hand to her stomach and marveled that something so small at this stage could make her so sick. And David was being so kind. The thought of upsetting this temporary truce between them bothered her, but she knew she had to tell him about the baby soon. Today was the day he would get the news that their lives would change forever.

She took a deep breath and slipped into her coat. She wrapped her scarf around her neck and headed out, giving Lisa a list of directives for calls and issues that might come up.

She walked down the steps of the courthouse and saw David's car pull up. He got out and walked around, opening the door for her and helping her onto the seat.

Today was the day. He had to know.

Lord, please let him be happy about this baby.

Chapter 6

David decided to do a few chores around the house while Kate napped. He was still in awe that she'd heeded his advice and left work. And she'd actually seemed pleased at this intervention and his concern. He settled her on the sofa in the living room with a blanket and a cup of hot tea. All he wanted was what was best for her. Was she finally starting to see that? He couldn't even pinpoint the moment when Kate had stopped looking to him for advice or support. Was it before she'd dipped her foot into politics and taken on the role of town manager? He'd certainly had no input in that decision, and while he wouldn't have stopped her from pursuing it, it would have been nice to have his opinion considered.

He walked out to the garage and saw John's car parked there. It was a good time to perform some maintenance on it before John returned to school. He was only home for the weekend and would make the two-hour drive back to campus tomorrow.

David slid into the driver's seat and started the engine, noticing as he did an envelope with what looked like a court seal tossed on the passenger seat. He picked it up and saw it was from the Franklin County District Court. The envelope was open, so he pulled out the letter. It was a summons for John to appear at court in January.

Why was John being summoned before a judge? David scanned the letter and found the charge listed at the bottom—shoplifting, a class E offense that could result in a $1,000 fine or up to six months in jail.

He gut clenched. John was being accused of shoplifting?

When?

Where?

And why hadn't his son told him?

David stuffed the letter into his pocket then continued checking John's car, but his thoughts were completely occupied by the situation with his son. John was in trouble and hadn't told them. That bothered him more than anything. He was certain the charge itself was a mistake. John was a good kid, and he had no need to shoplift. If he needed something, he knew all he had to do was ask.

David closed the car hood and headed back inside.

He didn't know what was going on with his son, but he was going to find out.

He poured himself a cup of coffee and stood out on the deck watching the sky as a gentle snow began to fall. Maine in winter was beautiful but could be brutal. A gentle snow could quickly become a thick blanket. He made a mental note to check their emergency supplies in case of a power outage.

Kate fidgeted on the sofa, and David walked back inside.

He knelt beside her. "Are you warm enough?"

"I'm fine, David. Thank you for taking care of me."

As she reached for her cup of tea, he saw her phone.

"Would you like me to put that on the charger for you?"

She shook her head. "Nope. I'm not going to need it." She picked it up and turned it off.

His eyes widened. "Are you certain this town can survive without you for a day?"

"They'll have to." She reached for his hand. "I have an idea. Let's put up the Christmas tree."

They had a tradition of waiting until a few days before Christmas, but he couldn't deny the enthusiasm in her face. . . or the fact that she was choosing to spend time with him over going back to work.

"That's sounds like a great idea."

He made certain she was warm enough as they piled into her SUV. He drove to the Christmas tree lot on the highway, and Kate picked out a large, full evergreen.

They managed to get it inside, and after much effort, the tree was in place in front of the big living room windows. Kate rummaged through the storage room and found the decorations, and together they went through them.

Kate ooh'd and ahh'd over each ornament the boys had made in their younger days, and David enjoyed the trip down memory lane. This might be the last year they would celebrate Christmas in the house, and this seemed a nice send-off.

He watched his wife in her socks and flannels as she reached to hang a handprint ornament Keith had made in second grade. She glowed with happiness. She curled up beside him on the sofa and leaned back into his arms, and they sat in silence for a while, watching the lights on the tree. He savored the moment, basking in the knowledge that she chose to be here with him.

"We've shared a lot of Christmases in this house, haven't we?" she asked.

"Yes, we have."

"Do you remember that year we bought both boys bicycles and we had to stay up all night trying to put them together?"

He laughed at the memory. The boys had been young then, only six and nine, and the store had wanted to charge thirty dollars a bike to put them together. Money had been scarce then and David had insisted on doing it himself. He'd finally finished around three Christmas morning. But it had been worth the effort when he'd seen the way his boys' eyes had lit up at seeing their brand-new bikes.

They were good memories, but he was thankful they weren't still at that point in their lives. "Can you imagine us staying up all night putting together bikes now?"

"It might be fun to do those things again."

"Are you kidding? I'm happy those days are behind us. You know, Mike dropped a bomb on me the other day. Tina's pregnant."

"Really?"

"Can you believe it? Starting over at their age? All I can say is I'm glad it's them and not us."

"Would it be so bad if it were us, David?"

"Are you joking? It would be the worst. Diapers, homework, adolescence. I'm not certain I could handle it all again."

She seemed to stiffen, and he realized his words sounded harsh. She was in a nostalgic mood, and although this had been an incredible day together, he suddenly wished they'd never taken this trip down memory lane.

He remembered the tickets in his pocket. Perhaps this was the perfect time.

"Besides, Kate, we're at the best time in our lives." He reached for his coat and pulled out the tickets. "Here," he said, handing them to her.

"What's this?"

"It's an early Christmas present for you."

Surprise covered her face when she realized what they were.

"They're tickets for a cruise next August. Isn't it great? Two weeks alone, just you and me. Won't that be wonderful?"

She stared up at him, tears wetting her brown eyes. "David, I—"

"You like them, don't you, Kate? We've always talked about doing this when the boys were older. Now's our chance."

"It's just that I'm not sure August is going to be a good month for me to get away."

"Why not?"

She took a deep breath. "There's something I need to tell you. David, I'm—"

The front door burst open and the boys rushed into the house, their noise cutting off whatever she was going to say.

"Cool," Keith said, looking at the decorations. "The tree looks awesome."

David asked about their night out, and Keith gave them a play-by-play of the basketball game they'd attended at the high school.

David motioned to John then reached for his coat. "Can I talk to you outside?" John followed him to the garage, and David pulled the letter from his pocket. "What is the meaning of this?"

John shrank back. "Where did you get that?"

"I found it in your car."

"You went through my car? Dad, that's not cool."

"John, it says you've been charged with shoplifting. What happened?"

John shrugged as if it were no big deal, but David could see the worry clouding his eyes. "I needed another pair of sneakers."

"Your mother bought you a pair when school started."

"They tore. I needed new ones, and I didn't have the money to pay for them."

"So you stole them?" He ran a hand through his hair, exasperated. "John, why didn't you call us?"

"I didn't want to bother you. You and Mom give me so much already. I didn't want to have to ask for more money for new shoes."

"John, you got arrested, and you still didn't call us. We're your parents. You can always talk to us, especially when you get into trouble."

"I'm sorry I didn't tell you sooner. And I'm sorry I took the shoes. I'll never do it again. Believe me, I learned my lesson."

David saw the anxiety in his young son's face. "We're not through discussing this, John, but you don't have to handle this alone. I'll drive up and make the court date with you."

"Thanks, Dad."

David hugged his son, and John walked back into the house.

It struck David that John needed him more than he'd realized. John might be in college, but that didn't make him grown. David was suddenly unsure how long it would be before he could ever stop worrying about his boys. Keith would be coming right alongside John next year, making his own bad decisions.

He would be more diligent about checking in on both boys from now on.

Chapter 7

Bethlehem Café had a rooftop deck that overlooked the bay. During the summer months, it was a wonderful place to sit outside and enjoy the Maine coastline, but during winter, Kate preferred the inside tables with the patio view.

Because of the early afternoon hour, the dining room was deserted, and Kate prayed it stayed that way. She needed some time alone to talk to David. . .assuming he showed up at all. She checked her watch. He was already ten minutes late. Had he gotten her text about meeting for lunch?

She should have just told him yesterday before the boys arrived home. Why had she hesitated? He'd given her the perfect opening. Why hadn't she just said the words?

I can't go on a cruise in August, David, because I'm going to be having a baby.

Why was it so hard to get those words past her lips?

She paced the floor, practicing how she would tell him her news. She wanted to soften the surprise, but she also wanted to let him know she was happy about having this child. She wanted to remind him that children were a blessing, a gift from God, even though she was certain he wouldn't feel that way in the beginning.

Murmurings downstairs alerted her attention. She heard someone call David's name, then his heavy footsteps on the stairs let her know he was on his way.

She'd arranged for a picnic-style lunch, complete with Italian subs and hot bowls of the soup of the day.

His gaze roamed the empty room and the arranged meal as he entered. "What's the special occasion?"

"Well, I was thinking about what you said the other day and decided you're right. I have been spending too much time focusing on this nativity and not enough time focusing on us." She motioned him toward a chair then took the one opposite it.

He sat down then reached for her hand across the table. "I know the nativity is important, Kate. I suppose I was feeling a little neglected. It seems as if things have been off with us recently. You seem so far away. That's why yesterday was so nice. I felt like you needed me again."

"I do need you, David. I don't mean to shut you out." She squeezed his hand reassuringly. She needed him to know how important he was to her. She would need him now more than ever. "I've been under a great deal of pressure lately. I suppose I've allowed my priorities to get messed up." She stared out at the ocean view, trying to summon her courage to tell him about the baby. "Do you remember when the boys were younger and we would take them to the ocean and they would run along the beach, looking for seashells?"

He smiled. . .a good sign. "It's hard to believe they were ever that small, isn't it? They've grown into fine young men."

"Yes, they have. We did a good job, didn't we, David?"

"I think we did." He sighed. "I confess, there were days when I wondered if we would make it. It was a long, hard struggle to get here."

She frowned. "It wasn't always a struggle. We had good times, too."

"Of course. That wasn't what I meant. I don't regret one moment of our life together. I only meant that it took us a long time to get here, to where we have a life more than kids. Do you remember the plans we used to make while we sat on those rocks and looked out at the ocean? We were going to sail away together one day, just the two of us, once the boys were grown. We're finally there, Kate. We can finally make that dream a reality." He reached into his coat, pulled out a folded picture, and handed it to her.

It was a picture of a sailboat.

"I spoke to the man selling this, and he's agreed to let me take it out on the water."

She was surprised by this turn of conversation. How had they gotten off her topic? "You want to buy a boat?"

"Yes." He reached out and took her hand again. "Think about it, Kate. You and me alone in the middle of the ocean. We could sail down the coastline when the weather here is bad then head back for the summer months."

"David, I have responsibilities here. I'm the town manager—a job I worked very hard to get."

"You don't have to work anymore, Kate."

"I love my job. I love politics. I would even like to go on to hold bigger offices, possibly even a state office."

"But our dream of sailing away. . ."

"We were kids. Dreams change, David. Plans change. No one still wants the same things they wanted when they were younger."

His face hardened at her words. "When you were younger, you wanted me. Has that changed, too, Kate?"

"David, no. You're my husband. Of course I still want you."

"I'm tired of playing second fiddle to everything else in your life—your job, the kids, the town. When does it get to be just us, Kate?"

She closed her eyes, wondering how to respond to that question. This baby meant it wouldn't be just them for a long, long while. But how could she tell him that?

She was still wondering when he got up and walked out.

∞

Kate ran into Tina Purvis in the church parking lot as they arrived for the nativity. Kate gave her a hug and greeted each of the kids.

"David told me about the baby. Congratulations. I'm so happy for you."

"Thank you. It was unexpected, but a nice surprise. I don't think David was too pleased with the news, however. I'm only sorry this upsets yours and David's plans to retire."

Kate laughed. "Retire? We're not retiring."

"Oh. . .well, Mike said David offered to let Mike buy him out of the agency."

Kate was stunned. They had never discussed retiring so soon. It seemed they hadn't been discussing a lot of things these days.

"I only hope if he finds someone else to buy him out that it will be someone who won't run it into the ground. They've worked so well together all these years, and it will be difficult to transition to partnering with someone else."

Kate nodded, reeling. David had been doing a lot of talking about looking forward to being able to travel, but she hadn't been aware before today that he was making retirement plans. First he was shopping for boats, and now he'd actually approached Mike about selling his share of the business?

What else had he done without consulting her?

She rubbed her stomach, realizing she'd been making plans of her own and hadn't yet shared them.

∞

Kate spotted David in the fellowship hall and was surprised to find him holding their friends' sixteen-month-old daughter. He was doing the tickle monster with her, and she was laughing and wiggling in his arms. It warmed Kate to see such a display and, more importantly, to see the enjoyment on David's face.

"Hi there, you two." She touched the little one's foot and soaked in the softness and the smallness of it. This would be their child in a couple of years. Would David be here, holding their child and playing tickle monster? And would she see the same enjoyment on his face as she did today with this child?

Kate smiled at him. "You're a natural with kids."

"It's easy to enjoy them when I know I can hand them back to their parents." He said it jokingly, but Kate felt the sting of his words.

"David, about this afternoon. . ." She hadn't seen him since the argument at the café, and she'd never gotten the chance to tell him about the baby as she'd planned. "There was something specific I wanted to tell you. Can we talk tonight after the nativity?"

The baby's mother came, and David handed her over. "I can't. I'm driving to Portland tonight to bring the boat back. I'm taking it out on the water tomorrow."

"You're still planning to buy that boat? I can't believe you would make that big of a decision without discussing it with me further first."

"I'm starting to realize that we've both been making decisions without consulting the other. When was the last time we agreed on anything, Kate?"

He marched past her toward the dining hall, where the church had provided a hot meal before the nativity. The tension between them was palpable, and she was certain others must feel it.

She spotted Mr. Samuels and his wife entering the fellowship hall and rushed over to assure him that everything was running smoothly again tonight.

"I hope you hired more officers to control the traffic," he grumbled. "Last weekend's traffic was terrible, and with the exposure we're getting throughout the state, I expect we'll see larger crowds tonight."

Kate was a little disheartened that the easygoing spirit of their last conversation had disappeared. She assured him it was taken care of, but truthfully, she had no idea what had been done to address the traffic issue. She scanned the hall for Myles and called him over.

"Mr. Samuels would like to know about the traffic situation," she said, and Myles jumped to the task, giving an outline of the newest measures they'd taken.

Mr. Samuels nodded but did not look pleased with the update. He marched away, tugging his wife behind him. Myles glanced at Kate, and she assured him that everything was fine before he rushed away.

She was perplexed. Myles was doing a wonderful job of staying on top of things. Kate didn't understand what reason Mr. Samuels would have to be upset, but she was certain she would hear about it from the selectmen.

As Kate entered the dining hall, she saw David seated at a table with several of their friends, including Mike and Tina. She fixed herself a plate then took the seat beside him. David dug into his meal, but Kate picked at her food then pushed her plate away.

"What's the matter, Kate? Don't you like the shrimp?" Mike asked.

"I'm just feeling a little sick."

"Tina couldn't eat much either. I thought each pregnancy was supposed to be different, but every time, all fried foods made her sick."

"And this pregnancy will be no exception," Tina said, laughing. "Just thinking about those onion rings is making me feel ill."

"Kate's was shrimp," David said. "With both boys, she wasn't able to eat it. But afterward, she devoured it."

"Well, she's not eating it now," Mike noticed. "What's the matter, Kate? Are you pregnant?"

David glanced down at her plate of untouched shrimp.

She could see his mind working, putting the pieces together, until the truth dawned on him. He stared at her, his eyes wide. She nodded.

Mike seemed to realize his comment had hit a sensitive spot, and he backed off. Tina, however, threw her arms around Kate. "Congratulations! We'll be pregnant together."

David pushed his chair back from the table, tossed down his napkin, and walked off. Kate rushed to follow him.

"This isn't how I meant for you to find out. I tried to tell you, several times, but you kept talking about how you were glad it was Mike and Tina and not us. I got scared, David." She caught at his arm. "Please, David. I'm very happy about this baby. I know it wasn't in our plans, but it is a blessing. We're going to have another baby. When I look at John and Keith and how well they're growing up, it makes me proud. I know it won't be easy, but we can do this. . .together."

He turned to face her, his eyes full of confusion and anger. "You should have told me sooner, Kate."

"I know. I tried. Stuff just kept getting in the way."

"Stuff has a way of doing that with us, doesn't it?" He stared down at her. "Why were you afraid to tell me?"

"I don't know. You've been dreaming about sailing away from here for years."

"I'm not going to abandon you, Kate."

"I don't want you to. I want you to stay. . .but I want you to stay because you want to, not because you feel some sort of obligation to me and this child."

"But I do have an obligation to you and this child. I can't ignore that." He ran a hand through his hair. "I thought we had our life planned out. I thought we both wanted to get away, to travel, to spend time alone together."

"That was always your dream, David. I love this town. I love my job. And I can't think of any better place to raise this baby than right here in Bethlehem, in our home."

Tears slipped down her face. This wasn't how she'd hoped this confrontation would go. "This doesn't have to change us, David."

"Something has to change with us, Kate, because I can't continue living this way. This is just one more thing to come between us."

He walked out, letting the door slam behind him. Kate didn't follow him. He needed to come to terms with the shock of this news. She knew David. He would do his duty to her and this child. . .but she also knew she wanted more from him than just duty.

⊗

David unlocked the door to his office then locked it behind him. He didn't bother turning on the overhead lights but chose instead to switch on the desk lamp. He didn't need to advertise that he was here to anyone who happened to drive by. He needed to be alone right now. He needed the peace and quiet to sort through the bombshell he'd just been handed.

He was going to be a father again.

He pulled his hands through his hair and fell onto the couch. This wasn't the plan. This wasn't where he'd imagined his life would go. He had plans for the future, plans to travel and enjoy life together—just him and Kate. They'd not had that since those very early few months of marriage. After learning about John's pending arrival, their lives had become focused on children, preparing for, providing for, caring for.

He stared at the photographs lining the walls of his office. He was proud of his boys. . .but was he ready to do it again? He wasn't sure he had the strength to go through all that again with another child.

Yet it no longer mattered what he wanted or whether or not he had the strength. A child had been created, and he was a father again. He would never leave Kate to raise it alone so he could selfishly go off and live his dream.

His phone beeped. He checked it and saw a message from Myles, wanting to know where he was.

He responded that he was on his way.

He'd never been the kind of man to duck out on his responsibilities. . .whether that meant playing the role of Joseph in the live nativity, or playing the role of daddy again.

He would do his duty to the best of his ability.

He made it back to the church in time to don his costume and meet Kate at Bethlehem Green. Her eyes pleaded with him to talk to her, but now was not the time for conversation. He wasn't yet sure he could deal with this, or what he could possibly say to make things right between them.

The time came for Kate to take the baby in her arms. David played his role, longing for the moment when he could find peace and quiet and time to think about how his world had been turned upside down.

But when he saw Kate, he felt a sting in his already open wound. He knew it was just a role, but to see her holding a baby only served to remind him of what lay in store. Diapers, nighttime feedings, years and years of money and commitments and doing his Christian duty to raise another child.

Kate had said she'd been afraid to tell him. Afraid of him? She had to know he would do his duty as this child's father.

The baby in her arms began to cry and Kate stroked his cheek. How many times had he seen her do that to their boys? How many times had she comforted a crying child?

He watched her now. She was so beautiful, and the child in her arms only added to her glow. She was a good mother—kind and gentle, generous and firm, training her children to love the

Lord with all their hearts and souls.

Still he held on tightly to his resentment. What would happen to them now? Would he have to work long hours, trying to juggle work and home and family?

Kate's odd behavior of late all made sense now. She'd been tired and irritable. She'd cried when he talked about taking the trip next year. . .and she'd been talking about how blessed Mike and Tina were to be having another child. She wasn't upset about Keith going away to college. She'd been afraid to tell him they were going to have another child.

Was this how Joseph felt when Mary broke the news to him about the baby Jesus? Had he felt the same betrayal, the same anger and resentment? He'd surely had plans of his own that didn't include a baby to raise that wasn't his, but he'd been able to let go of his bitterness and accept God's plan in his life. Could David do the same? In his heart, he knew God's plans were good. . .but at the moment, that didn't help him feel any better about the situation.

Chapter 8

Kate was heating up a cup of tea when she heard the garage door open and close. She held her breath, wondering if David had changed his mind about going to Portland. Had the news of the baby changed his decision to purchase the boat? A part of her had been surprised to see him jump into his truck after the nativity ended and head off. She had hoped they could talk now that he knew the truth.

Instead of David, the boys sauntered into the house. From the expressions on their faces and the way they stared at her, Kate suspected they had heard her news.

Keith confronted her. "Is it true? Are you having a baby?"

She stared at both her boys, so young, so confused about this new chapter in their lives. How she wished she had handled this differently and told them herself. She nodded. "Yes, it's true. I am pregnant."

She could see Keith struggling to wrap his mind around the idea. "That's so..."

"Weird," John finished for him, leaning against the back of a chair.

Keith nodded. "Weird."

"I know it's a shock, boys. It was for me, too. But this baby is a blessing. Everything will be fine."

"I overheard Mrs. Mitchell say women your age have a greater chance of having a baby with a birth defect. Is that true, Mom?"

Kate was shocked that Irene Mitchell would bring up such a subject with her boys around. But she sighed, realizing she shouldn't have been surprised they were being gossiped about. Everyone in the church had to have overheard her and David's conversation.

But when she saw the worry in Keith's face, she knew she had to address this topic. "It is a possibility, but not a certainty." She reached for Keith, gave him a reassuring hug, then looked at John. "Regardless, whatever difficulties this pregnancy may bring, we'll face them as a family."

John nodded. "You're right. Everything will be great."

Keith nodded his agreement as well, although he didn't seem quite convinced.

"Where's Dad? I want to congratulate him, too."

"Your father has gone to Portland to look at a boat. He'll get back late—it'd probably be best if you talk to him tomorrow."

The boys said their goodnights then headed to their rooms. Once the house was quiet again, Kate carried her tea to the table and opened her Bible. If she'd ever needed the reassurance that God had plans for her life, she needed it now. Tomorrow she would face the townspeople with their probing eyes and questions, but she would also face her husband and his doubts. Could he overcome them and be happy about this baby? She prayed he could. She wanted more for her family than a reluctant husband and father.

∞

The next morning, Kate responded to a summons from the selectmen wanting to meet her at her office as soon as possible. She dreaded what the meeting could be about, but she quickly dressed and headed downtown.

Lisa was already there. "They're waiting inside your office."

"Why are they here?"

"I'm afraid the word is out that you're pregnant."

"Even Mr. Samuels heard it already?"

"The scene between you and David at the church is all over town. This news is spreading like wildfire, and Mr. Samuels was not happy when he heard it."

"What business is it of his?"

"Oh you know him, Kate. He thinks everything is his business."

She nodded and thanked Lisa for the heads up. It was time to face this. She put on her best professional manner and walked into her office. "Good morning, gentlemen. What can I do for you?"

Murray Samuels was seated on her sofa. He motioned for Alex Littlejohn to do the talking.

"We have some concerns about how you've been handling the nativity. It seems you've been delegating a lot of responsibility to

Myles Sandford lately. We were under the impression that you were heading up this project. After all, it was your idea. You sold the idea to the town. Now it seems you've handed over the reins to Myles."

"Myles is perfectly capable of—"

"We didn't appoint Myles town manager," Mr. Samuels interrupted. "We gave that appointment to you."

"I realize that, but part of my job is to delegate, and that's what I've been doing. Part of being a good manager is to hire competent people and give them the opportunity to do their jobs."

Mr. Littlejohn nodded. "We understand some delegation is necessary, however it's our responsibility to make certain the town's best interests are being represented."

Kate was tired of tiptoeing around the truth and decided to confront them about the real issue. "This isn't really about my delegating duties, is it? You've learned that I'm expecting another child and you're concerned I can't handle the responsibilities of the office."

"Don't be ridiculous," Mr. Patterson said. "Our concern is that—"

"Can you?" Mr. Samuels stood.

She faced him. "I absolutely can. I've already raised two children."

"Your job performance over the past few weeks would seem to indicate differently. I've had calls about this issue. People are concerned, Mrs. Walters. They're concerned about their town."

Mr. Littlejohn strode toward the door. "We've called a town meeting for tonight to discuss this. We'll make our determination afterwards."

Lisa rushed in as the three men left. Her face was stricken with worry. "Kate, I'm so sorry. Should we call an attorney? This isn't the nineteenth century. They can't just boot you out because you're an expectant mother."

She could contact a lawyer and fight this in court, but dragging her town through a lengthy legal battle was not what she wanted.

She sat on the sofa and dropped her head in her hands. She was now in danger of losing her job.

This was not in her plans.

But her plans no longer mattered. Was this God's way of telling her that it was time to step down as town manager? She'd allowed this job to become so important to her—too important. She'd placed her duties here above her husband to the point that he no longer felt like he mattered in her life. That had never been her intention.

David's plans had to change because of this pregnancy. Wasn't it only sensible that hers had to change as well?

∞

David turned the boat toward the bay and headed out into open waters. He was still reeling from his conversation with Kate. Not that he had any real thoughts of taking off and leaving her to raise this child alone. He only needed to get away to clear his head and deal with the emotions that sat lodged in his gut. So much for his plans. So much for sailing away together. So much for time alone with Kate.

He drifted, enjoying the sway of the boat and the silence on the open water to sort through his emotions. Another child would alter their lives in ways he couldn't even imagine. He wasn't sure he had the strength to go through it all again. He wasn't sure he could shoulder the responsibility.

He thought of John and Keith. John had proven he was still in need of guidance with the shoplifting issue. And Keith was right behind him, waiting to go off to college. Who knew what choices he would make? David needed to be there to watch over them. He knew that. It wasn't as if he were planning to abandon them. He only wanted some time alone with his wife. Was that so wrong? He was tired of making plans only to have them changed or complicated by others' needs. He wasn't certain he could do it for another twenty to thirty years with a third child.

But what choice did he have? He was going to be a father again.

A thick fog rolled in, pulling David's attention squarely back to where he was. He turned on the onboard lights, but visibility was low. Then he switched on the electronic navigation, only to find it going haywire. He'd been too distracted by Kate's news to make certain all the systems worked before he'd launched.

Time had gotten away from him, and he had no idea how long he'd been gone or how far out he'd gotten. He searched the distance for any evidence of harbor lights, but between the fog and the darkness of night settling in, he couldn't even tell which way the shore was. He pulled out his phone and checked for a signal. Nothing. He was on his own, in a dire situation. If he drifted the wrong way, he could float out to sea. He needed to find that shoreline.

Suddenly, all the things he would be leaving behind flowed through his mind at the thought that something might happen to him. Who would watch out for John and Keith during their college years? Who would make certain they grew into the godly men he knew they could be? And what about Kate? Left to raise a baby on her own? How would she handle being a single mom?

He didn't want her to have to try.

He should have been thinking about his family instead of pouting like a child and storming off. He'd been thinking only of his own selfish plans, made a reckless choice, and placed himself in danger.

Lord, please help me find my way back to my family.

In the distance, he spotted a flicker of light. He aimed the boat toward it. As the fog moved, he didn't panic but kept moving forward in the direction he'd seen the light. He had no idea whether he was moving toward shore or away from it. Perhaps he'd only seen the light of a ship on the open water, but he had to take that chance. He had to try to reach shore. His family needed him. . .and he needed them.

As the clouds moved again, the light of the moon helped him to see the shoreline. He was headed in the right direction! He was going to make it home.

As he looked toward the shore, he saw a light high in the

night sky. He aimed the boat toward it. The closer he got, the thinner the fog got, and he could see the lights of the shore.

He finally docked safely and tied up the boat. He ran to his car, driving in the direction of the light, until it led him to Bethlehem Green. Then he realized which light he had been following—the glow of the nativity star, the star high in the night sky that led him toward. . .Jesus. . .and home.

What had Mike said to him that day in his office? Our plans aren't God's plans, but God's plans are always good.

David parked and ran to the manger, staring up at the star, his breath nearly gone and his heart racing, and his hands freezing from the cold. In the nativity story, God had used a star to lead the wise men to Jesus. . .and He'd used this star to lead David here, to the manger, to Jesus, to the baby, to the gift of God's love.

"Thank You, Lord."

Bill Mitchell appeared from behind the set and greeted him. "David, what are you doing out here?"

"I was looking at the star. Does it seem brighter to you?"

Bill looked up then shook his head. "It looks the same to me, although I did just replace the bulb."

With his breath finally beginning to return, David noticed how empty the street was. "Where is everyone?"

"Didn't you hear? The selectmen called an emergency town meeting. They're voting on whether or not to let Kate keep her position as town manager."

"What? Why?"

"Murray Samuels doesn't believe she can do her job if she's going to have a baby."

David shook his head. "That's ridiculous. If anyone can do it, my wife can."

"Well, they're meeting right now."

David turned and took off toward the courthouse.

It was time to take a stand. . .and he would proudly stand with his wife.

Chapter 9

Kate glared at Mr. Samuels. Why did he always have to make things so difficult for everyone? She couldn't win with him. Either delegating was a good idea or it wasn't—he couldn't have it both ways. Now she was on trial for doing her job and doing it well.

Was it God's will for her to give up her job? Was that why she'd been given this child? She still had no clear direction about what she should do. She knew how David felt—he'd made his resentment about her divided attention crystal clear. Should she fight for her job or quietly step down? *God, I need Your intervention here!*

She turned in her chair and saw John and Keith heading toward her. John took a seat beside her and gave her hand a reassuring squeeze. He was always so supportive.

"You've been a terrific town manager," he said. "They'd be crazy to dismiss you." Keith took her other hand. "Whatever they decide, Mom, we're here for you."

She was thankful for the support of her children, but what she'd really hoped for was the support of their father. She stared back at the door, praying he would walk through it, take her into his arms, and reassure her that everything would be fine. She hadn't seen or heard from him all day, and she'd worried more about that than about this mock trial.

What if he'd decided he couldn't handle the pressure and had sailed away without her? As ridiculous as she knew that fear to be, she couldn't stop thinking of the possibility and wondering how she could raise this child without him.

Mr. Littlejohn called the meeting to order and spoke for the selectmen. "Our one and only piece of business is to discuss our current town manager, Kate Walters. Would you come up here please, Mrs. Walters?"

Kate got up and stood in front of them. Her life, her future, her career, was in God's hands.

"We've looked over the preliminary numbers for the live nativity, and I don't believe anyone in this room could argue that it was anything but a success, even though we won't have official numbers for several weeks. This project was your idea, and we gave you complete authority over it. However, there has been some concern on the board"—he glanced toward Mr. Samuels—"and among the townspeople about your ability to continue to perform at this level, given your current condition."

Kate straightened to her full height. "I won't lie. I share some of those doubts, but I've loved watching this community come together to put on this nativity. It is one of the single greatest achievements of my life."

Mr. Samuels eyed her. "But how can you possibly give this

town the attention it needs and raise a child?"

John leaped from his chair. "She won't be alone. She'll have me."

Keith stood. "And me."

Kate marveled at her sons' dedication, and she appreciated their standing up for her.

"And she'll have me."

Kate's breath caught at the voice that echoed around the room.

David!

She turned to see her husband walking down the aisle of the courtroom. She couldn't stop the smile that broke out as he approached her. "I'm glad you're here."

He nodded. "Me too. This is where I belong." He glanced over at the boys then touched her stomach. "With my family." He pulled her into his arms. "Kate, there is no place I would rather be than in Bethlehem, with you. You were right. We belong here. And I won't see Murray Samuels run you out of a job you love."

He turned and addressed the council.

"You all know that I've grown a business in this town. Well, I didn't do it on my own. Along with my business partner, Mike Purvis, I had Kate helping me. She devoted her life to caring for our family while I pursued my plans, my dreams. And she did an amazing job raising our children. Now, it's my turn to do the same for her. She's devoted her blood, sweat, and tears to managing this town because she loves it. This is our home, the place where we've raised a family, built a life. No one knows better than I do the sacrifices Kate is willing to make for this town. Now, if you're unhappy with her work, with this live nativity and all the exposure and tourist money it's brought to our little town, that's one thing, but don't penalize her for something she hasn't done. She's the best town manager Bethlehem has seen in a long while."

Cheers and applause rang out. Kate knew she should be paying attention to the selectmen, to their responses, but all she cared about at the moment was David's presence. He'd come for her and stood up for her. Her David, so strong and loyal.

God had truly made His plans known.

⁓

Meet me on the boat.

The note David had left her that morning had Kate worried. Had he changed his mind and decided to buy the boat after all? He'd saved her job, and she'd believed everything was fine between them. . .then she'd awakened to find him gone and this cryptic note.

She walked toward the pier and found the boat. David helped her aboard. "It's a very nice boat," she told him, feeling like she should say something positive.

"It is a nice boat, but it's not mine. I didn't buy it, Kate."

"You didn't?"

"No."

"But your dream. . ."

"My dream wasn't about sailing away. It was about sailing

away with you. You're my dream, Kate. You've always been my dream. I suppose I'm selfish. I want you all to myself, but I can't have that, so I'll take you any way I can get you.

"I won't lie. I do feel an obligation to you and to the boys and to this baby. I would never abandon you. But more importantly, Kate, I don't *want* to abandon you. I've been worried that another baby meant going down the same road we've already traveled. But God is leading us down a new path, and I'm excited about it. It won't be like it was, because we're not like we were. Our situation is different. This child is different. I want to be there for this baby in a way I was never there for John and Keith."

"You were a wonderful father to John and Keith."

"I spent so many years worrying about those boys. Worrying about providing for them. But now. . .things are so different for us, Kate. The house is paid for. The business is thriving. You're thriving. God has given me a wonderful gift. He's given me the gift of time. This child will have a father that's involved in his or her life. And speaking of gifts, I have one for you." He took her hand and led her downstairs into the cabin.

Kate gasped when she saw a beautiful wooden cradle sitting in the middle of the room.

David wrapped his arms around her and pulled her tight. "I returned the cruise tickets and bought this instead."

"It's beautiful."

"And I was thinking, if we added on to the porch outside our room, we could build a nice nursery."

"I would love that, David."

"Kate, would you have a baby with me?"

She smiled and nestled herself into his embrace. "I would love to have a baby with you, David."

A CHRISTMAS PROMISE

By Sandra Robbins

Chapter 1

Bethlehem, Maine, no longer existed. Not in the way Emma Townsend had always known it. At least that's what she understood from listening to the town manager and the three selectmen for the last half hour as they outlined the plans emergency teams had put in place to tackle the cleanup and rebuilding of her hometown.

It had been years since a small tropical depression had developed into a powerful storm so late in the season and swept inland along the New England coastline. But that's exactly what happened a week ago when Hurricane Eleanor, a Category 2 storm with sustained winds of ninety-five miles per hour, roared ashore. Now the citizens of Bethlehem who hadn't sought refuge elsewhere sat quietly in the school gymnasium that had survived, and pondered the difficult task facing them.

Thankfully, no lives had been lost, but some of the shops and boutiques that lined Main Street had been blown away, and those left behind had suffered major roof damage. Some of the stately trees that lined peaceful streets had survived while others still lay tangled across the landscape like giant piles of pickup sticks. And fishing boats lay upside down in places where they'd never been before.

Now as Murray Samuels, the selectman who'd served the longest, stood behind a small lectern and continued his account of losses the town had incurred, the expressions on the faces of the townspeople grew more solemn. Mr. Samuels finished his speech and let his gaze drift over those in attendance.

"So, to sum up what I've just said, we have been declared a disaster area. That's why you've been seeing volunteers, along with emergency management personnel, coming in to help us get back on our feet. We're hoping electricity will be restored in a week, maybe two. Homes that are uninhabitable have already been identified, and we will keep the shelter open here in the high school and the one at Bethlehem Community Church for as long as they are needed. Thank goodness both buildings, as well as many of your homes, survived the storm. In fact, we should all be thankful that Eleanor weakened to a Category 2 storm before she came ashore. If she hadn't, most of us probably wouldn't be sitting here today." He stopped for a moment and took a deep breath. "Now I'll turn the meeting back over to Town Manager Kate Walters."

Kate rose from her chair and took her place at the lectern, gripping it with both hands and letting her gaze drift over the assembly. Lines of worry creased her face, and Emma frowned at how tired Kate looked. She could only imagine what the woman she admired so much had gone through ever since the weather forecasters had warned Eleanor's path had changed and was headed straight for Maine.

A weak smile pulled at Kate's lips as she brushed a strand of hair out of her eyes. "I want to thank our selectmen, who have worked so tirelessly ever since this emergency presented itself, and I want to thank you, the citizens of Bethlehem, for your dedication to your hometown. I'm sure if we all work together, we will soon have things back to normal around here. We ask for your patience until that happens. Now does anyone else have anything to add before we all get back to work cleaning up Hurricane Eleanor's mess?"

Michael Benson, better known to his congregation at Bethlehem Community Church as Pastor Mike, rose to his feet. "I'd like to say something, Ms. Walters."

"What is it, Pastor Mike?"

He rubbed his red-streaked eyes, and Emma's heart did that funny little skip it did every time she looked at her handsome unmarried pastor. She knew that he, too, had been working nearly around the clock with the volunteers who'd come to help, and he looked as if he were about to fall asleep on his feet.

Emma winced at the pained expression on his face. She wished she could put her arms around him and offer him some of the comfort he gave to his congregation all the time. Even though he was only a few years older than she was, and although she'd secretly hoped for months he'd ask her out, he'd never given her any reason to think she was special to him. In fact, he didn't treat her any differently than he did Mabel Harrison, who was eighty-five on her last birthday.

Pastor Mike cleared his throat. "This last week has been a real learning experience for me. I've watched TV coverage of hurricanes for years, but there's no way to understand it until you live through one."

Kate nodded. "I don't imagine they have many hurricanes in Illinois where you came from, but we've had our share around here." She paused and took a deep breath. "Those of us who've lived here all our lives know this is one of the hazards of being on the coast. I've seen hurricanes before, but I've never seen one like this so late in the season. Usually by October we breathe easier, knowing we've gotten by another year without a major storm."

Pastor Mike continued. "I know we have a lot to do before life gets back to normal in Bethlehem. But I have a question I think we'd all like to have answered today."

"What's that?"

"Like you said, this is the last of October. Christmas is only two months away. Ever since I arrived here, I've heard so much about the live nativity the town does that I could hardly wait to be a part of it this year. So, with all the storm damage, what are your plans for getting it ready?"

Kate looked in the direction of the three selectmen sitting at a table next to her. Two of them stared down at their hands clasped in front of them and remained silent, but Murray Samuels directed a steady gaze at her. When none of the three spoke, Kate sighed and turned back to face the assembled crowd. "I guess this is as good a time as any to tell you. We've decided to cancel the live nativity this year."

"What?" The word erupted all across the room, and several people jumped to their feet.

"You can't do that," John Roland yelled. "The live nativity has become a tradition in Bethlehem."

Kate shook her head, and Emma thought she saw a tear sparkle in the corner of her eye. "No one is more upset about this decision than I am. If you remember, I was the one who pushed for the nativity in the beginning. We have no choice, John. The building where the props were stored was blown away, and we have no idea where the contents ended up. Besides, we have other things to be concerned with. We don't need anything added to our worries right now."

Emma glanced at Pastor Mike. He looked as if he'd been punched in the stomach. She knew how much working with the nativity his first year in Bethlehem meant to him. He'd mentioned it often in his sermons. Before she realized it, she had jumped to her feet.

"Kate, please reconsider what you've said. The nativity may be just the thing this town needs to pull us back together. I know my girls' choir from the school will be upset if they don't get to perform the songs they've been practicing for weeks. And I'm sure I'm not the only one who's already been working to get ready."

Kate sighed and glanced at her fellow council members once more. "I'm sorry, Emma. Although the decision wasn't unanimous, the majority voted to cancel this year. At this point there's

CHRISTMAS COMES TO
BETHLEHEM, MAINE

nothing to be done about it." She took a deep breath. "There will be no live nativity in Bethlehem this year. Now it's time to close this meeting so all of us can get back to work cleaning up our town."

"But Kate," Emma shouted, but it was too late. Kate and the three selectmen had scurried out the side door of the building and disappeared from sight.

One by one the town residents began to walk from the room. Their slumped shoulders, grumbled comments about the town council's decision, and shuffling steps spoke volumes about how Hurricane Eleanor had affected their lives in the last week. An air of resigned doom seemed to hang in the air, and Emma brushed at the tears in her eyes.

She reached for her coat that hung on the back of her chair and was about to slip her arms in the sleeves when a voice interrupted her thoughts. "May I help you with that, Emma?"

Emma whirled around and gulped at the sight of Pastor Mike standing behind her. She swallowed the panic rising in her throat. "N-no, thanks. I've got it."

She pushed her arm in the sleeve of her coat, but somehow her fingers got tangled in the torn lining she'd been meaning to repair, and the coat wouldn't slide up her arm. Pastor Mike chuckled, reached behind her, and held the coat until she worked her fingers free and slipped the coat on. Then he stepped back and smiled. "There. That's better."

Her face burned, and she was sure her cheeks must have turned a bright red. With trembling fingers she buttoned the coat and tried to smile. "Thank you for your help."

He smiled again, and his blue eyes seemed to light up. "No problem. I can't have the star soloist in our church choir getting sick because she went out in the cold with her coat halfway on."

Emma's face grew warm. "I'm not the star soloist. I just like to sing."

He nodded. "I know. The joy music gives you is written on your face every time you sing."

Emma's mind raced for something to say, but it was as if her brain had suddenly shut down. She glanced around the room and realized they were the only two left. She swallowed and turned to leave. "There's nothing I enjoy more than singing God's praise. Now I think I'd better be going. I told Lucy Parker I'd come back to the church to help serve lunch to the people who are staying there. I'll see you later."

She turned and hurried out the front door but had only taken a few steps when Pastor Mike caught up with her. "I'm going there, too. I'll walk with you."

Emma hesitated a moment before she responded. Other than complimenting her on a solo she'd sung with the church choir, he'd never initiated any other type of conversation with her. What would she say to him all the way back to the church?

Come on, Emma, it's not like the guy's asking you for a date. You just happen to be going to the same place.

She shook her head and frowned. So much for thinking like a silly schoolgirl instead of a schoolteacher. Pastor Mike had no interest in her, and she needed to quit hoping he did.

As dedicated as he was to his ministry, it wouldn't be long before he'd be noticed by a larger church in some big city, and he would be gone. And she'd still be right here in Bethlehem, where she was born and raised.

Emma took a deep breath and smiled. "I'd love to have some company, but we'd better hurry. Lucy will be wondering where I am."

Her heart did that funny flip again when he returned her smile. "Then we'd better get going. I'd hate to be the one to cause a problem between two of our most dedicated church members."

His eyes danced from the teasing she heard in his voice, and for the first time since the hurricane roared ashore she felt some of the tension ease from her body. She glanced up at the sun beating down on the snow that had fallen last night and said a quick prayer of thanks for good weather after what they had endured. It was a perfect day for a walk in Bethlehem, and she couldn't think of anyone she'd rather share it with than Michael Benson.

Chapter 2

An hour later Mike stood in the church kitchen and stared across the filled tables in the fellowship hall. There seemed to be more people today than yesterday. At last count they'd had over a hundred people staying in the church, and more showed up every day. He said another quick prayer of thanks that God had spared their building so they could offer shelter to those whose homes had been destroyed or damaged in the storm.

As he glanced across the room, he caught sight of Emma Townsend moving between the tables, a coffeepot in her hands. She'd been one of the first on the scene after the storm moved inland, and she'd worked ever since to see that the refugees were fed and comfortable. He couldn't take his eyes off her as she poured coffee, all the time smiling and chatting with those who'd been displaced because of the storm.

As she bent over to fill an empty cup, her brown hair sparkled in the light coming through the window. His pulse raced, and he took a deep breath to slow his pounding heart. He'd felt an attraction to Emma since beginning his pastorate in Bethlehem, but he couldn't bring himself to ask her out. What would the congregation think about him dating a member of the church? The committee who hired him hadn't mentioned anything about that, but this was his first pastorate and he didn't want to do anything to jeopardize his position. Besides, he might not even like her if he got to know her. But still, there was something about her that drew him to her.

He groaned and raked his hand through his hair. Maybe his reaction to the pretty schoolteacher had something to do with how lonely he'd been since he arrived in Bethlehem. Not that the church members had ignored him. They'd been wonderful, but they all had their own families. And he'd spent a lot of time by himself.

Today when Emma jumped to her feet and asked about the nativity, he'd sensed they did indeed share some of the same ideas about the importance of certain things in life. That was what had given him the courage to ask if he could walk back with her to the church. Maybe the time had come to find out if they had other things in common.

She finished pouring coffee and started back to the kitchen, and he moved to intercept her. "Emma," he called out before she could exit the dining room.

She stopped and turned to face him. "Yes?"

For a moment he couldn't remember what he'd intended to say. His tongue seemed to have plastered itself to the roof of his mouth, and he couldn't speak. Not with the way she tilted her head and stared at him with just the hint of anticipation in her chocolate-colored eyes.

"Uh," he stammered, "I—I appreciate your help on catching me up on all the family connections in our church and in the town while we were walking back here. Even after six months, I haven't been able to figure out who's related. Now I think I have a better understanding."

"You're welcome. I was glad to do it. I know it's hard when you move to a new place to learn everybody's names and how they're connected. Not that I've ever had to do it. I've lived here all my life."

"It's wonderful to have roots like that," he said. "My family moved around a lot with my dad's job. I think it would be great to live in the same house all your life like you have."

She smiled and nodded. "Yes, it is. My grandfather built my house, and he always said it could withstand a Category 5 hurricane. Now I know it can make it through a Category 2, but I'd just as soon it not be tested any further." Her eyes darkened. "But I was sorry the house our church provided for you was lost to the storm. Maybe some of your belongings will be found during the cleanup."

"I keep hoping, but nothing yet. I guess I'll be staying in my office here for a while, but that's no problem. That old couch in there is comfortable enough."

Her eyebrows drew down across her nose. "I'm surprised you've slept any at all. It seems you've been working day and night for the last week."

"No more than everybody else. You've been busy yourself. I

appreciate all the work you've done here at the church to help the people displaced by the storm."

"It's been my pleasure." She smiled and glanced down at the coffeepot she still held. "And I'd better get back to work."

She turned to walk into the kitchen, but he reached out and caught her arm. "Emma, wait a minute. I wanted to talk to you about something else."

She glanced down at his hand on her arm, and he released his hold on her. "What is it?"

He cleared his throat and shifted his weight from one foot to the other. "I was just thinking about what you said at the meeting today."

A puzzled expression covered her face. "Oh? What did I say?"

"You know, that part about the nativity might be just the thing to pull this town back together again. Do you really believe that?"

She set the coffeepot on a table and nodded. "I do. I looked around the room, and everybody there seemed so sad, like they didn't know how to face what had happened. I thought maybe if we had a project like the nativity, we could work for a common cause. That could give us hope that no matter what we encounter, we can overcome it if we all work together."

He stared at her for a moment before he nodded. "I think you're right. I've been thinking about that ever since we left the meeting. Right now, I believe the most important thing we can do to give hope to our town and help us move past what's happened is by uniting everybody in putting on the live nativity."

Emma frowned. "But you heard what Kate and the selectmen said. They don't want to do it."

"I know. They have enough to do getting all the city services back up and running, not to mention removing all the debris and begin rebuilding. But what if our church took the nativity on as its project this year?"

Her eyes lit up, and she smiled. "You mean, do it ourselves?"

"Yes. What do you think?"

She was silent for a moment before she spoke. "I think it would be a big undertaking, but I know we could do it if we all gave of our time and worked together. But how can we get the town council to go along with this?"

"They can't decree what a church wants to do. If we decide to do a live nativity, they can't stop us. Besides, I don't think Kate would object. She seemed really upset that it had been canceled. The one who might object the most would be Murray Samuels, but he's a member of our church. I think I can reason with him."

Emma leaned toward him and smiled. "Do you really think we might be able to pull it off?"

"I'm sure we can, but we're going to need someone to direct the overall operation of the project. I'll be glad to do it if you'll agree to help me."

Her mouth gaped open for a moment before she swallowed and blinked. "You want me to work with you on this?"

"I do."

She smiled. "Oh, Pastor Mike, I would love to help you organize this. I've been so upset ever since we left the meeting today.

It won't seem like Christmas if the nativity is missing."

"I agree. I'll bring up the idea to the congregation at the Sunday morning service and get their feelings on whether or not they want to do this."

"I have no doubt you can get them as excited about the idea as much as I am, Pastor Mike," Emma said. "But we have a lot of work to do between now and the first performance if we're to make it happen."

"I know. But Emma, there is one more thing we need to do."

Her eyes grew wide. "What's that?"

"We're probably going to be spending a lot of time together in the next few weeks. I'd feel more comfortable if we were on a first name basis. What do you say we forget the pastor title and you can just call me Mike?"

A smile curled her lips, and Mike's heart fluttered. She picked up the coffeepot, turned toward the kitchen, and glanced over her shoulder. "I'd like that. . .Mike."

Chapter 3

Emma couldn't remember a more beautiful Sunday morning service. The congregation was smaller than usual, since so many of the members had left Bethlehem after the storm. Those in attendance, though, appeared determined to show they had come to give thanks to God in spite of the terrible destruction that had blown through their town a little over a week ago.

There was still no electricity, and candles burned brightly around the sanctuary. But it was the church's stained glass windows that captured Emma's attention. Somehow those beautiful panes of glass had resisted the winds of Eleanor, and they sparkled from the sunbeams that lit them.

Now with the service coming to a close, Emma wondered when Pastor Mike, or Mike, as he had asked her to call him, would tell the congregation about his idea. She didn't have to wait long to find out. With the last words of their parting hymn sung, he asked everyone to take their seats again.

As the gathered worshipers stared at him, he began to speak. "As you all have probably heard by now, the town council decided to cancel the live nativity this year. I spoke to a few of our members this week, and no one wants to see us discontinue this tradition that has come to mean so much to the town. I wanted to ask you this morning what you thought about our church taking on this project."

For a moment no one spoke then John Roland rose to his feet. "Pastor Mike, I've been a volunteer on the nativity ever since it started, and it's a big job. Do you really think we can do this? After all, our congregation has never taken on something as involved as this."

Murray Samuels stood. "I commend you for thinking our church could do this, Pastor Mike, but obviously you haven't thought this thing through. We have no costumes or props. And our church treasury is already struggling to meet our monthly bills, such as your salary. I don't think we can undertake such a big project."

Mike nodded. "I know we're going to have to step out on faith if we're to do it. But isn't that what we're required to do all the time as Christians? I believe that if we dedicate our efforts to God, He'll bless the results. I'd like for us to do this."

Mr. Samuels shook his head. "We can't do it," he said. "Although our church was spared in the storm, we lost a lot of shingles. You need to be more worried about getting the roof fixed than putting on a nativity that no one has the time to work on or even wants to see."

Emma jumped to her feet. "I want to see it. And I'll make the time to see that it happens."

John Roland raised his hand. "And so will I."

"Yeah, I will, too."

The voice came from the back of the church. Before Emma could identify the speaker, other voices rang out as people jumped to their feet and called out their commitment to the project.

Mike smiled at her and held up his hands to quiet the crowd. "Thank you, but I think we need to vote on this. If you agree that our church should assume the responsibility of the town's live nativity, please say yes."

"Yes!" The roar was almost deafening.

"Those opposed, please vote no."

"No."

Emma's eyes grew wide as Murray Samuels cast the dissenting vote. She turned and looked at him, but his attention was directed toward Mike.

Mr. Samuels's face had turned white, and he glared at Mike. "I knew this was going to happen when we hired a pastor with no experience in running a church. On top of that, you have no idea what we need in this community. We sure don't need somebody from the outside coming in here and telling us what to do. Go ahead and try to do your nativity if you want, but don't expect me to help. I've got all I can manage right now trying to get life back to normal for this town."

Mike didn't flinch from the anger evident in Mr. Samuels's voice. His reply reminded Emma of a parent trying to reason with a child. "I understand, Mr. Samuels, and I'm sure I speak for everyone when I say we appreciate all you've done for the town.

Now what we need to do is pray that God will bless the efforts of *everyone* who is trying to restore life to normal around here."

Mr. Samuels's face turned from white to red, and he bit his lip. Then he straightened to his full height and looked about to speak when John Roland beat him to it.

"Pastor Mike, how do we get started?"

"Emma Townsend is going to be helping me oversee this project. Please see her before you leave here today and sign up for whatever area you feel you could help with. I'll let her tell you what we need."

He nodded toward Emma, and she held up the papers in her hands. "We're going to need seamstresses to make the costumes, carpenters to build the sets, actors to fill the roles, musicians, people to be responsible for the animals, and set decorators. My girls' choir will sing, but we need other special music also. I'm sure we'll think of other things later on, but this is a good start. I'll put these sheets on the table at the back of the sanctuary, and you can sign up before you leave. And please know how much we appreciate whatever you can do to help us."

Mr. Samuels shook his head and glanced around the congregation. "It all sounds good while you're talking about it, but you're going to find out it's a bigger job than you thought once you get started. Just remember I tried to warn you."

Mike smiled. "I'm sure we'll all remember that. Now, why don't we have the benediction?"

Ten minutes later Emma picked up the papers from the table and glanced over the names of those who'd signed up before she walked to where Mike stood shaking people's hands. He turned toward her when the last ones left.

She held up the papers. "Nearly everyone signed on to take a job. I think this is going to be the best nativity we've ever had."

Mike rubbed the back of his neck and frowned. "I hope so. I just wish Mr. Samuels would be more supportive."

Emma chuckled. "Don't worry about him. I've known him all my life, and his bark is much worse than his bite. He really does love this town, and I'm sure he's worried about all that needs to be done right now."

"I like it that you can see the good in people. That's a wonderful quality for a person to have."

She shrugged. "It's nothing special. Besides, I know the people around here. They always pull together when it comes to our town. And Mr. Samuels will, too."

"I don't know about that. He didn't seem like he wanted to be involved today."

"He will be. Just wait. . ." Emma pulled the paper from the bottom of her stack and stared down at it.

"What is it?" Mike said.

She held up the sheet. "This is the sign-up sheet for actors. All of the roles are taken except for the three wise men. Nobody signed up for those parts."

"Don't worry about that. I'm sure we can convince someone to take those roles."

"I hope you're right. Everybody's gotten so used to the same men playing the part, they probably didn't think about having to get other actors this year."

"Why do we have to get other actors?"

"Because one of the men who's played the part for years died in March, another left to live with his daughter in Florida, and the third one moved into a retirement home in Bangor. They were all perfect in the role. With so many of the residents gone from town, I can't think of anyone else to play the parts."

"It can't be as bad as you're making it sound. I'm sure there are three men in this town who would be perfect, and we'll find them. Don't go looking for problems before we get started like Mr. Samuels did."

She frowned and shook her head. "He'd be happy if we abandoned the whole performance, but. . ." Her eyes grew wide, and she snapped her fingers. "That's it! I know who can play the roles."

"Who?"

"The three selectmen. They'd be perfect, and it'll be a way of getting them to support the nativity."

Mike looked at her like she'd lost her mind before he laughed. "You've got to be kidding. How do you think you'll convince Mr. Samuels to play a part in a nativity performance that he opposes?"

She arched an eyebrow and propped her hand on her hip. "Are you saying that you think I can't do it?"

"Well, not exactly. But you have to admit it sounds like wishful thinking."

Both eyebrows arched, and she gave a playful gasp. "Why,

Michael Benson, you sound as if you don't have faith in my abilities. Are you forgetting that it's my job to coax middle school kids into doing what they don't want to do?"

A slow smile pulled at his lips. "No, but I think getting Mr. Samuels to agree to this may be a little tougher than dealing with a thirteen-year-old."

She crossed her arms and stared at him. "I see that I'm going to have to prove myself with you. But just for the fun of it, I'd like to make this more interesting."

"Interesting? How?"

Emma thought for a moment before she replied. "You always compliment me when I sing a solo. But I've noticed that you barely open your mouth when the entire congregation sings."

He smiled. "That's because I can't carry a tune. Never have been able to."

Emma tilted her head and nodded. "You may think that's true, but it isn't. I had a voice teacher once who told me that if you can talk, you can sing. Maybe not like what you'd want to sound like, but you can at least make a joyful noise. And your overly long sermons certainly show you can talk."

"Overly long sermons? Nobody's told me that before."

Emma waved her hand in dismissal. "Well, maybe not all of them are too long, but sometimes you do get carried away. So let's say that if I can get Mr. Samuels to agree to be a wise man, you'll sing a solo in church."

His mouth gaped open and he stared at her in disbelief. "No way am I going to sing in front of the whole congregation."

"Aha!" she said. "Then you think I can convince him?"

"I didn't say that."

"So why would you be afraid that you'll have to sing if you're so sure I can't convince him?"

He stared at her for a moment before he smiled and nodded. "Emma, I'm seeing a side of you that I didn't know existed, and I must say, I really like it. I still don't think you can convince Mr. Samuels, though, so you need to promise to do something I want if you can't get him to agree."

"Something horrible, no doubt," she scoffed.

"No, nothing like that. I'll show you that I'm not such a bad guy. I'll give you something easy. Something you wouldn't mind doing."

"And what would that be?"

He bit down on his lip as if he was in deep thought, then smiled. "If you don't get him to agree, you'll sing a song in church that I choose as a solo."

"What would you choose?"

" 'His Eye is On the Sparrow.' It was my grandmother's favorite hymn. I'd like to hear you sing it."

Emma blinked to keep the tears from filling her eyes at the memories of hearing her mother's voice drift from the kitchen singing that song as she cooked supper. "I'd be glad to sing it no matter what happens. Shall we shake on it?"

He reached out and wrapped his fingers around hers. He held her hand for a moment before he shook it and took a deep breath. "Have you thought about how you're going to get Mr.

Samuels to agree to be one of the three wise men?"

Emma glanced down at his hand still holding hers and gently pulled free. "I don't know, but God does. I think I'll leave that up to Him."

Chapter 4

Three weeks after Eleanor, Emma sat at the desk Mike had set up for her in a corner of the church fellowship hall and stared at the names on the papers she held. It had all seemed so simple that day in church when she asked for volunteers and everyone had been ready to jump in and join the effort to stage the nativity. Now things didn't look as hopeful, or as easy.

"Good afternoon, Emma."

Mike's voice jerked her from her thoughts, and she glanced up to see him standing next to her. She dropped the papers onto her desk, closed her eyes, and massaged her temples with her fingertips. "I hope you're here to tell me your day has been better than mine."

He slid into the chair in front of her desk and leaned forward. "What's the matter?"

She sighed and crossed her arms on the desk. "I'm running out of actors for the nativity. I just got word that Jim and Karen Morrison have gone to stay with his parents in Pennsylvania. So now I don't have Joseph, Mary, or baby Jesus."

"I'm sure we can find others to play those roles."

She suppressed a small groan. "If only it were that easy. Half the people who volunteered aren't even in Bethlehem anymore. A lot of them whose homes were badly damaged have been evacuated to the emergency shelter the state set up at that big hotel in Augusta. What are we going to do?"

"We knew from the beginning this wasn't going to be easy. I hope this doesn't mean you're giving up."

She sat up straight and shook her head. "Giving up? No way. It's just that this last bit of news hit me at a time when I was thinking about the carpenters at my house. I haven't checked on them in three days because I've been so busy here."

"I know what you mean. I haven't gotten anyone to repair the church roof yet either. Every contractor I talk with is busy, and all they can do is put us on the list. Maybe Mr. Samuels was right. This may have been too much for us to take on."

"Don't you say that, Mike. We may be having a weak moment, but we're not going to quit. I really believe that if we can give our community the nativity, it will help to pull everybody out of their despair."

His gaze traveled slowly over her face, and Emma's heart did that funny little flip she'd come to associate with being around Mike. "You're right, Emma. You are such an inspiration to me. We just need to keep our eyes on the goal and do whatever it takes to make the nativity happen." He stood and came around the desk to stand beside her chair. He leaned down and studied the papers in front of her. "Now, what's our biggest problem?"

She tried to ignore the tingle that raced down her spine at his nearness, but it was no use. She found it harder and harder to think straight when he was around. In an effort to clear her mind, she directed her attention to the papers and shuffled through the lists. "Well, let's see. The men who signed up to build the props are busy repairing their own homes, the material I ordered for the costumes is back-ordered and won't be here for at least two more weeks, and I still haven't approached Mr. Samuels about getting the selectmen to be the three wise men."

He grinned. "So I'm not in danger of having to sing that solo yet?"

She propped her elbows on the desk and rested her chin in her palms. "Not yet, but don't think you're safe. I've been thinking about how to do it. I just need to come up with a plan. If I could get him to support the idea of the nativity, maybe he would pitch in and help us. But so far he remains just as set in his decision as ever. I've prayed and asked God to change Mr. Samuels's attitude, but so far nothing has changed. I keep telling myself to remember that God's in control, but we're running out of time."

Mike shoved his hands in his pockets and backed away from the desk. "All kidding aside, I want you to know I really admire you for wanting to change Mr. Samuels's mind. If anyone can do it, you can. I've watched you over the past couple of weeks, and the way you've approached this project and how you've worked with everyone has inspired me. You're quite a woman, Emma Townsend."

Emma's face warmed, and she stared down at her desk in an effort to avoid looking into his eyes. "Thank you, Mike. I keep telling myself to trust God, that it's all for His glory. Whatever He decides will be best for our town, and I'll be thankful for it no matter what."

"Then how can we fail?"

Emma rose to her feet. "We won't; so from now on I'm going to take a step back and get out of God's way." She smiled up at Mike. "It's going to be fun seeing what He has planned for us, isn't it?"

He didn't say anything for a moment, and then he reached out and covered her hand that still rested on the desk with his. "Thank you, Emma. I've really enjoyed getting to know you better these past two weeks. I'm sorry I didn't do it sooner."

Now the tingle raced up her arm as well as her spine. "It's been good for me, too. I'm glad you're more than my pastor now. You're also my friend."

He smiled and squeezed her hand. "Then how about having dinner with me tonight?"

"Where? There isn't a restaurant in Bethlehem that's opened up yet."

He glanced around the fellowship hall. "I've come to really like the cooking here. How about sharing my favorite table with me tonight at the hottest spot in Bethlehem right now? The Community Church Bistro."

She laughed and leaned closer. "That sounds like a wonderful place to eat. I believe if you're not in line at six o'clock, you're out of luck for the night. So I'll see you then."

"I'll look forward to it."

Emma watched as he walked from the room. Her heart fluttered, and she pressed her hand against her chest. Dinner with Mike Benson. She'd dreamed about it for months. Of course, she'd envisioned them sitting in some elegant restaurant, not the church fellowship hall. But the place really didn't matter. It was the company that made the evening, and she didn't know anyone else she'd rather spend it with.

∽

The hands on the fellowship hall clock clicked over to six o'clock just as Emma walked in the door. Mike paused from placing chairs at the additional tables they'd added that afternoon and stared at her. Even though she had to be tired from the hours she'd spent at the shelter today, there was no hint of it in her appearance. In fact, he thought she'd never looked more beautiful.

Her gaze swept the room, and she gave a small wave when she spotted him. The ladies helping in the serving line stopped what they were doing and watched as she walked toward him, her long hair brushing her shoulders and her eyes sparkling. One of the women whispered something to another, and they both smiled before they directed their attention back to the people waiting in line.

Mike's pulse raced, and he wondered what the woman had said to her friend. Was that a look of disapproval they'd sent his way? He shook the thought from his mind. In the last two weeks he'd come to know Emma better, and he liked her. A lot.

It didn't matter what anyone else thought. All that mattered at the moment was that he enjoyed Emma's company, and he thought of her constantly whether she was around or not. He took a deep breath to calm his emotions.

Emma stopped beside him and glanced at the serving line. "There are more people tonight than usual."

"A few more families checked in this afternoon. Apparently the electricity isn't on everywhere yet."

Emma's gaze drifted over the crowd and stopped on a young couple at the back of the line. A smile lit her face. "There's Don and Sue Baker. When did they get here?"

Mike pulled his attention away from Emma and studied the young couple. They looked to be in their late twenties. The man towered over the woman, who had a carrier strapped to the front of her body. A baby inside the carrier snuggled against its mother's chest.

"I don't know them. Where do they live?"

"Outside of town. She taught with me at the middle school until she had the baby. She's on leave now. I haven't seen the baby since he was born. Come on, and I'll introduce you." He followed her across the room, where she stopped next to the young couple. "Sue, Don, how are you?"

They turned, and a big smile flashed on Sue's face. "Emma! I was hoping I would see you here. We're as well as can be expected after living through Eleanor. How about you?"

"I'm fine. I've been helping out here since the hurricane." She glanced at Don. "It's good to see you. Was there much damage out at your farm?"

He nodded. "Yeah. We lost our barn and several animals. The house wasn't damaged too badly, but they haven't gotten the electricity restored yet. We stood it as long as we could, but one of our neighbors came by and told us the temperature was supposed to drop tonight. We decided we couldn't keep the baby there, so we packed a few things and thought we'd stay here for a couple of days. Maybe the electricity will be restored then, and we can go home."

"I see." Emma glanced from Don to Mike. "Don, Sue, I'd like you to meet our pastor, Mike Benson. Mike, this is Don and Sue Baker."

Mike stuck out his hand and shook Don's. "We're glad to have you here. Stay as long as you want. This center was set up to help those in need during this time." He leaned forward and peeked at the baby. "That's a cute baby you have. How old is he?"

"He's six weeks old now," Sue said.

Emma smiled. "I do believe he looks like his daddy."

Sue laughed, and her eyes softened as she looked at her husband. "I only hope he grows up to be as good a man as his daddy is."

"Do you attend church anywhere?" Mike asked.

"Yes. We've been going to a small church near our farm, but it was destroyed when the storm moved inland. I guess we'll have to find another place to worship for now."

"Then feel free to join us any time. We'd love to have you."

"Thank you, Pastor Mike," Sue said.

Mike pointed to the serving line. "I think they're ready to fix your plates. Get your supper. I hope you enjoy it."

They turned toward the line, but Emma reached out and touched Sue's arm. "One more thing, though. I don't want you staying here with the baby. There's very little privacy. I want you to come stay at my house."

Don frowned and shook his head. "We couldn't do that."

Emma arched her eyebrows. "Why not? I have a large house, and the electricity has been restored. Thanks to the repairmen who came today, I now have heat. I won't be there much, because I'm busy working on the nativity, but you can use the kitchen, too. In fact you can make yourself at home for as long as you need. If you won't do it for yourselves, please consider what's best for the baby."

Sue and Don stared at each other for a moment before Don smiled. "When you put it that way, how can I refuse? But we should pay you for staying there."

"No way," Emma said. "I don't want your money."

Don crossed his arms and inhaled a long breath. "Then you're going to have to come up with some other way."

Emma smiled. "Maybe there is a way you can help me. You know I said I'm working on the live nativity. I found out just today that the Morrisons, who were to play Joseph, Mary, and baby Jesus, have left town. I need three new actors. Do you think the Baker family can fill in for us?"

Don laughed. "Us, actors? Sue can do that all right, but me? I've never been in a play in my life. I don't know if I could learn the lines or not."

"Oh, you don't have to say anything. You just have to stand there while someone else speaks and while the musicians tell the story in song."

He nodded. "I think I can handle that."

"Good!" Emma said. "Then go eat your supper, and I'll take you to my house later."

Mike watched the young couple get their plates and walk to a table before he turned to Emma. "That was very kind of you to offer your home to them."

Emma waved in dismissal. "I like Sue. We always got along well at school. I can't stand to think of that baby being in the middle of so many people here. He'll be better off in the quiet of my house."

Mike stared at her for a moment and wondered why he had ever thought that he might not like her if he got to know her better. Now all he could think of was how much time he'd wasted when he could have been enjoying her company for months.

He reached out and wrapped his fingers around hers. "You showed Christ's love to that young couple, and God solved one of your problems for the nativity. I can't wait to see how He's going to take care of the rest of them."

She glanced down at their hands and squeezed his fingers. "Neither can I."

Chapter 5

Thirty minutes later Emma swallowed the last bite of chocolate cake and moaned. "Nobody can bake cakes like Sarah Davis. Eating one of her masterpieces can sure put you in a good mood."

Mike set his coffee cup down and smiled at her. "The one she baked today seems to have put everyone in a happy frame of mind. I haven't heard this much talking in the dining room all week."

Emma's gaze drifted over the crowded tables. "Everybody seems happier tonight. Maybe we're all beginning to come out of the shock from the storm."

"I hope so."

"What are you hoping for?" A voice echoed through the room.

Emma tried to mask her surprise as she stared into the face of Murray Samuels. As far as she knew, he hadn't been in the emergency shelter since it had been set up.

"Mr. Samuels? How good to see you here tonight. Would you like something to eat?"

"No, thank you, Emma. I just dropped by to give Pastor Mike a message."

Mike rose to his feet, grabbed a chair from the next table, and pulled it toward them. "Have a seat and let us know what's on your mind."

Mr. Samuels shook his head. "I don't have time. The city council is holding an emergency meeting in a few minutes. I stopped by to give you some news."

"What is it?"

Mr. Samuels took a deep breath. "I got a call today from a TV station over in Augusta. They're sending a reporter here tomorrow to do a story on how our town is coming back to life after Eleanor. Kate wants to bring her by here to see how the church has set up an emergency shelter for those whose homes were damaged."

Mike's forehead wrinkled. "Do you know when they plan to be here?"

"She said it will be in the early afternoon. Why? Is there a problem?"

"No, it's just that Emma and I have a meeting set up in the morning with all the committees that are working on the nativity. But we should be through before lunchtime."

"That's good, because we want to show this reporter we're on our way to building our town back."

Emma smiled up at Mr. Samuels. "The whole town owes the city council a big debt of gratitude for all your hard work in the last few weeks. I've been meaning to ask, though. Do you have any idea when Bethlehem Green will be cleaned up?"

"That's not one of our priorities at this point. Why do you ask?"

"Because that's where the nativity is going to be, and we need to begin building the sets."

Mr. Samuels shook his head and sighed. "I'd hoped you'd given up that harebrained idea. I'm sorry, but at this point we don't have the manpower to put anybody to work on the park."

"But, Mr. Samuels, this is important—"

He cocked an eyebrow, held up his hand to interrupt her, and shook his head. "Emma, I thought you understood how the council feels about this. It's nothing personal. I like you. I always have. I respected your parents and felt a great loss when they died. But my responsibility right now lies with restoring this town to normal."

She rose to her feet and faced him. "I understand that, Mr. Samuels, but the town is more than buildings and electricity and businesses. It's also the people who make up the community. They need to know that no matter what happens, God is going to be there for them. We need to nourish their souls with hope and love so that they can look forward to the future."

"I understand what you're saying, Emma, but I still disagree. Now if you'll excuse me, I have to go."

He turned to leave, but she reached out and touched his arm. "There is one more thing I'd like to ask you."

"What?"

"Would you talk to the other two selectmen and ask them if they'd join you in being the three wise men for the nativity?"

His eyes grew wide, and his mouth gaped open. "Are you serious?"

"I am."

He cast a look of disbelief at Mike before he faced Emma again. "I've just told you what I think about staging the nativity. Why do you think I'd take an active role in it if I'm opposed to having it in the first place?"

Emma realized this was the opportunity she'd been waiting for, and it might not come again. Even though her heart felt as if it were in her throat, she flashed the most winning smile she could muster. "Because you're a good man. Everybody in Bethlehem knows that, and we know you love your hometown. You've been working night and day to get life back to normal around here. But the citizens of Bethlehem need something more than just the physical things in life. They also need comfort for their hurting souls."

"And how do you think the selectmen can do that?"

"By showing your faith in God and reminding us how He can get us through the worst of times. And by giving us hope that He will always be here for us, no matter what comes against us. And you can give our town those gifts by the retelling of what happened in another Bethlehem two thousand years ago. Won't you help us?"

Mr. Samuels stared at her. A puzzled look flashed in his eyes. Then he shook his head and chuckled. "Emma, you always were quite a talker." He took a deep breath and turned toward Mike. "The film crew should be here about two o'clock tomorrow afternoon."

He darted one more look at Emma, turned, and strode from the room. When he disappeared through the door, Mike looked at her. "I must say, that was a surprise. When did you come up with that speech?"

Her words had been as much a surprise to her as they were to Mike. She shook her head. "I have no idea. I just opened my mouth, and the words came out."

"Do you think it helped?"

"I don't know."

"At least he didn't say no. Now if you'll excuse me for a moment, I think I'll go ask Sarah Davis to make sure there's cake and coffee tomorrow afternoon for the film crew's visit."

Emma watched him walk away before she sank down in her chair. She raised a shaking hand to her forehead and wiped at the perspiration that had suddenly appeared. What made her say those things to Mr. Samuels? It had seemed right at the time, but now she wasn't so sure. Had she ruined the project for all those involved?

Tears welled up in her eyes, but then she straightened her shoulders and smiled as Mike's words flashed in her mind.

At least he didn't say no.

No, he didn't. Maybe God had wanted her to say those things. If so, maybe something good would come from it. She would just have to wait and see.

❧

The next morning Mike glanced at his watch as he hurried down the hall to the room where Emma was meeting with the church members who had volunteered to head the committees for the nativity. He'd told Emma he'd be there at ten, and here it was almost ten thirty. But he hadn't expected his landlord to show up at his office this morning to tell him that the house and furniture he'd rented to Mike was now considered a total loss. Added to his growing list of things to do now was find a place to live.

He paused when he arrived at the closed door of the meeting room. From inside he could hear raised voices, and they didn't sound happy. Quietly he opened the door and slipped into the room. Emma stood at the front. A relieved look flashed across her face when she saw him.

"Pastor Mike," she said, "I'm so glad you're here. There are some concerns being shared."

Mike walked to the front of the room and faced his church members. "Is there anything I can help with?"

Chester Dyer stood and pointed to his brother Dwight, who sat beside him. "Everybody in town knows that the Dyer brothers do the best carpentry work around. That's why Emma wanted us to build the set and the props for the nativity."

Mike nodded. "And is there a problem?"

"There sure is. How do you expect us to get anything done down at Bethlehem Green? Every path is blocked with downed trees. We've gotta have the nativity somewhere else."

Mike shook his head. "Where would you suggest? There are trees down everywhere. I know there have been a lot of volunteers to help the emergency workers, but it's going to take time to get everything back in order."

"I know that," Chester said. "We've talked to the crews doing the cleanup, but they say Bethlehem Green is one of the last places on the list to be cleared. They don't know if they'll get to it by the first of December or not, and that's when we need to start building the sets."

"I'll talk to Kate Walters and tell her we need the park cleaned up in the next three weeks. Maybe she can get them to redirect their efforts."

Chester smiled. "That sounds good. That'll give us plenty of time."

Mike darted a glance at Emma and flashed her a weak smile. "Then that will be our goal."

Chester sat down, and John Roland stood. "I'm in charge of the music and the sound. The generator we've used in the past didn't survive the storm. I thought I might be able to borrow one, but so far everybody I've talked to is using theirs. We need to buy a new one, and that'll be a big expense."

"That's something I hadn't thought about. We'll add it to the list."

"And about the musicians," John continued. "Will we have the school choir sing, or have all their families left town?"

"Emma's working on that, John," Mike said. "She should have an answer for you in a few days."

Janet Burgess jumped to her feet. "Well, it don't make no difference whether we have a set or music or anything else if we don't have the costumes for the actors. Emma, when is that material gonna be here?"

"I called the company again yesterday, and they said they shipped it last week. They're trying to track the order and see where it might have ended up. If they can't find it, they will replace the material."

Janet propped her hand on her hip and stared at Emma. "Do you know how long it took us to make those wise men's robes? We spent weeks on each one with all the jewels and sequins we used, and we hand sewed every one of them." Her glasses perched on the end of her nose bounced a little as she shook her head. "And we don't aim for these costumes to be cheap looking. After all, our seamstresses have their reputations to uphold."

Emma breathed a small sigh. "I understand, Janet. Everybody in Bethlehem knows that your sewing circle makes the most beautiful garments of anybody in town. You'll have the material. Just try to be patient for a few more days."

Janet arched an eyebrow. "Okay. We'll give you a few more days."

Gordon Brown stood up when Janet sat down. "I have a question, Pastor Mike."

"What is it, Gordon?"

"It's about the actors. I'm in charge of that, and I was wondering who's going to play the wise men. I haven't been told yet."

Mike glanced at Emma, and she swallowed. "We're working on that, Gordon. I just need a few more days to finalize it."

Gordon nodded. "Just asking, Pastor Mike. Let me know when you find out something."

Janet jumped back up. "And we need to fit their costumes

to them. That is, if we ever have any material to make their costumes with."

"And what about the animals?" Chester asked. "Are we going to be able to get them?"

"As you know, Dr. Norwood, our local vet, takes care of the animals. Our contract is with a provider out of Portland, and as you can imagine, it's expensive to ship exotic animals this far and then care for them once they get here. We're still trying to find the money to pay for that."

Chester shook his head. "And now we have to add a generator to the list. Without the funds from the town council, we may not be able to come up with the money."

The committee members frowned at each other. Several muttered comments under their breaths that Mike couldn't hear. From the looks on everyone's faces, the meeting seemed to quickly be headed toward something akin to a mutiny.

He raised his voice above the din. "Don't worry, folks, I know things look bad now, but it's going to work out."

Emma held up her hands for silence. "Please don't give up. We've come this far. We have to keep going. We just need to have faith. The Bible tells us that if we have faith the size of a mustard seed, we can move mountains. I think all of you are mountain movers, so let's put all of this in God's hands and let Him show us what He can do."

"I agree with that," Mike added as he glanced at his watch. "It's getting close to time for lunch to be served in the fellowship hall. Why don't we all go get something to eat and think about how great this year's nativity is going to be."

Chester and Dwight stood up, and Dwight shook his head. "We won't stay to eat. We're gonna get on back home and do some work cleaning up around our place. We'll see you Sunday."

Janet and her sewing circle ladies along with John Roland got to their feet and followed them out of the room. Mike heard them start chattering the minute they reached the hallway. He glanced at Emma and smiled. "Are your ears burning?"

Gordon Brown was the last to leave. He stepped up to Emma and smiled. "I heard some talk around town that you wanted the selectmen to be the three wise men. How's that coming along?"

"Not too well, I'm afraid."

He chuckled and put his hat on. "Don't worry about them, Emma. They'll come around."

Her eyes grew wide. "Do you really think so?"

He winked at her and nodded. "I've been knowing you since you were a little girl. I never had a better friend than your father, and he always said when you set your mind to something, it happens. Besides, I've been praying they'll give in and join us."

Tears welled up in Emma's eyes, and she grasped Gordon's hand. "Thank you, Gordon. I appreciate that."

He glanced at Mike. "See you Sunday, Pastor Mike."

Gordon stuck his hat on his head and walked from the room. When he'd left, Mike turned to Emma. Tears still sparkled in her eyes, and he smiled. "It's going to be all right, Emma. God will get us through this."

"Three weeks, Mike. If we don't get the green cleaned up by

then, we won't have enough time to get ready for the nativity."

"I know."

She took a deep breath and smiled. "But God created the world in six days and rested on the seventh. Just think what He can do in Bethlehem if He has three weeks to work with."

Mike threw back his head and laughed. "Emma, you are delightful."

She tilted her head. "And hungry. Ready to eat?"

For a moment he was frozen in place as he watched her move toward the door. Then he hurried forward and caught up with her as she headed to the fellowship hall. When he'd come to Bethlehem, he thought God had brought him to his first pastorate in a small congregation to give him experience in dealing with people, but now he was beginning to think God had something even better in mind for him. And her name was Emma Townsend.

Chapter 6

Emma propped her hands on her hips and stepped back to survey the table of refreshments that awaited the film crew scheduled to arrive at the church any minute. Sarah Davis had outdone herself by baking the most mouth-watering chocolate cake Emma thought she'd ever seen. But Sarah hadn't stopped there. She'd also made some open-faced sandwiches and added a plate of her famous peanut butter cookies.

Emma was just about to check the coffeepot and make sure it had finished brewing when Mike pulled the door open and stepped back for several people to enter the room. Kate Walters walked in, followed by a young woman Emma had seen on the nightly news for the last two years and a man with a camera in his hand.

Kate smiled when she saw Emma and headed toward her. "Emma, I'd like for you to meet our visitors from Augusta." She stopped beside Emma and turned toward the young woman. "This is Kelsey Warren and Tanner Hodges. They're doing a story on how the East Coast is cleaning up after Hurricane Eleanor, and they stopped by to check out how things are progressing in Bethlehem. They're in a hurry to get on to the next town, but I persuaded them to take a detour here for some cake and coffee before they leave."

Kelsey Warren looked at her watch and frowned. "But I'm afraid we're going to have to skip the cake. It's getting late, and I want to get this story on tonight's news segment."

Emma smiled and held out her hand. "I'm sorry you have to leave so quickly, but I'm very glad to meet you, Ms. Warren. I watch you on the news every night. It's an honor to have you in our town."

The petite young woman's eyes sparkled as she grasped Emma's hand. "Please, call me Kelsey. This is my first time to visit Bethlehem, but I'm impressed with how your town has responded to this emergency."

"Are you sure you don't have time to drink a cup of coffee at least?"

Tanner Hodges shook his head. "I'm afraid not. We've just spent time with Mr. Samuels, and he told us everything we needed to know for the story. But Kate insisted we come by the church to check out the shelter you've opened here."

Emma pointed to Mike. "The credit for that goes to Pastor Mike. He's worked around the clock since the storm to make sure every family has a place to stay and good food to eat. He's been so busy taking care of everybody else, he hasn't had time to do anything about his house that was damaged during the storm. He's been sleeping on a couch in his office."

Kelsey's eyes grew wide. "Really, Pastor Mike? How many people have you housed here since the storm?"

Mike's face flushed, and he glanced at Emma before directing his attention back to Kelsey. "I'm not sure of the total number at this point, because we've had so many come and go. Right now we have about a hundred people staying here."

"And Pastor Mike sees that the needs of every one of them are met. The volunteers do, too." Emma pointed to the chocolate cake on the table. "One of the church ladies has spent every day baking. The children love her peanut butter cookies, and she always has a huge supply of them. But Pastor Mike is always there to give encouragement when someone needs it. And believe me, we've all needed it at times. We're fortunate to have a caring pastor."

Mike shook his head. "Emma's making me sound like some kind of hero, but I'm not the only one who's worked hard. She's been helping here at the shelter every day. She's even opened her home to a family who lost theirs in the storm. And on top of that, she's working to make sure we have the live nativity this year."

Kelsey and Tanner exchanged glances. "What live nativity?" Kelsey asked.

"Bethlehem has a live nativity every year," Emma said. "It's a big production, and the whole town gets involved in it. We don't want to skip this year. In fact, we need it this year more than ever."

Kelsey frowned. "Why more than ever this year?"

Emma thought for a moment before she answered. "We wanted to find a way to let the people of Bethlehem know that God hasn't forgotten about us. Even though there may be moments that it seems like He has, He's still watching out for us and caring what happens. We decided that we need to be strong and not give up the way Bethlehem celebrates the birth of Christ. It's something we need to do together to heal from the storm."

Kelsey stared at Emma. "But how are you going to have a nativity with Bethlehem in such a shambles?"

Emma laughed. "We're not sure how it's going to end up. All we know is that we've turned it over to God, and we're letting Him work it out."

Kelsey didn't say anything for a moment before she pulled her cell phone from her purse. "Emma, I think I'll take a piece of that chocolate cake and a cup of coffee after all. I'm going to call my producer and tell him we may be a bit late getting back to the station today. I want to hear more about this nativity."

Tanner frowned and shook his head. "Kelsey, we need..."

"To get the real story in Bethlehem," she finished for him. "So, sit down and have some cake while I make this call. Then we'll talk with Emma and Pastor Mike some more."

Tanner nodded and glanced at Emma. "It looks like we're staying. And I must say that cake looks good."

Emma laughed as she sliced a piece and put it on a plate for him. "You won't be disappointed. Sarah Davis has won a lot prizes for her baking."

"And help yourself to the sandwiches and coffee," Mike added.

Later, after the cake was eaten and the coffee cups drained, Kelsey stared down at the notebook where she'd been writing comments while they ate and talked. She shook her head and directed a smile at Emma. "I have to say, you're quite brave to attempt doing the nativity this year. Where do you plan to have it?"

"We've had it downtown in Bethlehem Green in the past, but I don't know if that's going to work this year."

"Why not?" Kelsey asked.

"Because the Green is littered with fallen trees, and there are fishing boats that washed inland sitting underneath a lot of them. I hope the cleanup crews can get to them in the next week, but it's beginning to look like they might not be able to get to it in time."

"Oh, that's too bad," Kelsey murmured. She glanced down at her notes again. "It looks like you need a lot of help just to stage the nativity. The green needs to be cleaned up, it's beginning to look like the material for the costumes was lost in the mail, and all your props were destroyed in the hurricane. On top of that you need actors, a generator, and money to rent the live animals. Does that about cover it?"

Kate winced at the list of problems Kelsey rattled off. "Those are the ones we've identified. We don't know what else we may encounter."

Kelsey's eyes grew wide, and she leaned forward. "Then how do you possibly think you can pull this off?"

Emma glanced at Mike, and his gaze didn't waver as he smiled at her. She relaxed and turned back to Kelsey. "I can't."

Kelsey frowned. "Then how. . ."

Emma held up her hand to stop Kelsey. "I can't, but God can. I don't know how He's going to make everything come together, but I have faith that He's going to."

Kelsey stared at her for a moment before she smiled. "And what are the dates of the nativity?"

"This year we're going to do three nights, with the last one on Christmas Eve. Next year we'll return to our regular schedule."

Kelsey wrote in her notebook for a few minutes before she closed it and smiled. "I think I have everything I need for my story. We're going to film some shots around the church then we'll come back inside and get some of you two before we leave."

Kate, who'd remained silent during the meeting, rose to her feet. "I'll show you around outside."

Emma watched them go before she stood, picked up the plates Kate had stacked after they finished eating, and walked toward the kitchen. She'd just placed the plates in the sink when Mike came up beside her and set some cups down.

"I was impressed by the things you told Kelsey."

She shrugged. "I hope I didn't come off as some holier-than-thou person. I just want people to understand how important it is to put their trust in God."

He reached down, grasped her hand, and smiled. "You did great. I was very proud of you."

They stood like that for a moment before Emma pulled free and reached toward the faucet. "I'd better get these dishes washed. The ladies will be here any minute to start dinner, and

I don't want to leave a mess for them."

"Need any help?"

"You can dry if you'd like. The dishtowels are in that drawer over there."

Fifteen minutes later Emma handed Mike the last cup, and he was drying it when a voice from the doorway startled them. "That's perfect. Just what we needed."

They turned to see Kelsey at the door, along with Tanner, his camera aimed toward them. Emma reached for the dishtowel Mike still held to dry her hands. "We didn't hear you come in."

Kelsey chuckled. "We didn't expect to catch you washing dishes. The two of you seemed very intent on what you were doing, and we didn't want to interrupt. But I think we have all we need now, so we're heading out. Kate's already left to go back to her office." She walked toward them and held out her hand. "It was good to meet you, and I wish you the best of luck with the nativity."

"Thanks," Mike said. "We appreciate your coming to Bethlehem. Is there anything else we can help you with?"

"Yes, there is one more thing. Kate said cell phone service has been restored, so I'd like your number in case I need another quote from you for the story."

"Sure." Mike rattled off his number, and Kelsey entered it in her phone.

When she'd finished, she smiled once more and glanced from Mike to Emma. "It was a pleasure meeting you, and I hope you're able to pull off the nativity."

"We do, too," Emma said. "And thanks again for coming to Bethlehem."

"No need to thank us. We were just doing our job, and you've helped us with a lot today. Maybe we'll get back this way soon to see how the cleanup's going."

"We'd like that," Mike said.

Kelsey turned to Tanner, who stood at the door. "I guess we'd better get back," she said as she strode from the room. Tanner gave a small wave before he followed Kelsey.

After they left, Emma realized she and Mike were alone again. He appeared to be studying her intensely. What was he thinking? They'd been talking minutes ago when they were washing dishes, but suddenly she felt shy and couldn't think of anything to say. She turned back to the sink, folded the dishtowel Mike had handed her, and laid it on the counter.

"I guess I'd better be getting home," she said. Her voice trembled, and she wondered if he noticed.

Mike leaned against the counter next to the sink and crossed his arms. "Have dinner again tonight with me?"

Her face warmed, and she stared up at him. "T-tonight?"

A small frown wrinkled his forehead. "Yes, tonight. Is there something wrong, Emma?"

"N-no, but we have been spending a lot of time together."

"Haven't you enjoyed our time together?"

"Of course I have."

"Then what is it?"

She bit her lip before she directed her gaze toward him. "I

was just wondering what the congregation might think."

He reached for her hand and held it in both of his. "I have to admit I've wondered the same thing, but I've come to believe that they want me to be happy. And you make me happy."

For a moment Emma thought her heart might burst open in her chest. No one had ever said anything to her that thrilled her as much as Mike's words did. She blinked back the tears that threatened to spill from her eyes. "You make me happy, too."

"Then you'll have dinner with me?"

"Yes."

He straightened and smiled. "Good. I'll see you at six o'clock."

"I'll be here."

Mike squeezed her hand once more before he released her. "Then I think I'll go work on Sunday's sermon. I'll see you later."

When he'd left, Emma sank down in a chair and raised a shaking hand to her forehead. She could hardly believe it when he said she made him happy. She made Michael Benson, pastor of Bethlehem Community Church, happy?

Her heart beat like a bass drum in her chest. She clasped her hands together in her lap and leaned forward until her head touched them. If she made Mike happy, then maybe there were even better things to come. She was going to enjoy discovering each and every one of them.

Chapter 7

A week later Mike sat at the desk in his church office that had become his home since Eleanor had blown in from the sea. He stared out the window at the afternoon sun sinking slowly in the west. He tapped his pencil on the desktop and wondered how much progress was made today in the downtown cleanup that a volunteer group from New York had worked on.

His overhead lights flickered, and he glanced up at the small fixture above his desk. At least they now had electricity, thanks to the teams of electricians from all over New England who had poured into town after the storm. Cell phone service had been restored, but it was going to take a bit longer for the telephone company to get their landlines back in service.

Mr. Samuels had told him that another group of volunteers from Texas was arriving tomorrow to help with clearing the debris that still littered the streets. The town selectmen appeared excited about all the volunteers who'd come to get the town up and running again, but they still hadn't publicly added their support to the nativity. And nobody had tackled Bethlehem Green yet.

With all of the work taking place around town, a few more people had returned to try to get their homes back to what they'd once been. With so many buildings destroyed, Mike had no idea where he would find a place to live, but that could come after everybody else was taken care of. As long as he had the couch in his office, he at least had a place to sleep.

He'd seen Emma every day, and she was trying to put up a brave front. But he knew she was approaching the breaking point. When she'd come by the shelter early this morning, she'd looked tired. She bristled a bit when he suggested that perhaps she needed to take the day off and get some rest.

"I can't rest," she said. "Even though the school isn't open yet, I've contacted the girls in the choir who are still in town. We're having practice at ten o'clock, but I don't know if we even have enough to sing. Then I've got to find someone to clean up the green, and I need to call the company about the material for the costumes. If we don't get it delivered in the next week, the ladies may not have enough time to get them finished."

With that she'd hurried out the door. He'd tried to call her back, but she didn't turn around.

Mike glanced at his watch and opened his door. It was almost time for the volunteers to begin serving the evening meal. He made a practice of being there at that time in case people needed him for anything. As he took his first step outside his office, his foot hit something, and he stumbled.

Surprised, he looked down, and his eyes widened in shock. Three white crates with the words "United States Postal Services" stamped on them sat on the floor. They were overflowing with mail. All of the envelopes he could see were addressed to Bethlehem Community Church, Bethlehem, Maine. He frowned, picked up a letter with a postmark of Colorado on it, and ripped the envelope open. Why would someone in Colorado be writing to his church?

He pulled out a white piece of stationery, unfolded it, and sucked in his breath when three twenty-dollar bills met his eyes. He read the short note:

Dear Pastor Mike,

I saw the news report on television about how your church is trying to have Bethlehem's traditional live nativity even though Hurricane Eleanor nearly destroyed the town. I wanted to have a small part in helping your congregation. Please accept this gift and use it wherever you have a need.

Sincerely,
Molly Southerland
Silverton, Colorado

"News report?" he whispered. "In Colorado?"

He pulled out several letters from each crate and stared at the postmarks. California, Texas, North Carolina, Minnesota. Why were people all over the country writing to his little church in Maine? He opened several of the envelopes, and like the one from Molly Southerland, they each contained a short note of support for the nativity and either cash or a check. He mentally added the total from the opened letters and gasped.

"That's over a thousand dollars from those few envelopes," he whispered.

"What are you mumbling about?" He whirled at the sound of Emma's voice and stared open-mouthed at her.

"What are you doing here?"

"I came to tell you Sarah Davis needs to see you in the fellowship hall." She took a step closer and frowned. "What's the matter? You have the strangest expression on your face."

He waved a hand in the direction of the mail crates. "I just found all this mail outside my door. Since the hurricane the mailman has been leaving the mail with the ladies in the fellowship hall, but he must've brought this to my office this afternoon. I was so involved in studying my sermon I didn't hear him."

Emma frowned and stared down at the crates. "Where did it all come from?"

He held up the letters he'd just opened. "They're from all over the country. Every one I've opened contains money to help with the nativity. I already have over a thousand dollars just from the ones I've opened."

Emma's eyes grew wide. "What? How do these people know about the nativity?"

"Molly Southerland said she heard some news report."

"News report? Do you think she means Kelsey's story? But that can't be right. Kelsey did that story for a Maine television station."

He nodded and held up the money. "I know, but that doesn't change the fact that people we've never heard of have sent us donations to help stage the nativity."

"Do you think all these other letters might contain money?"

"I don't know, but we need to open them soon. We'll have to keep good records so we can thank them." He picked up the crates one by one and shoved them inside his office then locked the door. "After we're through serving the evening meal, we can open them in the fellowship hall where we'll have more room."

"Okay."

They'd only taken a few steps when Mike's cell phone rang. He stopped and pulled it from his pocket.

"Hello."

"Hi, Pastor Mike. This is Kelsey Warren."

Mike smiled. "Hi, Kelsey. How are you?"

"I'm great. Still working to keep the public informed, but I had some news I wanted to share."

Emma leaned forward and whispered. "Tell Kelsey I said hi."

He nodded. "Emma says to tell you hi."

"Tell her the same for me. I think she's going to be excited about my news."

"What is it?"

"The story I did about Bethlehem was well received, and it caught the attention of someone at the network in New York. They passed it on to the national nightly newscast, and they gave it a big spot on the news that night and then repeated it the next day on their morning show. The story of how one little town is struggling in this economy to get back on its feet after being hit so hard and is determined to perform the yearly live nativity has touched people nationwide. You wouldn't believe the e-mails and tweets the network has received from churches about how they want to help Bethlehem with the nativity."

Understanding dawned on Mike, and he smiled. "Oh, that explains the crates full of mail the church received today. I've only opened a few letters, but they were from all over the country, and all of them contained money to help with putting on the nativity."

"Then I suspect the other letters contain money, too, because the story not only made the networks, it also hit YouTube. Youth groups across the country are discussing it on social media, too."

"You're kidding."

"No, it's true. Churches and Christian organizations are keeping their eyes on your town to see if you can pull off this nativity in the midst of devastation, and they want you to do it. There's no telling what you'll experience in the next few days. I just wish I could be there to share it with you and Emma."

Mike started to speak, but he choked up and had to clear his throat. He struggled to get the words out. "Thank you, Kelsey. This wouldn't have happened if it hadn't been for you and Tanner. We owe you a big debt of gratitude."

She laughed, and the sound echoed in his ear. "You owe me nothing, my friend. I've gained something I thought I'd lost a long time ago. I haven't had much time for God in the last few years, but coming to Bethlehem and seeing the faith you and

Emma have, I discovered that God hasn't forgotten me. I'm getting all kinds of recognition over reporting such a warm human interest story. Emma was right when she said she was waiting to see what God would do. It looks like He's starting to show us."

"I'm so glad, Kelsey."

"And, Pastor Mike, I intend to be standing in the front row during the nativity on Christmas Eve night."

Mike laughed. "That's great. We'll see you then."

"Oh, and one more thing. I met a group of men who volunteer to help clean up after hurricanes, tornadoes, and such when I went to the Gulf Coast after their last hurricane. They're from a church in Tennessee and call themselves the Nehemiah Crew. The leader of the group called me today and said they're heading up to Bethlehem to get the green cleaned out. They should be there in a few days."

Mike closed his eyes and propped his hand against the hallway wall. "I don't know why I'm so overwhelmed when I knew God could do it, but I am."

Kelsey laughed. "Maybe you're just thankful."

"That's definitely correct."

"I have to go now, but I'll be checking in to see how things are going. Bye."

Mike disconnected the call and tried to digest everything Kelsey had just said. When he didn't say anything, Emma grabbed his arm and shook it. "Aren't you going to tell me what Kelsey said?"

He reached out and took her hand in his. "You were right,

Emma. All we had to do was get out of God's way."

Her eyes grew even wider. "And what did He do?"

He watched her expression change from excitement to shock to happiness as he told her the conversation he'd had with Kelsey. When he finished, she was so excited she threw her arms around his neck and hugged him.

"Oh, Mike, I knew God would help us. Isn't He wonderful?" His arms tightened around her, and she suddenly stiffened and pulled away. Her face turned crimson, and she tried to break his hold on her. "I'm sorry. I shouldn't have done that."

He pulled her back to him. "Yes, you should have. It was exactly the perfect thing to do." He gazed into her eyes for a moment before he lowered his face to hers. "I've never known anyone like you, Emma. The times we've spent together in the last few weeks have been the best of my life, and I don't want it to end after the nativity is complete."

She directed a somber gaze at him. "Neither do I."

He smiled. "And that is very good to know."

Then he pulled her closer and pressed his lips against hers. A thrill like he'd never known rushed through him at her response, and he realized something. The last few weeks might have been the best he'd ever known, but what lay before them in the future promised to be even better.

Chapter 8

The next few weeks seemed to fly by with every day bringing them closer to staging the nativity. On the first Sunday in December, following the benediction, Pastor Mike asked those who planned to help with the nativity to remain for a short meeting. To his surprise the whole congregation sat back down, settled into their seats, and waited for him to speak.

"As you know," he said, "the nativity plans got off to a rocky start, but I'm so thankful for the members of this church who never gave up and persevered to make it happen." He turned and smiled at Emma in the choir. "Especially Emma Townsend, who kept reminding all of us that God could take our efforts and make them into whatever He wanted. When we got out of God's way, we saw that she was right. I thought it would be good if we went over our plans this morning and see what needs to be done before the first performance."

Chester Dyer stood and held up his hand. "Pastor Mike, I'll start off by letting you know everything is now on schedule. That crew from Tennessee arrived, and I couldn't believe how fast they worked. They had the downed trees cut up and hauled off in just a few days. Then they cleaned out the debris and got all the fishing boats towed back to the marina. Even with the snowfall last night, the green is in good condition and looks great. There were some damaged limbs on the trees that weathered the storm, and we cut them out just to be safe. Didn't want them falling on someone during the nativity. So everything looks good."

"That's good news, Chester. So is everything ready for you and Dwight to begin building the set?"

Chester nodded. "We plan to get started in the morning. It shouldn't take long now. And I saw Dr. Norwood yesterday, and he said he had the animals all lined up. They'll arrive in plenty of time for the nativity, and he has everything arranged for their care while they're here."

Mike smiled. "Wonderful." He glanced around the congregation. "Who's next? John, how about the music?"

John stood. "All the solos are lined up, and Emma has been practicing with her girls' choir. Quite a few families have left town, so we're going to have a smaller group than last year, but we'll have music."

"And tell the congregation about the generator," Mike said.

"I was worried we might not be able to purchase a new generator, but with all the money that people across the country have donated, we were able to buy a bigger and better one than we originally had."

"That's awesome news, isn't it, people?"

Heads bobbed and several shouted out a loud yes. Mike

glanced across the crowd and spied Janet Burgess. He smiled at her. "Janet, how about you? What's the word on the costumes?"

Janet got to her feet. "Pastor Mike, some of the material finally came in last week, but we found out that the material for the wise men's costumes—the very colorful, more fancy fabric—had to be backordered. We decided we'd do the best we could and scheduled a meeting for that afternoon to start cutting them out even though we doubted we could finish in time. We only have two sewing machines that survived the storm."

"Oh, I didn't realize that," Mike said.

"Well, it turned out it didn't matter. Right after lunch a delivery truck arrived with several big boxes addressed to the Bethlehem Sewing Circle. They were from an opera group in Pennsylvania. When we opened them, there was a letter inside one that said they performed the opera *Amahl and the Night Visitors* last Christmas, and they wanted to share some costumes with us."

Mike frowned and shook his head. "I'm not familiar with that opera."

"I saw it once when I was visiting family in New York. The story is about a boy who dreams he is a disabled shepherd boy who lives with his mother in biblical times. One night they have three visitors come by their house wanting a place to sleep. They are wise men who are seeking a baby that has been born, and they have gifts for him. Their robes are the grandest thing Amahl has ever seen." Janet caught her breath and waved her hand in dismissal. "Anyway, there's more to the story, but the point is this

opera group didn't have any use for the wise men costumes anymore, and they sent them to us. We're going to have the richest-
looking wise men we've ever had when they put on these robes."

Mike's eyebrows arched, and he turned to Emma. "You didn't
tell me about this."

She smiled. "Sorry. There's been so much happening. I guess
I forgot."

From the back row of the church Gordon Brown's voice rang
out. "I'm in charge of the actors, and I haven't heard anything
about who's filling the parts of the wise men."

Mike turned back around and faced Gordon. "I'm not sure
we know that yet, Gordon. Maybe we will in a few days."

"I'd like to say something, Pastor Mike." For a moment Mike
couldn't identify the speaker. He glanced across the congregation
and then sucked in his breath when Murray Samuels slowly stood.

Mike's first impression was that the man had aged at least
ten years in the weeks since Eleanor. That was no surprise,
though, since he'd been going nonstop ever since the storm
moved inland. "Of course, Mr. Samuels."

To Mike's surprise the selectman stepped out of the pew
into the aisle and walked toward the front of the church. He
didn't stop until he stood next to Mike. Then he took a deep
breath and faced the congregation.

"All of you know my position on staging the nativity this
year. I spoke out against it the first time Pastor Mike and Emma
brought it up. With the task of rebuilding our town facing us,
I didn't think we had any business distracting ourselves with

something that wouldn't help us get back to the way life was here before the storm."

Mike glanced over his shoulder at Emma. She arched her eyebrows as if to ask why Mr. Samuels was bringing this up again, and Mike gave a small shrug before he turned back to the selectman.

Mr. Samuels looked at Mike and gave him a weary smile. "But, Pastor, I want you to know I was wrong. Life can't get back to normal until we put all our faith in the One who gives life. Somewhere along the way I forgot that." He smiled at Emma. "Emma, you have been an example to all of us by making us see what God can do if we really trust Him. I want you to know that I wholeheartedly support the nativity, and the selectmen will be honored to be the three wise men in this year's production."

Mike almost laughed out loud at the stunned look on Emma's face. She clamped her hand over her mouth as tears trickled down her cheeks. The congregation rose to their feet and applauded as Mr. Samuels let his gaze drift over the people he'd known for years. The weariness that had lined his face moments before seemed to disappear.

Mike reached up and grasped Mr. Samuels's shoulder. "Thank you. The citizens of Bethlehem are fortunate to have you as an elected official. And we thank you for all you've done in the past few weeks."

Mr. Samuels smiled. "And one more thing. The council decided it wouldn't be Christmas without the tree-lighting ceremony. So we've ordered an eighteen-foot tree from a farm down in Vermont. It should arrive next week. Although there's a lot of damage downtown, it's going to be placed across from City Hall. We'll light it a week from tomorrow."

Another round of applause erupted from the congregation. Mike held up his hand for quiet. "I'd say the Lord has blessed us today. Let's thank Him before we go our separate ways." Everyone bowed their heads, and Mike began to pray. "Oh, Lord, thank You for what we've seen happen in our town in the past few weeks. You have raised us to stand above the despair that followed Hurricane Eleanor's arrival on our shore, and You have reminded us that all things are possible with You. Now be with us as we get ready for the production of the nativity, and keep us ever mindful where all our blessings come from. In Your blessed name. Amen."

Several "amens" echoed across the room as the people raised their heads and began to move out of the pews. Several men walked over to shake Mr. Samuels's hand as he tried to make his way up the aisle. Soon he was surrounded by people offering their thanks for all he'd done for them in the past few weeks.

Warm satisfaction flowed through Mike as he watched the selectman's face beam and heard him thank each person for their contributions in helping the town return to normal.

They all headed up the aisle toward the door, their lively conversation and laughter drifting across the sanctuary. Mike stood still and closed his eyes to soak in the sweet sound.

"What are you doing?" Emma's voice from behind startled him, and he turned toward her.

"Listening to what the end of services sounded like before

the hurricane. We've turned a corner in Bethlehem. We're beginning to heal."

She nodded and watched the congregation exit the building. "It's nice, isn't it?"

He took a deep breath and sighed. "There's something I'd like to ask you to do for me."

"Sure. What is it?"

"Remind me to never doubt you again."

She arched an eyebrow. "Why?"

"Because now I have to do what I vowed I never would, sing in public. So which Sunday do you choose?"

She grinned and looped her arm through his. "Whenever you're ready. But if it will make you feel better, I'll sing with you."

His heart raced at the playful look she directed at him. "I'd like that very much."

"Then we'll worry about your singing debut after the nativity is over. Until then, though, we still have hungry people who'll be in the fellowship hall for lunch. Are you ready for the next shift?"

He smiled and shook his head. "Did anyone ever tell you that you're a slave driver? I don't think I've had a moment's rest since we decided to stage the nativity."

She laughed and pulled him toward the door that led to the fellowship hall. "And you've loved every moment of it."

He stared at her, and the truth hit him. He had loved it. He'd talked to his congregation today about blessings. But now as he stared into her eyes, he knew God had given him a special blessing when He brought him to Bethlehem to meet Emma Townsend.

Chapter 9

Emma had never thought of herself as a nervous woman, but she had been antsy all day long. She couldn't sit still, and she flitted from one task to another, checking to make sure every detail was perfect for the first night of the nativity.

Now with only an hour left before the opening scene, her stomach continued to do flip-flops. She hugged her coat tighter around her and stared across the small crowd that had already gathered on the green. She'd worried that the morning snowfall might keep the crowd away, but at least some hardy souls had ventured out tonight.

"Are you ready for this?"

She glanced around at Mike, who'd stopped beside her. They'd hardly had a chance to speak today as they'd worked to make sure everything was on track for tonight. She smiled and glanced back at the set.

"Chester and Dwight did a great job. I don't think we've ever had a more beautiful set."

"They did," Mike said. "The stable is perfect, and the platform above it is just what we needed for the angels and the soloists. The only thing I'm worried about right now is the performance. Dress rehearsal didn't go too well last night."

Emma laughed and punched him on the shoulder. "You know what they say. A bad dress rehearsal means a really good opening night."

He winced and rubbed his shoulder. "I hope you're right." His eyes softened as he stared at her. "But then, I've found out for the past few months that you're usually right about everything."

Her face grew warm, and she glanced back at the gathered audience. "I don't know about that. I predicted a large audience, but it looks like the snow may keep that from happening."

He arched his eyebrows. "Since when did you quit having faith? And what does it matter how many people show up? The Bible tells us where two or three are gathered together, He is there."

"I know. I guess I'm letting my emotions run away with me. We've worked so hard for weeks, and I want everybody to see how much they're appreciated. We'll have to make sure they know that, no matter how many people show up tonight."

She'd just finished speaking when the lights that had lit the set suddenly dimmed and went out. Mike cast a startled look in her direction, whirled, and headed to the back of the set with Emma right behind him.

When they rounded the edge of the set, they saw Chester, a flashlight in his hand, on his knees in front of the generator. He glanced up as they approached.

"What happened, Chester?" Mike asked.

"I don't know. John is in charge of the generator, and he was back here a few minutes ago. When the lights went out, I came to check, but he wasn't here."

Emma's heart pounded. "Where is he? We've got to get this generator fixed right away or there won't be a performance tonight."

Mike turned to her. "Calm down, Emma. It's going to be all right."

Tears rolled down her cheeks at the sight of the new generator that had been working perfectly a few minutes ago now sitting idle. "This can't be happening. Forty-five minutes until we begin, and we don't have lights."

"Please, don't cry. I'm sure we can. . ."

"What's the problem, folks?" John Roland's voice rang out.

Emma whirled at the sound of his voice. "John, what's happened to the generator?"

"Nothing."

"What do you mean nothing?" Emma said. "It's not working."

John stared at her for a moment before he grinned sheepishly. "It's not working because I turned it off."

"You did what?"

John muffled a chuckle as he set down the large yellow can he was carrying. "Emma, when you have low temperatures like we do tonight, the fuel in the generator can gel and clog the filters. So you have to add an anti-gelling mixture to the fuel before you put it in the generator. I mixed some up this afternoon, and

I wanted to see if I had the ratio right. I've been letting the generator run, and everything seems okay. But because it's been running for a while, the fuel level was getting low, so I turned it off and went to get some more. I'll have everything back to normal in a few minutes."

Emma raised a shaking hand to her forehead. "I'm sorry I panicked. I feel so foolish."

"There's no need to think like that," Mike said. He gripped her shoulders and turned her to face him. Then he leaned close and stared into her eyes. "You have been so strong ever since we began this project. When everyone else wanted to give up, you were right there offering love and encouragement and telling us what God could do if we'd give Him the chance. You were right, and now we're about to see how your faith has affected this whole town. Are you ready for that?"

She looked up into his eyes, and her heartbeat quickened at the way his eyes bored into hers. She swallowed and nodded. "Yes. I let my emotions get the better of me. I won't do it again."

He smiled and grasped her hand. "Good. Now let's go back out front and see if the audience has gotten larger since we came backstage."

She let him lead her around the edge of the set back to the front. Her gaze drifted over the assembled people, and her heart warmed. "I see some people I don't recognize. So we have visitors, not just hometown folks tonight."

He turned to her. "And remember that we don't know the hearts of those who have come or the problems they're facing.

Maybe God has brought someone here tonight who really needs Him. If just one person is helped because of our efforts, it's all been worth it."

She nodded. "You're right. I'll remember that. . ."

She paused as she spotted a car stopped at the edge of the green where parking wasn't allowed. A frown pulled at her forehead, but it changed to a smile when the passenger door opened, and Kelsey Warren stepped out. Tanner Hodges crawled out from the driver's side. He opened the back door of the car and retrieved his camera.

"Kelsey, Tanner," Mike called out. "Over here."

Kelsey glanced around and smiled when she saw them. She said something to Tanner, and the two walked toward them. Kelsey reached out and gave Emma a quick hug when they reached them.

Emma shook her head in disbelief. "Kelsey, what are you two doing here?"

Kelsey laughed. "I know I told you I'd come for the Christmas Eve performance, but I decided I wanted to be here tonight for the first one."

"We're glad you are," Mike said. He pointed to the camera in Tanner's hand. "Are you going to record some of it?"

Kelsey nodded. "I thought there might be some interesting events taking place tonight that would make a good follow-up to the first story. Especially since it was so well received."

Mike smiled and swept his arm across the green and the nativity set. "God used that story to make it possible for us to have our nativity this year. We're grateful to all the people across the country who donated money or items for the nativity. We could never have done it alone."

"Hey, face the camera and repeat that," Tanner said.

Kelsey took Mike's arm and positioned him so that Tanner could record their conversation as she continued questioning him about how everything concerning the nativity had fallen into place after her story. The most satisfying of all to Emma was that Mike spoke from the heart about how God had used so many people to accomplish His will in Bethlehem.

"So, here we are tonight, our first performance, and we couldn't be more pleased to have you and your news team here with our small first-night crowd," Mike concluded.

Kelsey chuckled. "I think your crowd is about to get larger."

"What do you mean?"

The roar of an approaching vehicle cut through the night air, and Emma stared in surprise as a chartered bus drove up and stopped behind Tanner and Kelsey's car. Before she could ask what was going on, two more buses rolled to a stop behind the first one.

Tanner turned his camera on the buses as the doors opened and people began to stream down the steps. They headed across the green and joined the small group of onlookers who'd arrived earlier.

Emma stared open-mouthed at the crowd. "What's going on?"

Kelsey laughed. "I had a call today from a charter bus company in Portland. The man you rented the animals from is a friend of the owner, and he told him about the nativity and everything that had happened. The bus company owner decided to see if anyone was interested in coming, so he advertised a special nighttime trip to the Bethlehem Nativity. He had enough responses to fill three buses tonight and more for the other nights of the nativity. So get ready for a big audience every night."

Emma and Mike looked at each other in disbelief. Tears filled Emma's eyes. "If you have the faith of a mustard seed. . ."

"You can move a mountain," Mike finished for her.

He reached out and wrapped his fingers around hers. Her throat closed up, and she couldn't make her voice respond. She only hoped the love that had grown in her heart for him shone through her tears. She swallowed and tried again to speak.

"Mike. . ."

Before she could finish, the lights dimmed, and the crowd grew quiet. The melody of "O Little Town of Bethlehem" drifted from the sound system, and Emma closed her eyes to let the sweet strains soak into her soul. As the recorded introduction neared the end, she opened her eyes and smiled to see her girls' choir, dressed as angels, on the platform above the stable.

Although only half the members had been available to participate, Emma thought they had never sounded better as they began to sing the opening song. Their clear voices carried on the night air, and she felt as if she were being transported back in time to a night of miracles when angels sang and shepherds came to worship the newborn king.

As the performance progressed, Emma found herself being

drawn into the story of Christ's birth with a new understanding. The last two months had reminded her more than ever before of the importance of the event that took place in a stable in Bethlehem.

God had sent His Son that night, and He was still in control all these years later. All she had to do was look at the faces of the people who watched the drama unfolding in front of them.

All too soon the performance neared the end, and the introduction of a new song drifted from the sound system. Emma jerked her attention back to the stage. Her choir took their places again and began to sing "We Three Kings."

Slowly three camels emerged from the shadows beside the green and lumbered toward the set. Emma sucked in her breath at the regal appearance of the three selectmen who sat on the camels' backs. The jewels on their robes twinkled in the lights, and the attendants who accompanied each king carried gifts representing the gold, frankincense, and myrrh that were given at Jesus' birth.

The camels came to a stop, knelt, and the selectmen slid from their saddles. With their backs straight and heads erect, they approached the manger and bowed to worship the baby.

Emma glanced across the audience at the rapt attention directed toward the scene, and once again she was reminded of how God had brought them to this night. The same faith that led the townspeople had led the wise men so many years ago.

She leaned close to Mike, who stood next to her, and whispered in his ear. "I think we need to promise God that we'll always remember how He provided everything to make this night possible, and that each year we'll dedicate our nativity to Him for blessing us during very hard times."

Mike nodded. "A Christmas promise, that's what it will be. We pledge that each year we'll show those who come to see our production that nothing is impossible with God if you just get out of the way and let Him be in control."

He put his arm around her shoulders and drew her closer. She closed her eyes and said another quick thanks to God for something else that had blessed her life—Mike's coming to Bethlehem.

Chapter 10

An hour later Mike stood in the center of the town green, staring at the darkened set and letting his mind drift back over what had happened on this spot tonight. The people of Bethlehem had united in faith to let God lead them, and they had retold the familiar story of Jesus' birth two thousand years ago. But it hadn't just been an old story. It had been one that still carried the message of God's promises in the twenty-first century.

He heard the crunch of footsteps across the frozen ground, and he glanced over his shoulder to see Emma approaching. He smiled when she stopped next to him. "Did Kelsey and Tanner leave?"

"They followed the last bus out of town, but they said they'd be back for the rest of the performances to interview more people."

"What about the cast? Have they gone back to the church for hot cocoa and cookies?"

She laughed. "They have. Everyone was so excited about how well everything went tonight. They couldn't wait to get there and relive every minute."

Mike sighed and glanced at the darkened set once more. "It was a night to remember. Everything went great, but I must say my favorite part was when the selectmen rode in on those camels. After all Mr. Samuels's blustering about not doing the nativity, he turned out to be the biggest supporter."

"I know," Emma said. "I told him that you and I had talked about how we needed to promise God that the production would continue each year and serve as a reminder that anything is possible with God."

"What did he say?"

"He thought it was a great idea. He said just let him know what we needed from now on, and he'd see that we had it. Changing his mind may be the greatest blessing of all."

Mike grasped her hand and stared into her eyes. "I think there's something else that's a miracle."

She tilted her head and smiled. "And what's that?"

His heart hammered in his chest so hard that he feared she could hear it. "Getting to know you."

"I've enjoyed getting to know you, too. I've respected you as my pastor ever since you came to town, but now I feel much closer to you."

"I feel much closer to you, too." He swallowed and put his arms around her. "I'm just sorry we haven't had a chance to spend more time alone. Do you think we could do that now that we won't be working on the nativity anymore?"

She looped her arms around his neck and smiled up at him. "I'd like that."

"Me, too." He swallowed before he continued. "From the first time I saw you at church, I knew you were different than anyone I'd ever met before. I wanted to ask you out, but I was afraid to get close to you. I didn't know what the congregation would think if I dated a church member. And then I thought that I might not like you so much after I got to know you. I was afraid if it didn't work out, I would offend you and cause a problem in the church."

"So you chose to ignore your feelings," she said.

He bit his lip and nodded. "I did. I thought it was better not to get involved."

"And now what do you think?"

He hesitated a moment before he drew her closer. "Now I wish I hadn't waited to get to know how wonderful you really are. I could have been happier all these lonely months I've been in Bethlehem."

She smiled. "I'm glad you told me this. Ever since you came to Bethlehem, I've wished you would ask me out. I'd about decided it was a hopeless cause, though. Then we began to work together on the nativity."

He nodded. "We did, and I knew right away God had brought me here to meet you, Emma. You're the blessing He's been preparing me for. You're the one He wants by my side as I do His work, and you're the one I promise I'll love for the rest of my life."

Her eyes grew wide. "Are you saying you love me?"

"I do. More than I can ever tell you. I pray you feel the same about me."

She smiled, and her eyes sparkled with tears. "I've loved you for so long, but I'd about given up hope you'd ever notice me. I guess when I got out of God's way and let Him take control of the nativity, He decided not only to make it a success but to throw in a special blessing for me, too. I love you, Michael Benson, and I always will."

He smiled. "In that case, Emma Townsend, will you marry me and make me the happiest man in Bethlehem, Maine?"

"I will."

He lowered his head, and their lips met to seal the commitment they'd just made to each other. When Mike released her, he glanced back to the darkened nativity set and said a quick prayer of thanks for all the blessings that had poured down on their little town of Bethlehem since Hurricane Eleanor.

He hugged Emma close, and she rested her head on his chest. "We made a promise to God tonight that we would give Him the praise each year when we present the nativity, but I want to make another promise to Him."

"What?" she murmured.

"That no matter what comes our way in the future, you and I will get out of God's way and let Him take control. Can you imagine what He can do in our lives if we give Him total control?"

She snuggled closer. "I can't, but I'm looking forward to finding out."

ONE HOLY NIGHT

By Elizabeth Ludwig

Chapter 1

The door to the McElroy Veterinary Clinic whooshed open, ushering in a blast of frosty November air. Leesa ignored the accompanying chime of the doorbell, her attention focused on the cast she was applying to the leg of a temperamental schnauzer.

"Want me to see who that is, Doc?"

Leesa eyed the snarling schnauzer and then her assistant, Samantha "Sammy" Reynolds. "Okay, but make it quick. I can do without another complaint from this old guy, eh, Rupert?" She gave the schnauzer a pat on the rump with the back of her hand.

Sammy grimaced and peeled the rubber gloves from her fingers with a snap. "Complaint? Right. He about took my finger off the last time he 'complained.'"

She scowled at Rupert then circled the metal examination table and ducked through the door toward the reception area.

Smoothing the last strip of casting tape into place, Leesa smiled. Sammy was still in high school, but hiring her had been the best decision she'd made since opening the clinic two years earlier. Sammy worked well with both people and animals—even Rupert. It hurt her heart to think she might have to let her go.

She bent to whisper into the dog's twitching ear. "Lucky for you I need customers." He growled, and Leesa sighed. "And lucky for me, your mommy doesn't much care for old Dr. Norwood or his muzzle."

Stripping free of her latex gloves, she dropped them into a trashcan, one eye trained on the schnauzer. She'd given the dog a dose of acepromazine to calm him during the procedure, but that didn't mean he wouldn't lash out—an instinctive reaction to anxiety and fear.

She patted Rupert's trembling side and gently burrowed her fingers into his fur. "There, boy. Six weeks and you'll be good as new."

Sammy reentered, a bounce in her step. "All done?"

"Yep. Go ahead and call his mommy. Tell her everything went fine, but let her know I want to keep him a couple of hours for observation. I want to see how he'll do with the cast."

"Will do," Sammy said, already snuggling Rupert into a brown, fuzzy blanket adorned with doggie bones. Mindful of his teeth, she lifted him carefully from the table and turned toward the kennels off a hallway at the back of the clinic.

"In the meantime, you have a visitor waiting for you up front. Kate Walters."

Leesa tugged at the snaps on her lab coat. "What does she want?"

Sammy's mouth turned up in an impish grin. The pooch

cradled in her arms, she backed into the hall and disappeared.

Great. This probably won't be good.

Drawing a deep breath, Leesa deposited her soiled lab coat into a laundry bin on her way to the reception area.

Even with Leesa's rubber-soled shoes, it was obvious Kate heard her approaching. Nervously pushing her stroller back and forth, she straightened, squaring her shoulders before she turned to extend a greeting. "Morning, Dr. McElroy."

Not fooled by her bright tone, Leesa rounded the counter. "Morning, Kate. How's the little one today?"

The lines smoothed from Kate's face, replaced with a radiant smile as she peered down into the stroller. Motherhood agreed with her.

"She's just fine. Finally over her cold, thank goodness."

Leesa bent for a peek at the slumbering child. With her thumb tucked into her mouth, her cheeks flushed and rosy, she couldn't look more cherubic. Leesa slanted her gaze up at Kate. It hadn't been easy for her and her husband, David, to learn they were becoming parents again so late in life, but they'd made the transition and appeared blessed by it, despite the challenges.

"I'm happy for you, Kate."

The professional mask Kate wore as the Bethlehem Town Manager dipped slightly. "Thanks, Leesa. It hasn't been easy balancing motherhood with my job."

No doubt. Just thinking about trying to run the clinic while juggling marriage and a family made Leesa shiver. She gave an understanding nod then drew up her spine and crossed her arms. "Is that why you're here? Work?"

Kate slid back into her professional role. "Yes, as a matter of fact."

Leesa frowned. Just as she'd thought. "So what is Dr. Norwood complaining about this week?" She glanced at the flyer pinned to the bulletin board behind her desk. "Is it the rabies clinic I'm conducting next spring? I told him I'd be happy to coordinate with his office—"

Kate's forehead bunched in puzzlement. "Dr. Norwood? Oh. Right."

The confusion cleared from her face. Everyone in Bethlehem knew about the animosity between Leesa and the town's older, more established veterinarian, Andrew Norwood. He made it a point to inform anyone who brought up her name that he thought Bethlehem was too small for the two of them.

Kate shook her head. "It's not him this time. I'm here because I need to ask a favor." Her hand drifted to the stroller, and she resumed the nervous rocking. "You know the live nativity the town puts on at the green every Christmas?"

How could she forget? It was a highlight of the season and drew hundreds of visitors every year. Even Hurricane Eleanor, whose 95-mile-per-hour winds had battered the small town just a couple of years ago, failed to curtail the event. If anything, the storm had only strengthened the bond between Bethlehem's residents and their beloved nativity. "Of course. It's one of the reasons I fell in love with Bethlehem."

That, and it's hundreds of miles from Bangor.

Leesa shoved that thought into a remote corner of her brain. "Why?"

Kate's face brightened with a winsome smile. A politician's smile, Leesa corrected, her fingers tensing around a pen she picked up from the receptionist's desk. Why did she suddenly get the feeling this "favor" was going to require something big?

"As you know, there are a lot of animals involved in the production. Dr. Norwood is going to be out of town this year visiting family in Utah, which means we'll need someone to step into the role of caring for them while the nativity is going on."

Big.

"Of course, I thought of you. I'm hoping you might be interested in playing one of the shepherds. . ."

Bigger.

". . .and maybe speaking to Logan Franks?"

Biggest.

Leesa put up her hand. "Hold on there. . .Logan Franks? How did he get in on this conversation?"

A blush crept over Kate's cheeks. She checked on her sleeping daughter then took a step closer. "Listen, Leesa, where do you think we get the camels the wise men ride every year?"

Leesa gave a weak laugh. Truthfully, she'd never thought about it. "Camels-R-Us?"

Kate's echoing laughter flowed much more naturally. "I wish. No, we have to contract with a farm outside of Portland. Costs us hundreds of dollars to get them here, and with the economy being tight. . ." She shrugged her shoulders. "This year, it's just not in the budget."

"Okaaay." Seeing where this was going, Leesa bit her lip. "But Logan—"

"Logan Franks has hundreds of exotic animals, from camels to coyotes, and he's right here in Bethlehem. We'd save a fortune if we could work out a deal with him instead of having to ship them from out of town."

"Then why haven't you?" Leesa asked, frowning.

"We've tried. In fact, it was Dr. Norwood who spoke to him when we were putting this thing together years ago."

"He wouldn't do it?"

Kate shook her head.

"So what makes you think I'd have any luck?"

Her eyes took on a wily gleam. "You still in the singles class at Sunday school?"

Leesa took a defensive step backward. "Kate. . ."

Kate blinked, dispelling the gleam as quickly as it had appeared. "Besides, with Dr. Norwood gone, I thought you might like to try your hand. After all, it'd be quite a coup, considering *he* wasn't able to pull it off."

Honestly, the woman changed tactics faster than a Navy Seal. Leesa shook her head. "No fair throwing his name into this."

"It is if it works." Kate's shoulders lifted in a contrite shrug. "C'mon, Leesa. Please? You're always talking about how you never have time to get to know people. What better way than the nativity?"

Leesa turned her back, taking her time as she retrieved the receptionist's chair. Against the tiled floor, the wheels made a gentle clacking sound—something that wouldn't be heard if the kennels were full. But thanks to Dr. Norwood...

No, she chastised, Norwood was only part of the problem. The people of Bethlehem didn't know her, had not yet learned to trust her expertise. What Kate was offering was more than a chance to drum up business. It was a chance to take part in something the community loved—finally feel a part. But Logan Franks...

Her heart thumped just thinking about his imposing frown. The man could freeze a volcano with one of his glares. To have to actually ask him for something meant risking frostbite. Or worse. Like death from hypothermia.

Too bad he was also stop-you-in-the-street good looking.

Leesa sighed and plopped into the chair. Across the counter, Kate's eyes shone hopefully. To her credit, she'd held her tongue while she waited.

Leesa drummed the desktop once, twice, then blew out her cheeks and nodded. "I'll do it. I'll play one of the shepherds," she added quickly when Kate's face lit with excitement, "but you know I can't guarantee Mr. Franks will even speak to me."

"He will," Kate said, with far more confidence than Leesa felt at the moment. "He comes across as unapproachable, but you'd be surprised how kind he can be. I remember a time..." She dropped her gaze as though embarrassed by what she'd been about to say. "Anyway, let me know how it goes, will you? I'll need an answer fairly quickly, so we can start planning one way or another."

Leesa nodded, and after promising she'd get back with Kate soon, watched as she wheeled the stroller out of the clinic and down the street. What did Kate know about Logan Franks that Leesa didn't, and why hadn't she shared it?

The questions nagged her long after she'd gone home for the day. *Kind* and *Logan Franks* were not words she'd have strung together. No, she thought as she removed a plate of leftover meatloaf from the refrigerator for her supper, Logan Franks was more like this dish—cold and a little bit stiff.

The thought made her giggle, but it was his menacing glare she remembered later as she brushed her teeth and got ready for bed, and his scowl she saw when almost an hour later, she finally went to sleep.

Chapter 2

The sun peeking above the miles of rolling hills had yet to melt the frost off the trees or the grass under his feet. Logan drew a long breath of icy morning air and blew it out slow, like the steam from a locomotive. Funny how, on days like this, he could still be transported to his youth—for a moment, anyway.

His heart clenched, and he lowered his gaze to the pair of yellow eyes watching him curiously. "Right. Let's get moving. Too cold to stand here gathering wool."

The wolf's nose twitched in agreement.

Lifting the latch on a long, metal gate, he pushed through, waited for the wolf, then let it clang shut. On a typical day, feeding the livestock came first, but the wolf made the camels nervous, so Logan veered toward the aviary.

A high, tinny whistle carried on the air, mingling with bird songs. Not surprising. His hired hand, Pete, was an early riser for a college kid—earlier than Logan.

He entered the aviary, the wolf on his heels. Greeted by a blast of warm air, he unwound the scarf from around his neck

then directed a sharp glare at the wolf. "No tricks. Sit there and
be good."

As if to say that had been his intention all along, the wolf
dropped to his belly at the door and laid his head on his paws
with a long-suffering sigh.

Pete rounded the corner. In each hand, he lugged a large
bucket brimming with chopped fruits and vegetables, mixed
with seed. "Morning, Boss."

"Morning."

Logan relieved him of one of the buckets then followed him
to the center of the aviary, where they made short, silent work
of distributing the food. That was one of the things Logan liked
about Pete. He didn't feel compelled to fill up the quiet.

The two toiled side-by-side for almost an hour—cleaning
the aviary, changing the water in the bathing pool, sweeping out
leaves and debris. It was menial, mind-numbing work, but these
days Logan appreciated the simplicity. It filled his days, leaving
him with little time to think.

"I see Wolf's back."

Logan cut his gaze to the door, where the wolf's ears perked
at the mention of his name. "Yeah. He was gone longer this time.
I was starting to worry."

Pete shook his head. "Probably got himself a girl up in the
woods. That time of year."

"Uh-huh." Logan leaned against the broom handle.
"Speaking of the time of year, shouldn't the college be letting you
out for Christmas break soon? I assume you'll be going home?"

Even with Pete's head lowered, Logan saw the flush coloring his cheeks. The kid hunched deeper into his shoulders and cleared his throat. "Actually. . .I was kinda thinking about sticking around Bethlehem."

Logan clenched his jaw and went back to sweeping. "That'd make two years in a row, Pete. I'm sure your parents miss you."

"My parents won't mind, if they know I'm needed here," he blurted, his face reddening.

No, they probably wouldn't, considering how many prayer-filled cards and letters they'd sent. That still didn't excuse Logan from claiming their eldest son for a second Christmas. Finished with the broom, he stowed it and the dustpan in a small closet then twisted his wrist to read his watch. Almost seven thirty.

He clapped Pete on the shoulder. "I'll finish up. You'd better head to class before you're late. We'll talk about the break another time."

Though he said nothing, Pete looked almost as forlorn as the wolf. He bobbed his shaggy head—the kid needed a haircut, bad—then ducked out the aviary door and loped toward a beat-up Oldsmobile Cutlass.

A wry smile tipped Logan's lips. No wonder Pete had been one of Miranda's favorite students. He was a good kid. And he loved animals. He'd make a wonderful zoologist one day. Miranda always said so. . .

The usual pang that accompanied his wife's name rippled through his chest—a warm, familiar ache that Logan welcomed. Anything to be able to feel again.

Giving a whistle, he led Wolf out of the aviary, securing the door behind him, and turned for the barn. Though he was by no means tame, the wolf sat obediently when ordered and waited while Logan filled feeders and cleaned stalls.

The job took most of the morning. Stepping from the barn, Logan wiped the sweat from his brow and peeked at the sun high overhead. Almost midday. Time to eat. His body reminded him of the need for sustenance even though his mind tended to lapse into forgetfulness.

He headed for the house and was surprised when the hum of an engine rumbled up the winding driveway.

Pete back already? Class must've let out early. Logan waited at the gate, narrowing his eyes when it wasn't a Cutlass that rounded the curve a quarter-mile down the road, but a newer model Ford. White. The vet.

He scowled and crossed his arms. What did she want?

She pulled to a stop a few feet shy of him and climbed out of the car, her blue eyes wide and hopeful, a bright smile pasted on her lips. "Morning, Mr. Franks."

He resisted the urge to shoot a glance at the noonday sun. No need to be rude. "Dr. McElroy. What brings you out this way?"

Her mouth slackened at his directness, and her booted feet skittered to a halt on the gravel drive. "Well. . .I. . ." Her focus slipped past him to something beyond his shoulder.

Wolf. He heard the low growl before he turned to look. "Easy, boy."

The wolf crept to Logan's side, his gray head lowered and his gaze fixed on the intruder.

"My fault." Dr. McElroy retreated a step. "I'm in his territory uninvited. He's just doing his job as the pack leader."

"His job?" In spite of himself, Logan cracked a smile. Sounded like something Miranda would say.

Pang.

Huh. Twice in one day.

"You know wolves are a hot button issue in the state of Maine, right?" she continued and then stopped when he stiffened. "Sorry. Not why I'm here."

"No problem." Seeing her shiver and rub her hands over her arms, he gestured toward the shelter of the barn. "Come inside?"

Inviting her in was a definite mistake. She'd cut her visit short if she was cold. Still, he couldn't stand by and watch a person freeze. He swung toward the barn. This time, the wolf didn't follow. He sniffed the air as Dr. McElroy passed. Shooting Logan a deep look of disgust, he turned and disappeared into the woods.

"Lucky dog," Logan muttered, holding the door.

Dr. McElroy stopped at the entrance—far too close for comfort—and peered up at him. "Sorry?"

He shrugged and turned his face from her narrowed gaze. Edging toward the stalls, he rested his foot on one of the rails. Hopefully, the posture at least made him look unaffected by her presence. She was barely out of vet school and only a little bigger than a minute, so why he always felt so off-kilter around her. . .

No good, that line of thinking. He crossed his arms and fumbled for one of his reliable scowls. "What can I do for you, Dr. McElroy?"

Apparently, she came prepared. She didn't waver under his glare, and her smile only slipped a little when he deepened his scowl. If anything, she looked at peace, happy even, standing there in her yellow rubber boots and matching slicker. Her hand rose and she pushed the hood from her head. Disconcerted by the blond curls spilling around her face, he sought the cracks in the wood floor, the piles of loose hay drifting in the corners of the barn, anything but her eyes.

"I appreciate your talking to me today, Mr. Franks. I apologize for not calling first, but unfortunately, we don't have a lot of time, and I am really, really desperate."

He brought his head up at the urgency in her voice. She stood with her feet braced, hands on her hips. Except for the puckered lines across her brow, she looked perfectly at home in his barn.

He slid his foot from the rail with a thump. "Excuse me?"

"Your animals." She cast a glance around the barn. "You still have camels, right?"

"Yes, but—"

"What about sheep?"

"A few."

"Donkeys?"

"No."

She shrugged. "We'll make do."

"Hold up, what are we talking about?" Logan raised his hands, palms out. "Make do with what?"

"The sheep."

"The—" He stopped before he actually repeated "sheep." This time, it took very little effort to scowl.

A flush stole over her cheeks, and she settled into her boots with a sigh. "Sorry. This is not how I rehearsed it in my head."

Something about her contrite, pixie-like smile melted a corner of his heart. . .and the irritation seeping through his thoughts. He relented with a sigh. "Maybe you should start from the beginning."

If she'd thought to win his patience with a smile, it was dispelled by her next words.

"Mr. Franks, I've come to ask for your help. What would you think about playing a shepherd in the Bethlehem Live Nativity?"

Chapter 3

Logan Franks's face looked carved from a glacier. Responding to her instincts, Leesa jammed her hands into her pockets. Flailing her hands when she got nervous or scared was a habit that started when she was young, and judging by the tempo of her heart, she'd start swinging any moment.

"Mr. Franks?"

He dragged his fingers through his dark shock of hair. "A shepherd. In the nativity."

Leesa swallowed and began again, slower. "Allow me to explain?"

With disbelief darkening his features and his lips clamped in a firm line, he hardly looked in the mood to consider an explanation. She swallowed again hastily and launched into a monologue similar to the one Kate Walters had used, the words spilling so fast she barely registered them—something about Dr. Norwood being out of town, the cost of shipping camels, and the logic behind playing the shepherds. She hoped she made sense. She was certainly louder than Kate. And more passionate. And yes, more animated, given that somewhere during her discourse, her hands had slipped free from her pockets and begun flailing.

"So you see, Mr. Franks"—she spread her palms wide—"it is absolutely crucial that we enlist the help of Bethlehem's residents if we want to keep the nativity going."

Was that a hint of glacial melting she saw in his somber gaze? Leesa's heart pattered hopefully.

Mr. Franks gave a slow shake of his head. "Sorry, Dr. McElroy. I understand the need, but I'm afraid I won't be able to help."

Screech.

Her thoughts couldn't have ground to a halt any faster. "W-what?"

"I don't loan out my animals, and certainly not for something as public as the nativity. They're not trained for it."

"Of course, which is why I will be right there to—"

"I didn't realize you were skilled in handling large animals." He grabbed a pitchfork and began walking away.

Actually. Walking. Away.

Leesa gritted her teeth and followed. "What I meant to say, Mr. Franks, is that you and I would both be present to head off any trouble we see brewing. You see, it just so happens that one of the selectmen has the measles."

"So?"

"So with you playing a shepherd, one of the other actors could take his place, and you could oversee the care and control of your animals."

Her ire rose as she struggled to keep pace with his long

187

strides. Really? The man thought he could outrun her? She'd show him what an hour of cardio every morning did for stamina.

At a large, circular corral, she drew even with him then stepped around and in front before he could reach for the gate. She fisted her hands on her hips, her head tilted back so she could squint up at him. "Is this about the fight we had last summer?"

"Fight—?"

The confusion cleared from his brow. Propping the pitchfork against the hardened ground, he leaned on the handle. "You mean the town meeting where you communicated the dangers of bird flu so eloquently?"

Wary of his casual stance, she nodded. "They asked for an expert opinion."

"Oh, and you gave it. Quite willingly."

"That's not fair," Leesa protested. "I did go on to explain that outbreaks of highly pathogenic avian flu viruses occur mostly in domestic poultry in parts of Asia and the Middle East, and that there've been no reported infections in birds, poultry, or people in the United States."

His eyebrows rose. So frustrating, but even to her own ears, she sounded like a recording. She swallowed a growl of frustration and changed tact.

"You have exotic birds. It's only natural that there would be some concern." She settled back on her heels and crossed her arms. "If anything, I would think you would be glad that my research laid those fears to rest. After all, I was only trying to help."

Tick, tick. She watched as the twitching in his jaw intensified.

He straightened and reached around her to unlatch the gate. "You wanna help?"

Even hours of cardio couldn't calm the sudden racing of her heart caused by his nearness. She eased out of his way, caught a whiff of his aftershave, decided she still wasn't far enough, and retreated another step.

He shoved the handle of the pitchfork toward her. "Then follow me."

He strode off without waiting for her answer. Watching his broad back, she itched to put the pitchfork to use.

"Remember why you're here," she muttered then cast a glance heavenward and repented of her dark thoughts.

The corral wasn't exactly circular, she realized. What she entered was actually a large gathering pen. Opposite were two diagonal sorting pens and beyond that, a round forcing pen that fed into a curved, single-file chute.

She had to admit, it was a nice setup. Almost like he knew what he was doing.

"You coming?"

She startled, her cheeks warming as she realized he'd been aware of her scrutiny. "Right behind you."

He scoffed, a corner of his mouth lifting in a wry grin. Sweeping one arm wide, he allowed her to precede him toward a monster-sized hayrack. Correction—an *empty* hayrack. She eyed him over her shoulder. "We're filling that?"

He jabbed his thumb to his chest and shook his head. "Not me. . .you. I've got water troughs to fill."

She narrowed her eyes at him. He didn't really think she'd give up that easily? Judging by the smug grin, he obviously did. Swept by a mix of determination and anger, she gripped the pitchfork in both hands and thrust out her chin. "Well, then, we'd better get started."

Hesitation warred with the confidence on his face. He eyed her hands. "There are gloves—"

"I'll be fine, thanks." Honestly, what kind of sissy did he take her for?

She regretted the rash words when, an hour later, blisters had formed on the inside of her thumbs and on both palms. Glaring at him from the corner of her eye, she jabbed the pitchfork into the pile of hay and straightened.

Forget the cardio. The workout she'd just finished beat anything she could do in the gym. Despite the cool temperatures, she wiped a sheen of perspiration from her brow.

"Had enough?" A bottled water in each hand, he crossed to her and extended one.

She ignored the satisfaction she read on his face and took the water. "Hardly." Unscrewing the cap, she tipped her head toward the hayrack then took a swig. Icy cold water had never tasted so good, not to mention how soothing the bottle felt against her sore hands.

He nodded in grudging appreciation. "Nice work."

"Thanks." Watching him, she ran the back of her hand over her mouth. Surely he'd be ready to talk now that she'd proven herself. She cleared her throat. "So. . .about the nativity?"

His gaze lowered to the bottle in his hand. He took his time unscrewing the cap, which allowed Leesa to study the strong planes of his face. Dampened with sweat, dark tendrils clung to his wide forehead. He hadn't shaved, which gave him a rugged look that made her breath catch. And his lashes. . .

They flitted up and she found herself pinned by his rich-as-chocolate gaze. "Why you?"

Pain?

"W-what?" she stammered.

He blinked, and the anguished look disappeared, replaced by the glacial mask she knew so well. She braced for disappointment, but to her surprise, he gave a curt nod. "I'm still not sure this is the greatest idea, but I'm willing to give it a shot."

"Really?" She gave herself a mental shake and forced a smile. "You won't be sorry. I'll make sure you have input on everything that happens with the animals."

He nodded his thanks. "What about rehearsals? I think the more the animals are around people, the better. Get them used to the noise and activity."

"I agree. We start next week. I'll make sure you have a schedule." She paused. Though she hadn't told him, his cooperation meant a lot to her and the success of her clinic. She gripped the water bottle tighter. "Thank you, Mr. Franks."

His gaze fell. With nothing left to say, Leesa fidgeted and then turned to go. "I'd better get back. Thanks for the water."

Again, he nodded. When she reached the gate, he called her name. "Dr. McElroy?"

She turned. He stood with both arms loose at his sides, one hand clutching the water and a look on his face she could only describe as shuttered.

"Call me Logan."

Her insides melted like butter on a hot biscuit. Grasping for a clever response and coming up empty, she whispered, "Okay." Licking her dry lips, she smiled brightly and lifted her chin. "And I'm Leesa."

Rather than reply, he studied her a bit longer before offering a brief nod and disappearing into the barn. Only then, did she truly feel free to breathe.

Chapter 4

The bell above the clinic door chimed merrily. Expecting Sammy, Leesa kept her head lowered while she pulled one final stitch free, then gave the cat's head a gentle tickle. "There you go, Molly. Good as new."

The cat's growl said she didn't agree. Leesa chuckled then carried her, still wrapped tightly in a towel to keep her from clawing, toward an empty kennel. Inside, the cat scrambled for her freedom then scurried to the back of the cage, where she crouched, glowering at Leesa through the bars.

"I know," Leesa said, securing the door, "but you'll thank me one day."

"Sure about that? She doesn't look too happy."

Startled by the rumbling voice, Leesa whirled. Logan Franks stood with his elbows atop the counter. Smiling. An actual smile, not the lopsided grimace she was used to seeing.

Realizing she had the towel clutched to her chin, she yanked her arms down then spun and tossed the towel into the dirty laundry. A deep breath later, she faced him and returned his smile. "Jinkies! You scared me. I thought you were Sammy.

My assistant. From high school."

His eyebrows rose. "Jinkies?"

Embarrassment melted over her cheeks. She'd picked up the expression watching cartoons as a kid. She paced to the counter, scooped up the clipboard holding Molly's chart, and held it to her chest. "What can I say? Scooby fan."

"Me, too."

"Really?"

His grin widened as he hooked both thumbs under his collar. "Still have my orange ascot."

"Now I know you're a fan," Leesa teased, stowing the chart in a filing cabinet. "Only the original Freddy wore an ascot."

"A fact only a true fan would know."

Before she realized it, Leesa had returned to the counter and was laughing along with him, the awareness of which seemed to strike them at the same moment. Their mirth dissipated like mist under a hot sun. Awkward silence crept into its place.

The nativity practice. Leesa motioned toward a stack of folders on the desk. "So, you're probably here to pick up a copy of the schedule?"

"Uh..."

She rifled through the folders until she found the right one then tugged a copy of the schedule free. "I can't tell you how grateful I am that you agreed to do this. Honestly, I don't think we'd be able to pull off the nativity this year without your help."

A blush darkened his cheeks.

Leesa's breath caught. As if the man wasn't attractive

enough—now he blushed? Swoon. She lowered her gaze and concentrated on keeping the paper from shaking. No good. Logan Franks had a serious effect on her calm. She dropped the schedule onto the counter then backed up a step when he extended his hand.

Dark lashes swept down to cover his eyes. "Thanks. I probably would've forgotten all about it if you hadn't mentioned it."

She licked her lips nervously. "That wasn't why you came?"

"Actually, uh. . ."

The Adam's apple in his throat bobbed. So, he was as nervous as she? Her heart jumped.

He motioned toward her hands. "I brought something for your blisters. I thought. . .maybe. . ."

She turned her hands up and followed his gaze to her palms. The blisters were irritated and red, but in her line of work, she was accustomed to slogging through occasional pain.

"I should've insisted you wear gloves."

The regret in his voice drew her eyes. His jaw hardened as he fished in his coat pocket. He retrieved something then set it on the counter and backed up in a move similar to the one she'd used with the schedule.

She reached for the squat container. The oval label beneath a bright red lid read "Dr. Naylor." She fought a smile. "Udder Balm?"

"Uh. . .yeah. Miranda, my wife"—his voice lowered a notch at the words—"swore by the stuff."

She unscrewed the lid and took a whiff. "Not bad."

Her answer seemed to amuse him. His lips twitched.

"Okay, so I don't know what I expected." A chuckle escaped as she dipped her finger into the container and removed a pea-sized amount. Rubbing it into her palms, she was surprised by the relief the balm brought to her tight skin.

Pushing the container back to him, she smiled. "Thanks."

"Keep it. I've got plenty."

The bell chimed again, and this time, it *was* Sammy who swung through the door. "I'm back." She eyed Logan curiously. "Hello."

Clearing her throat, Leesa made the introductions.

"High school?" Logan asked, raising an eyebrow.

Sammy grinned and flipped a lock of hair over her shoulder. "I'm on Thanksgiving break."

Leesa nodded toward Sammy. "How was lunch?"

"Okay." She shrugged out of her coat and draped it over the back of her chair. "Sorry I'm late. The sub shop was packed, and then I had to swing over to Bloom's to pick up my mom's prescription."

Leesa shook her head. "No problem." She pointed toward the kennels. "I finished up with Molly. She's ready to go home. Will you call her mommy?"

Sammy swung that way. "Okey doke. I'll take care of it." Around the corner and out of Logan's eyesight, she paused and made an exaggerated face. Waving her hand as though to cool her cheeks she mouthed, *"Hott!"*

Drawing a breath, Leesa tried to ignore the stubborn

warmth determined to flood her and returned her attention to the hottie—er—Logan. "Sorry for the interruption."

He shrugged. "No problem."

He either feigned ignorance, or he truly was oblivious of the effect he had on women. Either way, it was incredibly charming. Mortified by the direction of her thoughts, she dropped her gaze and reached for the balm. "Thanks again for bringing this by."

He nodded then half turned, a look of indecision on his face. "Listen. . ."

"Yes?" She raised her chin, proud of the professionalism she heard in her tone.

He glanced at the door and back. "I. . .uh. . .I was just about to grab a late lunch myself. I don't suppose you'd care to come? If you haven't eaten, I mean."

"I haven't eaten."

She could've kicked herself for responding so quickly, yet couldn't help reaching for her coat. "Where you headed?"

A tiny grin lifted his mouth. "A place I know. You in a hurry?"

Worry wriggled through her. It was only half past two, but she was through with patients for the day. She shook her head and lifted one finger. "Give me just a second."

After instructing Sammy about the cat and locking up, she made her way to the front where Logan waited. A gentleman, she noted as he opened the door and waited for her to step through.

Not necessarily, another voice argued. Remember what happened in Bangor.

She pressed her lips together tightly.

Outside, feeble sunlight seeped through breaks in the gray sky. The forecast called for snow, but not until later that evening. She pushed her hands into her pockets, wishing she'd worn gloves, and waited for Logan to join her on the sidewalk.

She motioned toward the alley alongside the clinic. "My car's around back."

He shook his head. "It's close enough to walk. Unless you're cold?"

"Not even a little bit," she said, which became true under the heat of his scrutiny.

He inclined his head to the right, and she swung alongside him on the sidewalk. Though Thanksgiving was still a week away, the town had gotten an early jump on Christmas decorations. Bright red bows adorned every lamppost. Here and there, wreaths and garland festooned doorways and windows. By the time the nativity began, every home and business would be decked in holiday cheer.

Logan motioned toward a team of men fastening a silver star to the top of a tall tower. "That's what happens when you live in Bethlehem, I guess."

She'd been thinking the same thing. Smiling, she shoved her hands deeper into her pockets. "I was surprised to see you in town today."

His mouth twisted in a droll grin. "What, you thought I never left the castle?"

Humor. She liked it better than the glower he wore so often. She squinted and pretended to consider the idea. "Do you blame me? I've lived here for two years and I've only bumped into you a dozen or so times."

Immediately, she regretted the telling remark. If he hadn't been watching her with that curious gleam, she'd have smacked herself on the forehead. At least he seemed inclined to ignore her gaffe. He motioned toward Bay View Street and the direction of the marina.

Interesting choice. Bethlehem hugged the coast, and while there were bait-and-tackle shops aplenty lining the shore, she wasn't aware of any restaurants. Even Trapper's, purported to have the best seafood in town, lay in the opposite direction. Instead of questioning, she determined to enjoy the walk and let him lead.

"So what about you?" she asked. "How long have you lived in Bethlehem?"

"Eight years."

"Long time."

He shrugged. "We moved here right after my wife got hired on at the university."

"She was a professor?"

He nodded. "Zoology. She worked in Trenton for a while, at the Acadia Zoological Park, but then she decided she wanted to focus on wildlife habitats."

A tumbler clicked into place. Leesa slowed her steps. "So, the animals back at your house. . .?"

"Part of her research."

Resuming her pace, she mulled his words. Logan must have

loved his wife very much to have been so supportive of her work. And now? Why continue the feed and care of the animals? Was it only out of a sense of devotion?

Veering right, they left the bricked buildings of downtown for a row of brightly painted clapboard shops, pausing when they came to a particularly quaint building with butter-yellow sides and green trim. A sign above the door read HARVEY's.

Logan motioned toward the shop, a curious half grin on his lips. "Well, we're here. What do you think?"

Leesa looked at him askance. "Harvey's is a boat-repair shop. I know, because I came in here once looking for sailcloth I could use as a sling."

Undaunted, he reached for the knob and gave it a twist. "True, but the owner also makes a mean enchilada casserole. Oh, and I should warn you." He tipped his head toward the door. "They open before the sun rises so the fishermen have bait, which means they eat supper early." Moving to the jingle of a single brass bell, he swept aside and motioned her in. "You coming?"

She raised one eyebrow skeptically. "This I gotta see."

Shelves of boat supplies and parts lined the inside of Harvey's. The man himself was stooped beside a row of bins filled with an odd assortment of levers and hooks. He looked over a pair of wire-rimmed glasses at their entrance and then straightened completely when he caught sight of Logan.

"Well, if it isn't my old amigo, Logan Franks. Long time no see." He bustled toward them, swiping his hands on a white apron fastened around his waist. " 'Bout time you came around.

I was telling *mi esposa*, oh your pardon, miss"—he dipped his head toward Leesa—"I mean I was telling my wife that it's been too long."

Logan gripped the man in a firm handshake—the kind that spoke affection, with both men grasping the other's elbow at the same time—then flashed a broad smile. "It's good to see you too, Javier." He lifted his nose and sniffed. "Is that Lali's tortillas I smell?"

Javier's belly shook. "It sure is." He crooked an eyebrow at Leesa. "I hope you're hungry."

Leesa smiled as Logan stepped aside and motioned her forward. "Javier, I believe you've met my friend Leesa McElroy. She owns the veterinary clinic on Main."

Javier clasped her hand and gave it a warm shake—not quite as affectionate as the one he'd given Logan, but still nice. "Yes, we've met. How'd the sling work out?"

"Great," she said. "Thank you so much for all your help."

"It was my pleasure."

She glanced back toward the door. "So, the sign outside? I didn't realize you owned the place."

At her look of confusion, Javier shrugged. "Not too many people can pronounce Javier. Harvey is easier."

He grinned then wandered to the front of the store, flipped the closed sign, and turned the lock. Returning, he draped an arm about Logan's shoulders. "Business has been slow today anyway. Come to the back. Lali's going to be so happy to see you, Logan."

Leaving the boat shop was as simple and immediate as stepping through a door. On the other side of the threshold lay a comfortable home, clean and neat, and tastefully furnished. The trio skirted a wide living room with a large window that overlooked the bay, and wound toward the kitchen, where the aroma of fresh corn tortillas and grilled onions wafted.

"Look who I found," Javier announced before they were fully inside.

"Logan!" A plump woman with streaks of gray running through her raven hair clapped her hands and then flung a ruffled apron from around her neck. "Javier and I were just talking about you."

She circled a large red worktable to envelope him in a warm hug. Noting the moisture that rose to the woman's eyes, Leesa hung back. Obviously, these people cared very much for Logan. She wondered about their relationship and why he'd stayed away so long.

Lali's gaze swung to rest on her. She released Logan and offered a shy smile. "And who is your friend?"

"Lali, this is Leesa McElroy."

Lali extended her hand. "Lali Reyes. Pleasure to meet you."

"Pleasure's mine," Leesa replied, shaking the woman's hand.

She had a nice grip, confident and warm, but not so tight as to be intimidating. What Leesa found discomfiting was the odd way the older woman searched her face. Whatever she looked for, she seemed to find, for she gave a slight tip of her head and her lips tilted in a smile of approval.

"Welcome. I was just about to start supper. I hope the two of you are hungry."

"We sure are. Enchiladas?" Logan asked.

She crossed to a drawer and removed two green bib aprons. "It's Tuesday, isn't it?" She laid one apron on the counter and carried the other to Leesa. "I hope Logan explained." She quirked an eyebrow at him that said she knew he hadn't. "Around here, everyone pitches in."

Relief sagged Leesa's shoulders. "That's perfect."

How many times had she gathered around the kitchen table with her mom and sisters? How many dinners and batches of Christmas cookies spent poring over cookbooks and batter bowls?

But that was before she'd had her heart broken in Bangor.

Lowering her gaze, she took extra care knotting the apron strings around her waist. In her peripheral vision, she saw Logan doing the same while Lali chatted.

"You okay?"

His proximity surprised her. He stood mere inches from her, his attention focused first on her trembling fingers, and then on her face.

"Leesa?"

She swallowed and smoothed the apron over her hips. "I'm fine."

Lali withdrew a grater and large block of golden cheddar. "Good. Then you can grate the cheese."

Kindness shone from the older woman's steady gaze. She

nodded encouragingly as she held up the grater. Leesa accepted it gratefully.

"Hey, that's my job," Javier protested, shoving his glasses higher on his nose.

"Not today. Today, you chop the onions." Javier groaned as Lali removed a slatted cutting board and plunked it on the counter in front of her husband. Unphased, she laughed and turned to Logan. "And you. . ."

Logan raised his hands. "I stir the chili."

"Riiight."

"Somebody needs to keep it from burning."

She crossed her arms, a look of mock disgust flashing across her face. "Fine, but use a wooden spoon." She jerked her head toward a crock filled with utensils. "Over there."

He selected one then saluted Lali with it before turning to a large pot of chili bubbling on the stove.

After washing her hands, Leesa set about grating a generous portion of cheese then stood back to watch as Lali, Javier, and Logan began rolling up tortillas and filling a large pan with enchiladas, assembly-line style.

Dinner was casual and filled with warm conversation. Leesa envied the intimate relationship Logan shared with the couple—the admiration and respect she saw reciprocated between them. After the final dish was scrubbed and replaced in the cupboard, Logan grabbed their coats and invited Leesa outside onto a broad deck stretching out over the water.

"Go," Javier urged, pulling a metal coffee tin off a shelf while

Lali prepared a tray of cookies. "We'll join you in a minute."

Logan lifted an eyebrow. "Well?"

She smiled as she allowed him to help her into her coat, liking the way his hands lingered on her shoulders and the tingle that traveled her flesh when his fingers grazed her neck.

Outside, a nip sharpened the air, but Logan drove it back with the flip of a switch on a portable heater. He motioned to a bench near the water, and Leesa sat to look out over the waves.

For a while, neither spoke, enjoying the gentle lap of water against the deck pilings and the occasional moan of a boat horn.

Leesa jerked her chin over her shoulder toward the house then burrowed into the warmth of her coat. "I like them."

"Me, too." Logan's breath formed a smoky plume against the purple evening sky. "Miranda introduced us. Said they reminded her of her parents."

"They liked her, too. I could tell by the way they talked about her." Without sorrow or regret, Leesa noted silently. They'd spoken Miranda's name with hope. She shivered and folded her hands in her lap. "Hard to believe I've lived in Bethlehem for two years and never bothered to get to know them. It's a small town, after all."

Maybe it wasn't townspeople who'd never accepted her. Maybe she'd never accepted them.

Warm fingers closed over hers. Fleetingly. She had just enough time to cast a wondering glance at their clasped hands before Logan pulled his away. "It's never easy settling in a new place. It takes time getting to know people."

Her lips parted in surprise. Recovering, she pressed her mouth closed. "Very intuitive."

His eyes twinkled, and he turned to gaze out over the bay.

"What about you?" she prodded. Now that she'd caught a glimpse of the man behind the scowl, she couldn't resist. "Are the Reyes the only people in Bethlehem you're close to?"

He shrugged. "There have been others. But Javier and his wife are special. They were there for me after I lost Miranda."

Leesa's breath hitched at the sorrow twisting his features. It was no wonder he rarely smiled. This man bore a heavy burden. Instinctively, she lowered her voice. "Mind if I ask how she died?"

His lashes swept down to hide his gorgeous, soulful eyes. "Car accident. She was driving home late one night and lost control on an icy road."

She swallowed. "I'm sorry."

"Thanks."

He exhaled deeply, and she regretted having dredged up so much heartache. She was about to suggest they go back inside when he looked at her and smiled.

"I don't. . .talk about it much."

Her heart in her throat, she could only nod.

He turned to face her, so close their knees touched. "You know, I wasn't sure about this whole nativity thing at first, but now. . ."

"Now?"

Was it her imagination, or did he lean closer?

"Maybe it's time I put the past behind me and started living again."

The words loosed a rush of surging emotions. She licked her lips, uncertain how to respond, but certain she wanted to. If only she could do the same and forget Bangor. "Logan—"

The door crashed open and Lali rushed out, with Javier close at her heels. "Logan!"

He jumped to his feet. "What's wrong?"

She thrust a phone toward him. "It's Pete. He's at Bethlehem Municipal waiting for a flight. His father's had a heart attack."

Chapter 5

Dried corn rattled from the bucket in Logan's hand into a squat, wooden bin. Too late, he realized he'd passed the full mark. Kernels scattered in every direction, rolling into cracks in the floorboards. He groaned. His whole morning had gone much the same way, all because he couldn't keep his thoughts off Pete for more than two minutes at a time.

A low growl sounded, and Logan turned his head. Wolf chided him from the doorway, his shaggy head lowered in disapproval.

"I know. Focus."

He dropped the bucket and moved toward the closest stall. If it weren't for the animals—he opened the gate and stepped back to let the cow through—he'd have been on a plane to check on Pete and his father in person.

He worked the latch closed then reached for a broom. Pete would have arrived in Buffalo late. He'd probably driven to the hospital, gotten an update, and was now catching a couple of hours rest before he remembered to call Logan, which meant any time now—

His phone vibrated in his pocket. Logan snatched it out. "Pete?"

"Yeah."

"How is he?"

"Stable. He's out of surgery and resting. His doctor even sounded a little more optimistic this morning than he did last night."

"That's good."

"I guess. But Logan. . ."

"Yeah?"

Pete drew a shuddering breath. "Dad's going to have a pretty lengthy recovery. I know I said I was going to stick around for Christmas, but Mom—"

"Don't even think about it."

"The farm?"

"I can manage on my own for a while."

Pete blew out a sigh. Even with the miles separating them, anxiety thrummed along the line. Logan gripped the phone tighter. "He's going to be okay, Pete."

Why did he say that? He had no idea if Pete's father would be okay.

"I hope you're right." There was a pause, followed by, "I'm really sorry, Logan."

"Don't be. You're where you need to be."

Silence, and then a muffled, "Thanks. And about the plane ticket?"

"Think of it as an early Christmas present."

Pete sniffed. "I'll call you in a couple of days to let you know how he's doing."

"Sounds good. And don't worry about things here. Take care of yourself and your family."

"Will do."

They said their good-byes, and Logan hung up and replaced the phone in his pocket.

"Was that him?" Leesa stood framed in the barn entrance, the same spot where Wolf had been moments ago. She gestured to the phone. "Pete?"

Logan nodded and scanned the barn. Wolf had disappeared, but Leesa still looked at him, waiting. He gave her a quick update. "It'll probably be a day or two before the family really knows what they're facing, but at least they can be sure he's in good hands."

She dropped her gaze, fidgeted a bit, and then dragged a wool scarf from around her neck and looped it over her arm. "Poor Pete. This has to be hard on him."

Logan jerked his head toward the door. "I didn't hear you drive up. You just get here?"

"Yeah. I probably should've called first. I just thought. . .I mean, I figured with Pete gone. . ."

Her booted feet shuffled against the barn floor. Booted—as in work boots—not the sunny yellow things she'd worn the last time she came. His gaze traveled upward, past her jean-clad legs, over the brown Carhartt jacket, to the work gloves clutched in one hand.

She gave an almost embarrassed shrug. "I thought you could use some help."

His heart did a tiny flip. The woman did more to unsettle his calm than anyone he'd ever met, except for Miranda. He grunted a "thanks" and turned his back. Rude though it was, he needed a minute, and he took his time replacing the broom and securing the feed bucket before gesturing for her to follow.

The sheep barn was the oldest structure on the farm, but it was by far Logan's favorite. Whimsical in its way, the faded gray walls reminded him of his grandparents' home back up around Moosehead Lake and of summer days spent climbing through haylofts. He set the bucket by the door and lifted the latch.

"You came at a good time. This is where I keep the sheep. You can look them over while I feed and water 'em, maybe pick out the ones you want to use for the nativity."

He pushed open the door and prepared to let her pass before retrieving the bucket, but she grabbed the handle before he could reach for it and swung it from her fingertips.

"Is this for the sheep?"

He nodded. "This time of year, I add minerals to their diet. There are feeders in every stall."

"How much do you give them?"

"The sheep take what they want. I just make sure the feeders are full."

"Sounds easy enough. Where are the minerals?"

He pointed to a wooden box where he stored the bags of loose minerals. "But you don't have to—"

She strode off before he could finish. Watching her, Logan fought a grin. She was stubborn enough, that was for sure. And hanged if he didn't find that attractive as all get-out.

Blowing out a breath, he headed toward the automatic watering tubs. Temperatures at night were cold enough to allow ice to form. He removed the thin layer then went back to the barn to draw a couple of pails of hot water from a sink in the tack room. Once the troughs were full, he shut off the water to the tub and moved on to the hay feeders. All told, it was almost an hour before he headed back to the barn in search of Leesa. He found her huddled next to a sheep in one of the ewe stalls.

At his entrance, she looked up, a dream-like smile on her face. Logan's breath caught.

"This one's pregnant."

Feeling a touch guilty but helpless to resist, he rested his forearms on the top of the stall and enjoyed the view. "I know. Dr. Norwood said she's due next spring."

"Do you have any others due around the same time?"

"A few. I just keep Ella in here because she seemed a little sluggish. I wanted to make sure she wasn't coming down with something."

Leesa gave the sheep a pat and rose. "Good idea. I'll keep an eye on her the next few days."

Obviously, she planned on making a habit of her visits. Though it shouldn't have, something inside roused at the idea. He kept his gaze fixed to her as she crossed the stall to stand in front of him, and though he tried not to let it show, his breathing quickened.

"So?" She rose on tiptoes and flashed a saucy grin. "Do you name all your animals?"

Even with the stall wall between them, heat spread through his body.

Back away!

Reason screamed for him to move, add to the distance, yet he remained rooted, transfixed by her dancing blue eyes. "Most." He forced the word through dry lips. "Not the birds."

A crinkle formed between her brows. "Why not? What's wrong with the birds?"

"Nothing. It just,"—he gave a small shake of his head—"it tames them, somehow."

The teasing faded from her face, replaced by the barest of smiles. That, and the look of admiration that melted over her features, almost knocked him down.

"And you want them to remain wild."

Her voice had softened, yet it stirred something fierce inside him. He tore his gaze away. "We should head toward the house."

He spun, not waiting for her answer. Too bad there wasn't another icy trough around. He'd dip more than just his hands inside. Loosening the buttons on his coat, he strode up the hill, past the corral, toward the back door.

Confounded woman, anyway. What was it about her that kept him consistently off kilter? It was like he was back in high school and she. . .

She was the girl he'd spend the next few hours trying to pry from his thoughts.

Chapter 6

Adrenaline coursed through Leesa's veins as she pulled into the Bethlehem Community Church parking lot. The entire cast would be at the first nativity rehearsal tonight, including Logan.

Her heart thudded just thinking his name. A moment passed between them at the farm—a blistering interlude that made her insides quake and her knees weak. He'd felt it, too, if the look of panic that crossed his face were any indication.

She climbed from the car, her hand lingering on the handle. She didn't want to be attracted to Logan any more than he did her. To that end, she'd simply make sure things stayed professional—no smiling, no eye contact, no. . .flirting.

Squaring her shoulders, she wove in and around the other parked cars until she reached the church entrance. Many of the cast had already arrived, Kate Walters included. She beckoned as Leesa entered and motioned toward a row of half-full pews near the front. Someone handed her a list with names and phone numbers. Leesa added hers then glanced around the room as she passed it on to the next person.

No Logan.

Her stomach sank, a feeling she quickly and firmly quelled. If she reacted every time she saw him—or didn't—she could pretty much pack up any hope of maintaining an air of professionalism. Directing her gaze forward, she focused on the instructions Kate relayed.

"Now, if for any reason you cannot be at one of the scheduled practices, please let me or Pastor Mike know. Any questions?" She paused for responses, smiling brightly. "Okay, then I think the next order of business is for us to introduce ourselves. Why don't we begin at the back and work our way to the front? Betty, will you start?"

One by one, the cast introduced themselves, from Betty, who played the innkeeper, to the wise men, angels, and finally, the shepherds.

"Leesa McElroy. I run the veterinary clinic on Main—"

The door at the rear of the sanctuary swung open, and Leesa's head swiveled with everyone else's.

"Mr. Franks! Welcome." Kate's confident steps echoed throughout the sanctuary as she strode to the back. "We're so glad you could join us." She swept one arm wide. "Everyone, this is Logan Franks. He's agreed to loan us the use of his animals. He'll also be playing one of our shepherds."

Light applause sounded, and Leesa inwardly groaned. Logan would despise the attention. Indeed, he glowered like a thundercloud on a blustery day. She cleared her throat and stood.

"Excuse me, Kate, what about costumes? Will each of us be

responsible for finding our own?"

"No, no, not at all. We have several left from last year, but we will need to head to the costume room so Marge can get some measurements. If you will all come with me."

Light chatter swirled as the members of the cast rose to follow Kate from the sanctuary. Except for Logan. He lingered at the door as though he hadn't quite decided whether to stay or bolt.

The scowl slipped a bit as she approached. In fact—and she almost stumbled when she saw it—he actually smiled. "Hi."

"Hi." She resisted the urge to rub her palms on the legs of her jeans. "You made it. I thought maybe you forgot."

He shook his head. His gaze drifted in the direction Kate and the others had taken. "Thanks. . .for that."

She shrugged. "So. . .the animals?"

"I didn't bring them. I figured I'd better get a look at the size of the corral we'll be using first."

"Right. That would be Kate. I mean Kate would have to show you. The corral."

Stop. Talking.

She jammed her hands into her pockets. Just in time. Her fingers itched to flail. "We should probably go ahead and get measured."

"Right."

Though he agreed, he searched her face a moment longer. She yearned to ask what he looked for, but knew she'd never find the courage. Instead, she spun and headed up the aisle. Logan reached the door at the same moment. This time, she waited, and like before, he dragged it open and motioned for her to precede him.

The hall outside the costume room hummed with chatter as people gathered to sort through costumes, assembly-line style.

"Wise men?" a dark-haired man yelled, hoisting a labeled box over his head.

"Over here."

The box passed from hand to hand until it reached Fred Miller, who would be playing one of the wise men.

"More like wise guy," Betty quipped, which stirred a ripple of laughter.

"Okay, okay," Fred said, plunging his hand into the box and plucking out a jeweled turban. He plopped it onto his head and then preened in front of everyone. "Either way, it's a good look for me."

More laughter. Leesa's heart clutched. How good it would feel to be a part of this group, to join in their banter.

She glanced up at Logan. Like her, he seemed moved by the group's closeness. His face wore a bit of melancholy in the lines around his eyes and the sad smile on his lips.

"Excuse me." A youngish man—probably in his mid-to-late-thirties—stood with a box cradled in his arms. "Logan, is it?"

Logan nodded, and the man extended the box with a smile. "Here you go. Shepherds' robes. Staffs are in the costume room closet. Also, there are lanterns and other odds and ends tucked up on the shelves. Feel free to pick out what you want."

Logan took the box. "Thanks."

"Name's John Roland." He turned and smiled at Leesa. "Good to have you both with us."

Leesa smiled. "Thank you, John. It's good to be here."

"Listen, after we finish up here, a few of us are going to head over to Gino's for some pizza." He glanced between her and Logan. "You're welcome to join us. It's a good way to get to know the people you'll be working with, if you know what I mean." He grinned and jerked his chin toward Fred.

"Sounds good," Logan said before she could reply. As John moved off, he shifted the box to his hip, quirked an eyebrow at her, and added, "Unless you have other plans?"

"No plans," she squeaked. What was she, a mouse? She pointed toward the costumes. "Why don't we see what's in the box?"

His eyes twinkled as he dropped to his haunches. Next to him was far too close. Leesa chose to settle across from him with the box in between. Inside were plain robes of various sizes, belts made of rope and twine, and several linen towels.

Logan tugged one out. "What are these for?"

"Your head."

His eyebrows rose. She giggled and took it from his fingers. "It goes like this." Reaching over to him, she draped the towel over his head then fastened it with a length of cord. "See? Instant shepherd."

"I'll have to take your word for it."

"Good." She grinned and pushed back as though to stand.

"Uh-uh." Logan caught her hand.

"What?"

He pointed to her head. "Your turn." He fished through the box, found a towel in a hideous shade of orange, and held it high.

"No way."

"I let you pick mine."

True. She folded her hands in her lap and expelled an exaggerated sigh. "Fine."

She fought a swell of laughter while he fastened the towel to her head. Finished, he sat back with a wolfish grin. "Perfect."

"I doubt that."

"You'll have to take my word for it."

"Or I could just find a mirror."

"And ruin the surprise?"

He flashed a smile that made her insides melt. So much for keeping things professional. She swallowed a nervous knot as he dipped his head and went back to digging in the box. He pulled out a robe, eyed it critically, and then handed it to her.

"This one looks about your size."

She took it from him and stood. Laying hold of a second robe, Logan did the same. He held the garment up by the shoulders. "Shall we?"

Despite her trembling fingers, Leesa managed to slip the robe on. Poking up through the neck hole, she let the fabric ripple down past her shoulders, to the floor. "Mine's too long—"

Glancing at Logan, she broke off midsentence then clapped her hand over her mouth. He stood, arms jutting out from his sides, peering down at himself with a skeptical frown. The robe barely skimmed his wrists and fell to just below his knees.

"Uh. . ."

"It's perfect," Leesa said, swallowing a grin.

He narrowed his eyes at her. "Right."

"Okay, so maybe Marge will have to adjust the size a bit." A giggle tickled her throat. She grabbed the sides of her robe and lifted. "Or maybe we should trade?"

"Ya think?" He dropped his arms, splitting the seam on one of the shoulders. Horrified, he reached up. . .and succeeded in splitting the other seam.

It was too much. The giggle quickly erupted into laughter. A second later, Logan joined her.

Kate wove down the hall toward them, smiling. "Well, don't you two look great!"

Her comment only made them laugh harder.

"What'd I say?" she asked, propping her hands on her hips. Her gaze bounced from Logan to Leesa.

"Nothing," Leesa said, wiping a tear from her eye. She squeezed her lips together and somehow managed to keep a straight face.

"Okay, well, Marge is ready whenever you are." Kate eyed them skeptically then shook her head and moved back up the hall.

Warm breath tickled her ear. "Marge is ready whenever you are."

A bark of laughter exploded from Leesa's mouth. Whirling,

she dragged the towel from her head and used it to slap Logan's arm. "Stop."

"Why?" He ducked out of reach before she could smack him again. His eyes sparkled with glee. "I haven't laughed this hard since. . ."

He didn't have to say it. She knew when. And she hadn't laughed so freely since leaving Bangor and. . .

Rafe.

Her throat tightened as memories of pain and betrayal swirled through her. But then Logan's gaze fell, and she thought only of him. His feelings. His pain. He reached up and removed the towel he wore, but she grabbed his hand before he could turn away.

"Maybe it's time. For both of us," she encouraged softly.

For some while, he said nothing, only maintained his tight grip on her fingers. When he finally lifted his eyes, she thought she saw a glimmer of moisture there, rimmed with aching sadness.

"Sorry," he said, his voice gruff. "It sneaks up on me sometimes."

She nodded. After a moment, he took a deep breath and motioned toward the costume room.

"Ready?"

"Yeah."

Yes, she clarified silently. She was more than ready—to leave Bangor and its heartache behind. Her hand still tucked into Logan's, she moved with him down the hall, glad he'd trusted her with his grief, gladder still that he knew he could.

But she was terrified, too, she realized. Once before, she'd allowed another person space in her deepest heart. Two people. And they'd betrayed her.

She glanced down at the strong hand holding hers. Logan was nothing like Rafe. She could trust him, just as he'd done her, and they could move forward. Both of them.

Together.

Chapter 7

Gino's Pizza was packed for a weeknight. By the time Logan and Leesa arrived, the only places left to sit were a couple of spots near the end of the table. He helped Leesa with her coat then draped it over the back of one of the vacant chairs, thinking. Something had happened tonight. With just a smile and a moment of shared humor, she'd reminded him there was more to life than grieving.

He held her chair then sat next to her, glad for the comfortable hum of conversation and laughter.

At the head of the table, Pastor Mike was seated next to a pretty, brown-haired woman with sparkling brown eyes that watched him adoringly. His wife? He rose and held up his hand. "All right, everybody." He nodded his appreciation as the noise faded. "Thank you all for coming. I know many of you have done the nativity before, but for some, this is your first time."

Smiles flashed toward Logan and Leesa.

"We truly are looking forward to getting to know you all better, which is why Kate and I"—he nodded toward the town manager—"thought it might be a good idea to get everyone together for pizza and fun."

Kate rose and stood next to him. "The food is on us tonight, so please, enjoy getting to know one another, and thank you again for your time and commitment to the nativity."

The moment she finished, conversation resumed, louder than before and more cheerful. He'd missed time with friends, Logan realized with a glance around the table. Missed the camaraderie.

"I've missed getting together like this." Leesa's wave encompassed the table. "Most of my friends are back in Bangor."

He lifted an eyebrow. "I was just thinking the same thing."

"Really?"

He nodded and reached for his water glass.

A pretty blush colored her cheeks. "Guess we have something in common."

More than one thing, though he had yet to figure out the cause behind the flashes of sorrow he glimpsed in her eyes. He took a long drink from his glass. And earlier...when she'd taken the awkward attention off of him and put it on herself...

Warmth flooded him. He'd been more grateful than he could say in that moment. He cleared his throat. "Leesa—"

"Drinks?" A pert waitress waited at his elbow, her pencil hovering expectantly over her order pad.

His gaze flashed to Leesa.

"Diet Coke, please," she said.

"Same," Logan replied.

The waitress scribbled the order and moved on. Leesa placed a light touch on his arm, and Logan startled.

She tipped her head toward him and smiled. "You were going to say something?"

Amazing. He meant only to glance at her, but the moment their eyes met, he was snared. A lock of her hair slipped to lie against her cheek. Resisting the urge to tuck it back behind her ear, Logan rested his arms on the table and laced his fingers.

"I was just going to say I'm glad you talked me into this. Thank you."

Her warm gaze said she knew there was more he'd left unspoken, but she smiled anyway and accepted his thanks.

"We're all glad, actually," Betty said from across the table, obviously not embarrassed to be caught eavesdropping. "We couldn't have done the nativity without you this year."

"That's right," several others added.

Suddenly, the circle that had consisted of only him and Leesa expanded to include everyone.

Logan turned his attention to Betty. "I'm glad to help."

Curiosity sparkled from her brown eyes. "Kate tells me you have quite a collection of animals out there on your farm."

He nodded and leaned forward to brace his elbows on the table. "That's true."

"All exotic?"

"No, some are domestic—sheep, cows, a few birds."

"Really? What kind of birds?"

Their conversation had drawn the attention of others, but Logan didn't mind as much this time. He told them how he'd come to start the farm and the types of animals Miranda had

been interested in studying. Most of the questions were easy—
those pertaining to feeding and caring for the livestock. The
ones he found awkward were of a more personal nature—how
he and Miranda met and if he'd shared her love of animals.
Acutely aware of the woman sitting to his right, Logan shot her
a sidelong glance. Her gaze was fixed on him, her lips curved in
a sad sort of smile that made his chest hurt.

"I bet Miranda would love that you're taking part in the
nativity."

She hadn't whispered, yet Logan felt the words were meant
only for him. His face warming under her approval, he ducked
his head and reached for his water glass. Thankfully, the pizzas
arrived and he was given a reprieve as space was cleared for the
food and the blessing spoken.

"You ever thought about opening up your farm to visitors?"
Betty asked, reaching for a slice of pepperoni.

He shrugged and slid two slices of deep dish onto his plate.
"To be honest, I never really gave it much thought. Miranda and
I never planned for the place to be a petting zoo."

"Sure would be a shame to waste the opportunity. There are
plenty of kids in the area who would benefit from the experience
of seeing the animals up close."

"Betty is a retired schoolteacher," Kate said from her seat
farther down the table. "She's always looking for the educational
value of things."

"Retired or not, I still think children should spend more
time learning about things firsthand rather than reading about

them on the Internet," Betty protested.

"I can vouch for that." John's eyes lit with mischief as he lowered his glass and directed a questioning look at Betty. "Don't you still have my calculator?"

"No, I do not," Betty said above the hum of laughter following John's remark. "Though if I *had* taken your calculator, you certainly wouldn't get it back now, young man."

She glowered, but her eyes twinkled merrily, and Logan laughed along with the rest. From there, the talk shifted to reminisces of school days and past fiascos involving the nativity, all of which helped make Logan feel at home among the close-knit group. Even Leesa had to wipe tears from her eyes from laughing so hard.

Snagging a clean napkin, he handed it to her and then watched as she used the corner to dab the moisture from her eyes. No black streaks from too much makeup. No red imprint on the rim of her glass or powdery blotches on her nose. She was a natural beauty. Witty and smart. Perfect.

He balked at the last idea, but even when he looked for reasons to withdraw the adjective, he was hard-pressed to find one. Did he even want to? Giving in to the urge, he studied her from the tips of her long, capable fingers—which currently twisted the paper from her straw round and round—upward to the curve of her chin. And her mouth.

His stomach muscles tightened. Enough biology. He'd do better to concentrate on her words.

"I knew I wanted to work with animals, but it was the town,

the people, that made me want to settle in Bethlehem."

"Well, we're certainly glad you did," a good-looking man near the end of the table said. He flashed a smile that caused Leesa to blush and drop her gaze.

Logan wracked his brain for a name. Brian. He'd heard it spoken more than once over dinner by the single women of the group. His fingers closed tightly around his glass as Brian's gaze slid appreciatively over Leesa.

It wasn't a predatory glance. Not openly flirtatious or rude. Why then did Logan feel the urge to smash something?

Pushing away his plate, he gathered up his keys and coat, and rose. "Well, it's been a lot of fun. Kate, Pastor Mike, thank you so much for the pizza. I look forward to working with you both."

They nodded, and after a round of good-byes, Logan returned his gaze to Leesa. She watched him with an almost disappointed gleam. He cleared his throat and motioned toward the door. "Would. . .uh. . .you like me to walk you to your car?"

"I'd be happy to do it if you're not ready to go," Brian offered, his face brightening hopefully.

To Logan's relief, Leesa shook her head and stood. "Actually, I should probably be going, too. I've got an early day tomorrow. Thank you, though. Goodnight, everybody."

More farewells followed, and then Logan was escorting her out, his hand placed protectively on her back. And it was protective, he realized as he stepped forward to open the door. It was as though she were a wild, undiscovered land and he was staking a claim.

The walk to her car was over far too quickly. The alarm chirped as she pressed the button on her key fob. She peered up at him, her face illuminated by the glow of her headlamps.

"Thanks for walking me out."

"No problem."

The keys jingled as she wiggled them between her fingers. "I had a lot of fun tonight."

"Me, too." He should let her go, but he didn't want to. She looked cute snuggled inside her coat. He leaned one arm on top of the car. "So? Did you mean what you said in there about having an early day tomorrow?"

She smiled, crinkling her eyes at the corners, and shrugged. "No earlier than normal."

"Then you're not tired?"

She shook her head.

"Good."

Grabbing her hand, Logan led her through the parking lot to his pickup, parked a few rows away. She almost bounced on the seat as he climbed in next to her and started the engine.

"Where are we going?"

He grinned. "You'll see."

The drive up the coast passed quickly with Leesa beside him. They stopped only once for coffee before winding to a broad park overlooking the ocean. When they arrived, Logan cut the lights but left the engine running so the cabin stayed warm, and tuned the radio to his favorite jazz station. He bumped the volume down a little then sat back to admire the moonlight glittering on the waves.

"Nice place."

He took a sip from his cup. "Ever been here before?"

She nodded. "A couple of times, but never at night. It's really gorgeous."

Miranda had thought so, too, but for the first time, Logan didn't want to dwell on his memories of her. He glanced sidelong at Leesa. "Mind if I ask you something?"

Something in his tone must have betrayed his intent. She nodded warily.

He flicked the plastic tab on his cup. "Why'd you leave Bangor? I get the feeling it wasn't entirely by choice."

Her gaze flitted toward the passenger window, but not before he once again witnessed the spark of anger and sadness that tinged her blue eyes. For several moments, she said nothing, her teeth working her bottom lip and her fingers worrying the rim on her cup.

Resisting the temptation to soothe her fidgeting fingers, he slid his coffee into the cup holder on the dashboard then used both hands to grasp the steering wheel. "Sorry. I shouldn't have asked."

She shook her head. "I had a boyfriend in Bangor. A boy I met in college. We were both studying to be vets, so I thought we had a lot in common."

"You thought?"

She gave a one-shouldered shrug she tried to make casual, but which only stirred the protective feelings inside him.

He sat up straighter. "What happened?"

"It didn't work out."

But she obviously wasn't over him. Logan clenched his jaw. "How long did the two of you date?"

"Two years."

"Long time."

"Uh-huh."

"Long enough for you to think the relationship was going somewhere?"

Her slender throat worked as she swallowed. "Yeah."

Hurt for her squeezed his heart. He turned to face her. "Why'd he break it off?" Surely, that was what had happened for her to still be hung up on the guy.

"I broke up with him."

Surprise rippled through him. "Why?"

She looked at him, and all trace of sorrow disappeared from her eyes. "He found someone else."

"Someone you knew?" He was pressing, but he couldn't help it. He leaned toward her while he waited for the answer.

"Yeah, it was someone I knew."

She drew a sharp breath, and with the sound, Logan felt his stomach tense, saw his hand reach out as though to brace her.

"Her name is Emily, and she was. . .is. . .she's my sister."

Chapter 8

The drive to Logan's farm took longer than usual, or so it seemed. The clock on Leesa's dash testified otherwise. When at last she reached the winding road leading up to the stately manor, she hesitated, the clicking of her blinker the only sound cutting the frosty morning air.

Last night. . .

Her fingers tightened on the steering wheel. What propelled her to tell Logan about Rafe and Emily? Would things be awkward between them now that she'd bared her soul? Gratitude calmed the roiling in her stomach as she recalled the look that filled his eyes. Not pity—empathy. For the first time, she'd not been embarrassed confessing the details of her sad, sordid breakup. He even seemed to understand why she'd left Bangor and why she hadn't been back since, despite her mother's pleas.

A horn honked. Startled, Leesa checked her rearview and then turned up Logan's driveway. Awkward or not, she didn't regret telling him the truth. Maybe now that the reason for her coming was no longer hidden, Bethlehem would finally feel like home.

No activity ruffled the snowflakes falling gently over the barn and corral. Leesa gave a puzzled frown as she pulled up to the house and parked. Normally, Logan had the chores half done by the time she arrived. Today, it didn't even look as though a trail had been broken through the fresh snow.

The front door swung open as she climbed from her car. Her breath caught. Devastatingly handsome in a pair of worn blue jeans and flannel shirt, Logan waited barefoot on the covered porch, a steaming cup of coffee in each hand.

"Morning!"

She hurried up the wide steps to him. "What are you doing out here without any shoes? And good morning."

"I saw you coming up the drive." He extended one of the cups. "Coffee?"

"Yes!" She peeled off her gloves, shoved them under her arm, and accepted the mug thankfully. Taking a sip, she savored the warm, hearty brew.

"Hope you like cream and sugar."

"It's perfect." She grinned and shot a glance at his bare toes. "Playing hooky, or did you just forget to put on your boots?"

He ran his hand through his already tousled hair. "I overslept. I haven't done that for"—he paused, and a frown clouded his eyes—"actually, I can't remember the last time I overslept."

He shoved open the door and moved aside for her to enter. The house was bigger than Leesa had imagined. A broad hall emptied off the foyer, and two rooms split off both sides. Logan led her past a formal dining room and parlor to an expansive kitchen adorned with custom black cabinets and granite countertops.

She admired the stonework. "Nice."

Logan reached for the coffeepot and refilled his cup. "Miranda picked it out." He motioned toward two stools at the counter and took one, Leesa the other. "The house was in pretty rough shape when we moved in, but she loved the location, and the barn was in good condition, which was the important thing."

Leesa smiled. "Priorities, huh?"

He grinned back. "It was always about work with Miranda. One of the things I admired about her. You and she are a lot alike that way."

He fumbled to a halt, and her gaze drifted to his thumb, which he ran absently over the rim of his cup.

Clearing her throat, she tore her eyes away and took another sip. "What about you? What did you do before you moved here?"

The tender look on his face soured. "Corporate law. I made a good living at it, enough to retire early if I wanted, but I didn't love it. I never realized how miserable I was until I met Miranda. She had a passion for her job I found irresistible."

He studied the contents of his cup. "This farm isn't just about hanging onto her memory." His gaze cut to Leesa and back. "I mean, it was at first. . .just a reason to get up every morning. Now, I really do love the work. The animals keep me in touch with myself, you know?"

She did know. Instinctively, she reached out to cover his hand. "What about what Betty said last night? You think you'd ever consider opening up your place to visitors? Not a tourist attraction," she clarified quickly, "but an outdoor classroom-type thing might be nice. I bet Miranda would approve, considering she was a zoology professor."

Logan's brows dipped as he pondered the idea. "I never thought about it like that."

She shrugged and removed her hand from his. "So? What's the plan for today? More mucking?"

She faked a pained grimace and rubbed her lower back. Mucking the stalls had taken all day last time.

"Not today. Today, we're loading the livestock and driving them into town, not that I think you'd mind another eight hours of mucking manure." He laughed and shook his head then swiveled on the stool and stood. The move brought them mere inches from each other. She couldn't help it. She absorbed the scent of his spicy aftershave in one long draught.

Delicious.

Stop. It.

She jerked her head forward, not looking at him as he rounded the counter and dragged the coffee carafe from the warmer.

"Help yourself. I'll be back in a minute. Just gotta grab my shoes."

"Thanks."

Please. . .grab your shoes.

Something about the man in bare feet made her want to. . . she trimmed the thought before it could take root.

Despite the heat fanning her face, she reached for the carafe, filled her cup, and savored the coffee, black. With any luck, its stout flavor would bolster her flagging defenses.

Odd choice of words. Her cup clicked against the granite counter. She was cautious when it came to men. After what'd happened with Rafe and Emily, it was only wise. Yet she'd never thought herself defensive. When had that happened? And when, exactly, had Logan broken through?

"Ready?"

His deep voice, so vibrant and warm, sent a shiver down her back. Goodness, everything about the man elicited the same response—a mixture of instinct and anticipation that robbed her breath.

Arranging her features to be pleasant but not overly eager, she slipped off the stool and joined him by the door. "Ready. Thanks for the coffee."

"I have travel mugs if you'd like more."

He motioned toward the cupboard, but she shook her head before he could fetch one. "I'm good. Besides, I don't have a lot of time. Got a dog coming into the clinic this afternoon for his shots." She glanced at her watch for good measure.

Logan followed her gaze then seemed to shake himself alert. "Right. Sorry. I didn't even think to ask."

He grabbed his coat from the back of a chair and moved to the door, where he waited, his hand resting on the knob. On the floor next to him leaned a large—probably fifty pounds or more—bag of dog food. She lifted an eyebrow.

"It's for the wolf. When he does show up, he can really eat. Shall we go?"

Once again, Leesa thought about warning Logan against the danger of allowing the wolf to become too comfortable. People in Maine worried about danger from wolves and also from hybrids, since they tended to look no different from their full-blooded counterparts. But was it really her place to question without first knowing the facts? Besides, she and Logan had only just moved away from icy indifference, and polite was much easier to take. Shrugging, she followed him outside.

Once the animals were loaded on the trailer, she got into her car and followed Logan as he drove into town. She still had over an hour before her appointment arrived, so she parked next to the church and hopped out to help him back the trailer into the temporary corral.

"Thanks." He climbed from the truck, the door clanging shut behind him. Pulling a pair of leather work gloves from his pocket, he wrestled them on and motioned toward the trailer. "I can manage from here."

The wind nipped at her cheeks, and she burrowed deeper into her coat. "Okay. I'll see you tonight, then. At practice," she clarified softly.

He nodded, took one step toward the trailer, paused, and turned to look at her. "Listen. . .I was thinking, about what you said."

"What I said?" She shivered—from the cold. Not the earnest look in his eyes.

"About the farm. I think you're right. Miranda would approve of turning it into a classroom."

His gloved hand drifted to rest on the gate, and though his posture remained casual, she sensed he needed the support. Her heart melted and instinct took over. Crossing to him, she wrapped him in a hug then rose up on her tiptoes to press a kiss to his cheek.

"You can always change your mind," she whispered. "If it doesn't feel right or. . .if you decide you're not ready. People will understand."

He sucked in a breath, and she felt him tense. "Thanks."

Embarrassed, Leesa dropped her arms from his waist and retreated a step. "Okay. So. . ."

She lowered her gaze, heat fanning her cheeks. "See you tonight."

"Leesa—"

Whirling, she escaped to her car and quickly drove away. What Logan would make of her impulse, she didn't dare contemplate. She only knew what effect it had on her.

Anxiety birthed trembling in her limbs. Rafe's betrayal had hurt her, but Logan? Somehow, she sensed he could completely destroy her heart.

Chapter 9

The next few days passed in a blur. Despite Leesa's apprehension, no awkwardness lingered with Logan. In fact, he insisted she stop by the farm to help with the tours he'd arranged. She smiled with satisfaction as another group of children filtered through the barn.

Logan seemed pleased by the children's excited squeals as they raced from pen to pen to burrow their fingers in the sheeps' wooly coats. He stood with shoulders drawn back proudly as he explained each breed and the differences in their fur. When he finished, a man and his wife paused by the door to pump his hand.

"Can't thank you enough for this," the man said, a broad smile on his face.

"We plan on making this trip a Christmas tradition," the woman added.

When Logan merely smiled, Leesa eased to his side. "We're glad you enjoyed the tour. Don't forget about the live nativity next weekend. We'd love to see you there."

She gave them a flyer then waved good-bye as they bustled their children into a blue minivan and drove away. As the taillights faded from view, she lowered her hand to shield her eyes against the glare of the sun reflecting off a blanket of newly fallen snow. "That was fun, don't you think?"

She breathed a happy sigh, which quickly turned into a sharp inhale when warm fingers closed around her other hand. Heat radiated from Logan's gaze. . .enough to set her heart to thumping.

One side of his mouth lifted in a grin. "You were right." The sweep of his hand encompassed the barn and the animals inside. "Miranda would have wanted this, but I. . ."

He stepped closer, his grip on her hand tightening. Afraid to speak, she urged him to go on by squeezing back.

"I was too afraid of letting go of the past to even think about moving forward."

His voice roughened and he broke off, but for once, she didn't feel compelled to fill the ensuing silence. Too soon, he dropped her hand, his shoulders hunched into the folds of his jacket.

"Anyway, I just wanted to say thank you."

She hid a smile as he looked at the sky then down at the ground, anywhere but at her. Men and their pride. "You're welcome."

He cleared his throat. "So, ah, you hungry? We have a little time before the last tour comes through. I could fix us some sandwiches."

She feigned a disappointed frown. "What, no enchiladas?"

Logan chuckled and pushed open the barn door then followed her outside. "You'll have to see Javier for those, though I do think we're due for another round of Lali's cooking."

We're due. Pleasure spread through Leesa at his use of the plural. She liked the sound of it.

After a light lunch of sandwiches and chips washed down with a pitcher of iced tea, she and Logan returned to the barn just in time to see the first cars pulling into the yard. Children piled out, squealing with excitement.

Maybe next year we could add cookies to the tour, and hot choco-late. Maybe some fun crafts.

Next year?

She yanked her thoughts to a screeching halt. What Logan decided to do with the tours was his business, not hers. She had a clinic to run. Besides, she was only temporary help. Eventually, Pete would be back and things around the farm would return to normal. Wasn't that what she wanted?

Her disappointed heart said no.

Determined to find a distraction, she busied herself around the barn—helping dole out the corn Logan had provided to feed the animals, lifting the smallest children to see above the rails, demonstrating the various tools and equipment the cast would use during the nativity. Before long, everyone had filed through the barn and headed toward the camel pen with Logan, all except for a slender, dark-haired woman Leesa recognized from church. She appeared to be looking for something. Her head turned to and fro, a puzzled frown on her face.

Leesa draped the halter she'd been holding over a peg on the tack room wall and made her way over to her. "Mrs. Davis?"

The woman was older than Leesa by several years, pretty, and stylish in her black pea coat with silver buttons down the front. She looked up as Leesa approached, and the worried lines between her brows smoothed a bit.

"Dr. McElroy, thank goodness. Have you seen Hayden? He was here a second ago, but he seems to have disappeared."

Hayden. Leesa did a quick mental search and pulled up an image of an eight- or nine-year–old boy with dark hair and an impish grin. She motioned toward the camel pens. "Did he go outside with the others?"

Mrs. Davis wrung her hands. "To be honest, I'm not sure. There were so many people milling about, I suppose he could have. . ."

Smiling, Leesa gave her arm a pat. "Why don't we go check? I'll help you."

A bit of the tension seeped from the woman's posture, and she smiled. "Thank you. It's silly, I know, but Hayden has a way of finding trouble." They crossed the yard toward the circular camel pen. "My husband calls him his little daredevil."

"I take it he's pretty fearless?"

"Terribly." Mrs. Davis erupted in nervous laughter. "That child has given me more gray hair. . ."

Her words trailed off, and her eyes scanned the crowd gathered at the fence. Logan stood inside the corral, leading one of the smaller camels by a halter. Mrs. Davis reached for Leesa's arm and gave it a squeeze. "I don't see him. Do you?"

She shook her head. "What is he wearing?"

"A blue coat with red stripes on the shoulders and jeans."

"Okay." Leesa directed her toward the group with a gentle push. "Wait here. I'll let Logan know he's missing and we'll look together."

At her nod, Leesa whirled and lifted her hand to try to catch Logan's attention, but his gaze was fixed elsewhere, on the opposite side of the corral. At the same moment, a stirring started among the camels. They pressed against the pen, their round, flat feet pawing the hardened ground.

What was going on?

Leesa left the fence, her stomach twisting in a sudden, anxious knot. Pressing through the crowd, she emerged next to the gate. "Logan?"

His head swiveled at the sound of her voice.

At the rigidness of his features, her heart fell like a stone. He pointed toward the camels then looked opposite the pen toward the woods. Wolf stood there, his nose tilted toward the sky, sniffing the air. His gray fur nearly blended with the barren trees. In fact, had he not chosen that moment to howl, she might not have seen him at all.

The sound unleashed a tide of restless pushing and stomping. She turned to look at the camels, her mind ringing with something Logan had said during one of their many conversations.

"The wolf makes the camels nervous. "

It was then she saw the blue coat.

Chapter 10

"Hayden!"

Mrs. Davis's scream rent the air. In the same moment, Leesa dove through the gate and made a beeline for the camels. Logan beat her there. He shoved the small camel's reins into her hands.

"Try and get the camels moving toward the stable. I'll get Hayden."

He whirled before she could respond. Her breath caught as he disappeared into the swirling mass of hooves and fur, but then a plaintive cry rose that turned her blood to ice and she reacted on instinct. Raising both arms, she flailed them harder than she ever had in her life.

"Hyah, camels! Move!" Despite her fear of being stomped by their enormous feet and powerful legs, she surged forward, dragging the young camel with her, until the entire herd began to move.

Suddenly, men surrounded her, all of them waving their arms and shouting, "Move!"

After what seemed an eternity, the animals parted and Leesa

saw them—Logan with his arms around Hayden, huddled on the ground. Though they were dusty and Hayden's face was streaked with tears, they appeared unhurt. She exhaled on a whoosh. Her arms went limp and the reins slipped from her fingers, but she didn't care. All she could see was Logan. He stood, swept Hayden up into his arms, and carried him from the corral. Once he'd returned the boy to his mother, he searched the crowd.

For her?

She stepped from the corral. "Logan?"

The moment he caught sight of her, he strode forward to grip her by the arms. "Are you all right?"

She nodded. "You?"

"Yeah." He raked his fingers through his hair, breathing heavily. "The wolf—it never occurred to me—"

"Me either," Leesa said. "He's been gone so long, I forgot all about him."

"He does that sometimes. . .disappears for weeks or days, then shows up out of the blue."

"It was probably the people," Leesa said, lowering her voice. "He saw and smelled them and it confused him."

Logan craned his neck to see past her to the woods. "Did you see which way he went?"

"No." She shook her head. "I was too busy—" The words "worrying about you" died on her lips. "No, sorry."

His gaze returned to her face, concerned, earnest, searching. He blinked then gave himself a shake. "Can you do me a favor and help me get these people out of here?"

"Of course."

His lips pressed together, but she recognized the gratitude that flickered in his eyes. He turned and lifted one hand for silence.

"Folks, I'm very sorry for what just happened. No doubt we all realize it could have been much, much worse. Rest assured, I'll be taking precautions before we host another tour out here at the farm."

Mrs. Davis stepped forward muttering profuse apologies, but Logan dismissed them with a wave. "I'm just glad Hayden's all right."

After thanking him again, she spun toward the vehicles, clutching her son's hand.

Over and over, Logan and Leesa repeated their apologies as the visitors took their leave. No one seemed outraged by the incident. Instead, most offered gratitude for Logan's generosity and praise for his quick action in saving the boy. Finally, only a handful of people remained, but their faces showed concern. One of the men stepped forward to shake Logan's hand.

"Mr. Franks, my name is Allen Rushing. I work for the Department of Inland Fisheries and Wildlife. Could I speak with you a moment?"

Logan nodded and gestured toward the shelter of the barn. Though Leesa wanted to follow, she wouldn't, not uninvited. When the two men reached the door, Logan looked back at her and lifted an eyebrow.

"Coming?"

Heat flamed her cheeks as she nodded. "Be right there."

She ushered the last few guests to their cars and then hurried toward the barn. By the time she entered, the men were deep in conversation.

". . .law requires them to be registered, micro-chipped, and neutered to prevent reproduction," Mr. Rushing was saying.

Logan stood facing him, both hands braced on his hips. "Wolf isn't a pet. I told you, he just started showing up after my wife passed away. As for him being a hybrid?" He shrugged and shook his head. "I have no way of knowing."

"Which actually makes this situation all the more dangerous." Mr. Rushing lowered his gaze and rubbed his fingers over his jaw. "Mr. Franks, you do realize if anyone had been bitten—"

Her heart thrumming, Leesa stepped forward. "What's going on?" She extended her hand to Mr. Rushing. "Leesa McElroy. I own the veterinary clinic downtown."

A bit of the concern cleared from Mr. Rushing's countenance. "Dr. McElroy, good. I'm sure you're aware of the law that was passed a couple of years ago regarding wolves as pets."

As a veterinarian in the state of Maine, she had to be. Still, she cast an uneasy glance at Logan before responding. "I'm aware, though I thought it dealt specifically with hybrids."

She risked another peek at Logan. Warmed by the gratitude on his face, she pressed on.

"Besides, the law does not prohibit people from owning mixed breeds."

"That's correct," Mr. Rushing said, "but as I was explaining to Mr. Franks, the intent of the law is to protect people from the vicious attacks to which this type of pet are known. To do that, the state requires that the animals be registered."

Relief shot through her. Maybe she could help clear some of this up. "Mr. Rushing, Wolf isn't a pet. True, he's accustomed to having people around—well, just Logan, er, Mr. Franks, but to consider him tame—"

"Does he feed him?"

Her thoughts flashed to the dog food by the kitchen door. "On occasion, but—"

"What about shelter?"

She sought Logan for help, but his face was hard, unreadable. "I couldn't say for sure," she replied slowly.

His gaze fell.

She looked at Mr. Rushing. Though she read an underlying empathy in his steady gaze, it was countered by resolve.

"Please understand," he said, "it's people's safety I'm concerned about. Wolves with no fear of humans can be very dangerous, not only to people and domesticated animals, but to themselves."

"What do you mean?" Logan asked.

"If it's a hybrid, and it bites somebody, the law requires that it be put down," Leesa said quietly, her stomach twisting.

Logan stared at her. "You knew about this?"

She nodded, a knot of misery lodged in her throat.

"Why didn't you say something?"

"I thought about it—"

"And," Rushing said, "the animal's head would have to be sent to Augusta to be tested for rabies."

Logan huffed out a sigh. "So what do you suggest?"

He looked at Rushing, not at her. Leesa jammed her hands into her pockets and kept quiet.

"Our first step would be to file a report with Animal Control. They'll relocate him if they can. If he's too used to being around people to release into the wild, they'll find him a permanent home."

Logan scoffed. "Like in a zoo."

"It's better than the alternative," Rushing said quietly.

"Which is?"

Putting him down. Rushing didn't speak, but the answer rang like a clarion in Leesa's head and, she was certain, in Logan's.

Rushing took a card from his pocket and handed it to Logan. "My number's on the back. Give me a call after you've had a chance to think about it. In the meantime, I'm going to look into scheduling a meeting at the town hall."

Logan's head jerked up. "What kind of meeting?"

Rushing met his gaze steadily, his dark eyes somber. "The locals will want to take precautions for their children and pets until we figure out what to do."

Logan nodded reluctantly, and Leesa walked Rushing to the door. When he'd left, she lingered at the entrance, wringing her hands. Logan paced the floor, as restless as the wolf. Why, oh why, hadn't she said something? She should have warned him of the dangers of allowing the animal to become too accustomed to his presence. An apology ready on her lips, she stepped forward.

He spoke before she had a chance to voice it. "We can't let them relocate Wolf."

The agony in his voice tore her heart. Though she wanted to, she didn't reach for him. "I don't like it either, but—"

Still pacing, he shook his head. "Wolves mate for life, right? I think I read somewhere that they're as monogamous as humans."

She hesitated, the familiar itch to flail tingling in her fingers. "N—not exactly."

He drew up short and stared at her.

"I mean. . .that is an accepted train of thought, but in reality. . .what I'm trying to say is there has been some discussion regarding—"

At the look of exasperation he tossed at her, she fell silent. He didn't want a lesson on animal reproduction. She crossed to him.

"Logan?"

The muscles in his arm quivered beneath her touch. He was holding himself in check, but barely. She dropped her hand.

He cleared his throat. "The wolf. . .I told you, he disappears sometimes."

She nodded for him to continue.

"I've never seen a female, but I always thought. . .I mean, if that's where he's been going, relocating would split them up forever."

Her heart lurched. This wasn't so much about the wolf as it

was what the wolf had come to mean to him. "He'll find another mate, Logan," she said softly. "It is true wolves will choose one mate and remain with them during breeding, but if one were to die, the other *would* move on."

"He wouldn't be dead." Logan whirled and strode the length of the barn. "He'd be cooped up in a cage somewhere. And it'd be my fault."

She widened her eyes. "Your fault?"

"I never should have listened to you. I never should have let you talk me into turning this place into a petting zoo."

"Logan, we were only trying to—"

"The wolf showed up to help me. Somehow. . .he knew I needed. . .something. . .and he stayed even when. . ."

He trailed off, his hands clenching and unclenching into fists at his sides, his eyes storm-filled and cold. Though he stood mere feet away, his next words told her just how far the distance between them had grown.

"I'm sorry, Dr. McElroy. I know you were only trying to help, but I think it'd be best if you stayed away while I try to figure out what I'm going to do."

Dr. McElroy?

Leesa's heart clutched. She had to at least offer to help, yet the words refused to come. And then. . .Logan whirled and walked away. This time, she didn't follow.

Chapter 11

A light snow had begun falling, but inside the Bethlehem town hall, the air was stuffy and warm, thanks to the hundred-or-so bodies packed into the narrow space. Logan took a seat near the back, content to remain invisible, or nearly so, for a while longer. For several minutes, he merely listened. Definite sides had formed—from conservationists who believed people had no right to infringe on the local wildlife to people frightened for the safety of their children, and many who fell somewhere in between.

And Leesa.

Logan sucked in a breath at the sight of her standing near the front, her hair pulled tight into a ponytail and her face devoid of makeup. They hadn't spoken for days. He couldn't take back his last words to her, but he'd beaten himself up ever since speaking them. Before the night was over he'd tell her it wasn't her fault Wolf was in this mess. It was his. For one brief moment, their eyes met, and then she looked away.

Drawing a deep breath, he focused on what Kate Walters was saying. Her back was turned, but she stood with shoulders squared, facing three men seated behind a long table. Rushing was also there, seated near the end, but only volunteering information when he was asked.

"Bottom line, Mr. Samuels, unless this animal is a proven danger, I think it would be a mistake acting too quickly."

Logan scanned the faces at the table and settled on a dour-faced man he'd seen around town. Selectman Murray Samuels. Great. The battles between him and Kate were legendary. It appeared tonight would be no different as he rose to address the crowd. For nearly five minutes, he railed about everything from wolves to Kate's job as town manager.

"What is your point, Mr. Samuels?" Kate interrupted, a scowl creasing her lips.

"My point, Mrs. Walters, is that thanks to you, we do not have the money to spend on finding out whether or not the animal is a legitimate danger. Thanks to you, our best bet will be to either shoot it or have it shipped to one of the local zoos. Isn't that right, Mr. Rushing?"

"I hardly think we can blame Mrs. Walters for the economy," one of the other selectmen replied before Rushing could speak. A cutting glare from Samuels quickly silenced him.

"Like it or not," Samuels said, "responsibility for a town's resources ultimately falls to the manager. After all, it was Mrs. Walters who pushed to trim the budget, and by so doing, cut the number of city staff in half."

"Only after we all agreed it was necessary," another selectman said. "And that's beside the point anyway. What we're deciding tonight is what's best for this one animal, not the entire wildlife population of Maine."

The wildlife population of Maine.

Those words lodged in Logan's brain, blocking out the ensuing argument between Samuels, Rushing, and the other selectmen. For years, local wildlife had been Miranda's only concern. It was why she'd left her job at the zoological park and transferred to the university...why she'd insisted they settle in Bethlehem...

"It was wildlife habitats."

Stirring resulted around him, and Logan realized he'd spoken aloud. He met a few embarrassed gazes then turned his eyes toward the front, and Leesa. She was looking at him, her beautiful face bunched and worried. This time, he didn't glance away.

He stood. "Um...could I say something?"

Kate's back was still turned. Leesa motioned to get her attention then pointed at Logan. When at last the room fell silent, Kate beckoned him forward.

"Mr. Franks, I'm glad you could be here tonight."

She looked anything but glad—more like apologetic. Logan managed a reassuring nod before turning to address the audience.

"Before I start, let me just say that I am truly sorry. My wife studied animals her whole life. I think I can safely say she would have been pretty upset with me right about now."

A few people offered awkward chuckles. He paused to clear his throat against a sudden rush of emotion. From the corner of his eye, he saw Leesa give a nod. Bolstered by her silent encouragement, he continued.

"Miranda spent the last few years of her life studying wild-life habitats. She also taught, because she wanted to share her passion with others. I forgot that for a while. After she died. . . well. . .I pretty much forgot everything she stood for. Until a couple of weeks ago."

He directed his attention to Leesa. "I told someone recently that I was wrong to have turned my farm into a petting zoo. I meant that."

Despite the tears that rose to her eyes, Logan forged on. "It should have been a wildlife habitat."

Murmuring started around him again. He ignored it and took a couple of steps toward Leesa.

"I'm sorry." He lowered his voice. What he said now was only for her anyway. "I was stupid and angry, and I turned it on you, when really, I was only upset with myself."

She started to speak, caught herself, then dropped her gaze. "Logan—"

He shook his head. "I was wrong, Leesa. Wrong to forget everything Miranda worked for, to shut myself off for so long, but most off all"—he closed the last small gap between them and took her hand—"I was wrong to have blamed you for trying to make me see what was right in front of my face."

Amazingly, she didn't tug away, but instead squeezed back. "I was wrong, too, Logan. We both were. I should have warned you."

Later. They could talk that out later. Right now. . .

He turned to Kate, who was looking a bit desperate as she was bombarded by questions from both the selectmen and the audience. Rushing was talking, too, though it was doubtful he could be heard above the noise.

Logan lifted his hand. "Please, everyone, if I could have your attention for just a moment longer."

Gradually, the talk simmered down, and Logan seized the opportunity. "I realize I don't have nearly the knowledge that my wife had regarding wildlife habitats, but I think the local authorities might be willing to work with me." He directed a questioning look at Rushing, who nodded for him to continue.

Kate frowned. "I don't understand, Logan. Are you saying you would be willing to fund a wildlife refuge right here in Bethlehem?"

A slow smile spread over his face. Why hadn't he thought of it sooner? It was what Miranda would have wanted, and with Leesa's expertise—

He glanced at her. After all they'd been through, would she be willing to help? "We'll need a vet," he said quietly. "Someone to help run things—"

"Of course," she said before he could finish.

Joy sparkled from her gaze, flooding Logan's heart with gratitude. . .and something else. Something deeper.

He blew out a breath and looked back at Kate. "Obviously, it will take some time to work out the details. I'll have to contact the authorities—"

"I can help with that," Rushing said, rising.

Logan nodded his thanks. "The main thing will be putting off a decision about the wolf until we can finalize the details."

"Which should not be a problem, seeing as how he hasn't been a threat before, or since," Kate replied firmly.

Samuels slapped his palm on the table. "Now wait just a minute," he said, but Kate quickly drowned him out. This was followed by excited chatter about the idea of a wildlife refuge in the community.

No wonder Samuels didn't like her. She was one tough lady, and she definitely could handle any argument he dished out, especially now that public opinion seemed to have swung in her favor.

Giving Leesa's hand a gentle squeeze, Logan led her through the town hall and outside. A decorative awning protected them from the falling snow, which had intensified since he'd arrived, but it did nothing to cut the chill. He shrugged out of his coat and draped it gently over her shoulders.

"Thanks," she said, still shivering.

"Thank you." He jammed his hands into the pockets of his jeans. "You could've blasted me in there, and I wouldn't have blamed you a bit."

Her lashes swept down, hiding her eyes when all he wanted was to gaze into them. She bit her lip and then, finally, looked up at him. "Did you mean what you said in there about needing a vet?"

"I did." He shrugged. "I admit, it's a crazy scheme, and it only just now came to me. I have no idea how much will be involved—the laws, the funding—it'll be a massive undertaking."

"Miranda would've approved." She smiled. "Much better

than a petting zoo." Gradually, her smile faded, replaced by lines of worry. "I meant what I said in there. I'm so sorry for everything that happened, Logan."

Logan's heart hitched inside his chest. Reaching out, he grabbed the edges of his jacket and pulled them gently around her, snuggling her inside. "You know, I asked myself once why it was you who came to my door to ask me to be part of the nativity."

"You did?"

He heard the waver in her voice and felt her trembling breath against his cheek. He nodded. "Now I know."

"The habitat."

"No, it was more than that." His mouth went dry as she tipped her head back until their eyes locked. Mustering his courage, he ground out the words that had been clamoring for release since the first time he laid eyes on her back at the farm. "It had to be someone who could shake me from my shell. Someone like you, with enough passion and spirit to challenge me and remind me what it felt like to live. Someone. . .I could love."

She said nothing for a moment, only stared at him with a look of shocked disbelief that made his heart pound. Then, she blinked. "D–did you say. . ?"

It was now or never. Before she could finish, he cupped his hands to her cheeks, dipped his head, and kissed her. At first, she remained perfectly still, her mouth rigid beneath his, but then she was kissing him back, and Logan forgot everything and everyone but the beautiful woman in his arms. When finally he pulled away, she remained cradled in his embrace, her eyes closed and her breath coming in soft little gasps that only made him want to kiss her again.

"Leesa?" he whispered, pressing his lips to her forehead. "Did you—?"

"I love you, too," she said, cutting him off before he could ask if she'd heard. Her eyes drifted open. "I think I always have, though I was too afraid to admit it."

"Afraid?" Logan loosened his hold enough to peer into her face, where he saw an old pain reflected.

Of course.

"Because of your sister."

She nodded.

"And Rafe." Just speaking his name made Logan's muscles tense, but she quickly dispelled his unease with a shake of her head.

"Rafe was a mistake Emily and I *both* made. What I felt for him is nothing compared to what I feel for you."

And yet. . .he sensed a hesitation in her gaze, unresolved conflict that needed to be addressed before either of them could move forward.

"You need to talk to her," Logan said softly. "Make things right while you still can."

Tears filled her eyes, but she nodded.

"Do you want me to go with you?" He could be there for her, just as she had been for him, tonight.

"I. . ." She licked her lips and then shook her head. "I don't think so. I think this is something I need to do alone."

He understood, but a part of him ached for the agony she would face. He did kiss her then, only this time he poured as much love, as much encouragement and support as he could marshal, into one gentle touch.

It would have to be enough.

Chapter 12

Leesa squeezed her car into the only parking spot she could find—a narrow slot two streets away from the Bethlehem Community Church. Jerking the rearview mirror toward her, she did one last check before exiting the car and hurrying up the sidewalk.

She was late. Logan was probably pacing the hall. Her heart thumped. She hadn't stopped thinking about him since he'd kissed her. In fact, it was his kiss that had driven her to return to Bangor...

She pushed through the door to the church and was immediately assaulted by noise.

"We can't wait any longer! We need to get everyone moving."

"We can't move! We're one shepherd short."

She rose up on her tiptoes. "Here I am!"

"Leesa!" Kate Walters hurried over to her. "Thank goodness." She eyed her costume critically, gave a satisfied nod, then shoved a staff into Leesa's hand and pointed her in the direction of the hall. "That way. Logan and the others are waiting."

Hitching her robe and staff in one hand and holding her

headpiece in place with the other, Leesa wove through the throng until she reached the less-crowded hall. Betty, already sweating in her heavy innkeeper's garb, reached her first.

"There you are." She grabbed her arm and dragged her forward. "Where have you been? We missed you at practice last night."

"I was in Bangor." Together, the two of them pressed farther up the hall.

"Bangor! What in heaven's name were you doing there?"

"Looking up my sister. We had a lot to discuss."

"Leesa!" John joined her and Betty in the hall. "Thank goodness. Logan's outside. I told him I'd holler if I saw you. Where've you been?"

"She was in Bangor," Betty said.

"Bangor." John lifted an eyebrow. "Everything okay?"

Leesa blew out a sigh. "Never mind. I'll explain later." Holding her staff high, she used it like Moses to part the sea of costumed nativity actors. Finally, she burst through the rear door of the church into the night air, John and Betty trailing in the wake of her robe. Logan waited near the corral, his back to them as he checked the animals.

"Logan, she's here," John called before Leesa could speak.

He turned, and her breath caught. Even in a shepherd's costume, the man was gorgeous. He shot her a questioning look, which he cut quickly to John and Betty. "Are we ready?"

John nodded. "Kate is lining everyone up now." He pointed. "Here come the wise men."

Logan had worked extensively with the three men on handling the camels. For the most part, they would merely stand next to them with reins in hand, but it warmed Leesa's heart to see the extra precautions he had taken. Two metal gates blocked the rear of the corral, and a shoulder-height wall of hay blocked younger children from climbing inside. Also—and this part shocked her most—Pete acted as lead handler. Sammy worked next to him, and the two of them looked quite cozy.

As they took their places, Leesa elbowed Logan in the ribs. She jerked her head toward Pete. "What's he doing here?" she whispered.

"Came back early," Logan whispered back. "Said his dad is doing better than expected. I'll tell you about it later. How did it go?"

"I'll tell you later." She tried to look awestruck as they wound their way toward the makeshift stable near the back of the town green. Sheep were bleating, wise men followed the star, and next to the manger sat Mary holding Jesus, Joseph at her shoulder. It was a beautiful scene, really, and there, in the front row taking it all in. . .

She caught Logan's gaze and gave a subtle gesture. His eyebrows lifted and he mouthed, "Is that. . .?"

"My sister. Long story," she mouthed back.

Yet, how could she put into words the tearful pleas or heartfelt apologies? Who but God could explain the chasms crossed or wounds mended? Fresh tears rose to her eyes as she remembered the look of joy that had crossed her sister's face upon seeing her.

They still had much to work out, but with God's grace, tonight was at least a start.

People wound past the stable, many commenting on the manager, the animals, the beautiful costumes. Several times, Leesa saw tears reflected in the eyes of the onlookers and felt her own eyes brim. Logan's, too, she noted, as more than once he lifted his hand to brush across his face.

"It's beautiful, isn't it?" she whispered.

"More than that, it feels. . .holy."

His throat worked, and Leesa couldn't help herself—she reached out and touched his fingers, curled so tightly around the shepherd's staff that his knuckles shone white.

Holy.

It was a perfect description for the events leading up to this night, and a perfect description for what the nativity meant to her and the people she loved. It was holy, and tonight. . .this was indeed, one holy night.

THE LAST ANGEL SONG

By Lorraine Beatty

Chapter 1

Callen Grant shoved his hands deep into the pockets of his heavy coat, scanning the main street of the town. Bethlehem, Maine. Small town America. Population, 9,000. How could a place that small be known for having the quintessential live nativity in the whole of New England? And why was he here to cover it?

A quick inventory of the snow-lined street offered no surprises. Bakery. Bank. Veterinary clinic. Pharmacy. Dress shop. All the requisite retailers were present, complete with white-steepled church across the green.

Hunching his shoulders against a stiff breeze chasing down the street, he folded his collar up, seeking warmth. He could have been in Florida, with palm trees and sunshine and temps in the eighties. It should have been a no-brainer—take the reporting job in Clearwater. Instead, he'd delayed his decision and ended up here.

He set his jaw and started forward, his boots sloshing through the rapidly melting snow. Maybe if he could get rid of the headache that had plagued him all morning he could think clearly.

With his assignment as adventure/travel author for the Wilcox Communications Group at an end, his boss had offered him a temporary position at the Boston office and given him the task of writing a lifestyle piece on the Bethlehem nativity. He'd been promised a hard reporting job as soon as one opened up, but Callen wasn't sure he wanted to remain with the company. He was looking for something more, and Wilcox had a habit of not keeping their promises.

He'd been offered the reporting job with a Florida paper, but it meant starting at the bottom, and he wasn't sure he wanted to fight that battle again. So he'd come to the wilds of Maine and tacked on a few weeks of vacation, intending to use the time to sort out his future. Should he take the Florida job and work his way up, or stay with Wilcox and hope they found a job for him soon?

The door to Bloom's Pharmacy opened as he reached for the handle. An elderly woman with a scarf wrapped around the collar of her bulky winter coat ambled out. He smiled. She stared and kept on going. Callen shrugged off the slight in favor of the warmth beckoning him inside.

The warmth quickly chased the chill from his shoulders and the familiar mixture of aromas eased his headache. Perfume. Medications. Candy. Magazines. The intriguing combination of smells that accompanied a drugstore.

Callen unbuttoned his coat as he scanned the directories hanging above each aisle. Spotting the sign for painkillers and cold remedies, he strolled toward the left, turning down the second aisle. He frowned at the vast assortment of choices. His peripheral vision picked up movement to his right, and he glanced at the woman coming toward him. He looked away, only to jerk his head around again and stare.

It couldn't be. Why would she be in this small town? And what were the odds of finding her here, after all this time?

The woman looked past him until he turned to face her. It had to be her. He'd know those hazel eyes anywhere. The eyes that changed color with each outfit she wore. The eyes that had a tiny blue streak in the left and a spot of green in the right.

She met his gaze. The hazel eyes widened. He smiled. "Angie? Angie Silkowsky?"

"Callen?" She rushed forward, hands outstretched. "I can't believe this. What are you doing here?"

He opened his mouth and found his voice lodged in his throat. She was as beautiful as he remembered. The twelve years since he'd seen her last had only added to her loveliness. He cleared his throat and tried again. "I'm here on a working vacation. What about you?"

"I live here. And my name is Angie Monroe now."

A cloud passed over her face and he sensed her slight withdrawal. "In Maine? Why? And what happened to you? You were hitting the top of the charts; your last album went platinum out of the gate. Then you disappeared. The whole country was looking for you."

Angie took a step back. The withdrawal physical now. "I'm not in the music business anymore. I, uh, have a daughter. Lily.

She's three. I wanted a normal life for her. Not touring on buses and dragging her from concert to concert." She shrugged. "You know how it is."

He didn't know, but the life she'd described was the one she'd dreamed of her whole life. So why had she walked away? No. Vanished at the height of her success? "Angie, why—"

She smiled and moved another step back. "Where are you staying, Callen? Oh, must be at the Stoval-Mills House. It's the only bed and breakfast in town. Is Edna treating you all right?"

Callen's reporter antennae quivered. Angie was as tense as a too-tight guitar string. What was she hiding? "Yeah. It's great. She spoils me like a doting mom."

She nodded. "That's Edna."

"So I'd like to catch up. It's been a long time. Why don't we have dinner? I'll be here for several weeks."

She blanched, one hand coming to rest at her throat. "Sure. Fine. I'd like that. Of course, I'm really busy at the moment, with Lily and all. She takes up most of my time. Then I'm the director of the live nativity this year. That's a huge job. But I'll see what I can do."

Callen took a step toward her, smiling. "You're the director of the nativity? That's why I'm here. I'm covering your event for an article on the top Christmas attractions in New England. In fact, I'm meeting with the editor of the paper in a few minutes."

Angie's ivory skin turned an odd shade of gray.

"You're a reporter?"

Callen narrowed his gaze. What was wrong with her? Her

voice was husky, her posture defensive. Not at all the vibrant, full-of-life woman he'd fallen in love with long ago. He noticed she was holding a small box of cold medication. Maybe she was ill.

He nodded, deciding to give her space to explain. He slipped his hands into his pockets again and leaned back slightly, assuming a casual stance. "Don't sound so surprised. It's all I ever wanted to be. Remember?"

"Yes. Of course. I just didn't expect. . ." She blinked and met his gaze, her hazel eyes filled with confusion. "I thought you wrote those travel books. I used to see them everywhere." She moved her hand through the air like a banner. "*Granted: Adventures in Travel by Callen Grant.*"

"Yeah. They did really well. But those are done. I'm just finishing up on my contract. I've been offered a reporting job in Florida. It's a chance to do some serious news stories." Callen frowned. The pulse in Angie's neck was beating so rapidly he wondered if she might pass out.

"Well, it's been great to see you again. I'll call when I have a free evening. I've got to—" She stared at the medicine in her hand as if seeing it for the first time. "I need to get this home to Lily." She pushed past him and disappeared around the corner, leaving him puzzled, worried, and filled with memories he didn't want to visit.

What had happened to Angeline Silkowsky? She said her name was Monroe and she had a child. Had she married someone from here? Suddenly he had a lot more things to look into besides a live nativity.

❦

Angie Silkowsky Monroe swiped her debit card, her fingers tapping the counter impatiently as Betty rang up her purchase. She shot the woman a stiff smile as she took the receipt then glanced over her shoulder to make sure Callen wasn't watching. She could see his light brown hair over the top of the shelving.

Pushing open the door, Angie rushed outside, inhaling the cool, crisp winter air, the chill of it penetrating deep into her lungs and settling the nerves in her stomach. She took a moment to decide her next move. Turning north would take her to the Bethlehem Community Church. Turning south, to Edna at the Stovall-Mills House. A quick check of her watch showed she had nearly an hour before she had to pick her daughter up from preschool at the church. Plenty of time to get some questions answered. She turned south.

Edna Burrows was seated at the round kitchen table, a cup of steaming tea in front of her as she read a magazine. Angie tapped on one of the small window panes and waved.

Edna motioned her inside, smiling. "You're a sight for sore eyes. I haven't seen you in weeks. Where you been hiding? You want some tea?"

Angie nodded, pulling off her coat and taking a seat at the cheery table. Simon, Edna's husband, passed through the room with a nod of his head, and exited out the door. Simon was a man of few words. Probably because Edna talked enough for both of them. If you wanted to know about anything or anyone in town, Edna was better than the Internet. Which is why Angie had come.

"Plantation mint, your favorite." Edna placed the teacup in front of Angie and sat down again. "So what brings you here on a late afternoon? Shouldn't you be picking up that cutie of yours? That child is so adorable. Bright. Friendly. Full of energy. I don't know how you keep up with her."

Cradling her cup between her hands, Angie waited for Edna to take a breath. "You have a new guest." She held her breath, her stomach twisting in knots as she waited for the answers she dreaded hearing.

Edna grinned. "You mean that handsome, six-foot hunk of masculine charm, Callen Grant?" She sighed and placed her hand at her throat with a sigh. "If I were thirty years younger, and Simon wasn't the love of my life. . ." She winked. "He checked in this morning. What about him?"

Angie's heart thumped wildly in her chest. "Do you know why he's here?"

Edna's smile widened as she leaned forward. "Indeed I do. He's here to write an article about our live nativity. You know the attention has died down a good bit from our grand rebirth after the storm. It wouldn't hurt to put our nativity at the front of people's minds again. And since you're in charge of the whole thing. . ." Edna set her cup down with a clatter into the saucer, her eyes wide with sudden realization. "Oh my."

Angie rubbed her temple. "Oh my, indeed."

Edna waved off her concern. "Well, no need to worry. He'll never figure out who you really are. My goodness, you don't look anything like you did when you were a music star. You have different hair, different clothes, even a different name. Don't you worry; we all promised when you came to live here that we'd protect you." She reached over and patted Angie's hand reassuringly.

"Callen knows who I am. We've known each other since high school back in Ohio. He's not only a reporter by trade, but by nature. He'll want to know why I'm here, and he won't stop until he finds out."

"Then maybe you should tell him. Get it out in the open. If he's an old friend, maybe he'll agree to support your decision."

Angie prayed her friend was right. If not, her whole world could come tumbling down.

❧

An hour later Angie was still praying Edna's words would prove true as she picked Lily up from school. "Did you have fun today, Pumpkin?"

Lily held up a crumpled piece of paper displaying colorful crayon scribbles and glitter. "We made a sparkle tree."

"I love it. Let's put it up on the refrigerator, okay?"

Lily smiled and nodded. " 'Kay."

Thoughts of Callen swirled like a fierce winter wind in Angie's mind as she prepared supper. Mac and cheese, pears, and little green balls—peas . All of Lily's favorites. Angie tried to eat, but the food tasted like paper. Lily gobbled her food with delight, leaving behind an orange and green mess on the booster seat. By the time Angie had tucked the little girl into bed and headed back downstairs, she'd decided to follow Edna's suggestion and take the offensive in dealing with Callen. She'd meet with him, tell him what was going on, then she'd offer to be his guide and grant him full access to the nativity and any questions he wanted to ask. She'd tell him she left the music business to be a mom to Lily, that her name change was to protect them both from publicity. She'd be open and forthright, he'd accept her explanation, and she'd call on his friendship to keep her world intact. Picking up her phone, she scrolled down to Edna's number and dialed, ignoring the pricking of her conscience. She would tell Callen only part of the truth. He didn't need to know everything.

⌘

Callen Grant stared out the large window of his room at the Stoval-Mills house, barely registering the lights that decorated every charming home along Spruce Street. The B&B was tucked away around a corner from the main thoroughfare on a quiet, tree-lined street. Bethlehem was a living postcard of the idyllic Christmas village. Every place he'd wandered this afternoon had been more picturesque than the last.

Heat from the fireplace warmed his back, drawing him away from the window. He ran his palms down his face and lowered himself into the comfy love seat facing the fire. All that New England charm was lost in the memory of coming face to face with Angie Silkowsky. Known to the world as Silky Blaine. The girl with the voice like silk. Smooth, strong, able to wrap its dulcet tones around your nerves and touch your soul with sweetness.

The way she'd touched his heart from the moment he'd met her in English class in tenth grade. Quiet, shy, and pretty, she hadn't been one of the popular crowd. They'd sat beside each other at the back of the class and were an item all through high school. He'd fallen in love, but Angie was more interested in a singing career. She'd even cancelled their prom date to sing the national anthem at a Cincinnati Reds game.

Callen rubbed his forehead then reached for his hot cocoa. A part of Edna's hospitality. He'd had the ring in his pocket the night Angie received word she'd won the *American Star* talent search. She'd left for Nashville that next morning, and he'd never seen her again—except on television and on covers of magazines—but he hardly recognized her. She'd been transformed. New hairstyle and color, new clothes, and new name. Angie Silkowsky had become Silky Blaine, country music's hottest new star.

He'd never begrudged her the opportunity. She'd worked hard and achieved her heart's desire. But the hole she'd left in his heart had never healed, and he'd never found anyone else who could fill it.

The old-style rotary telephone rang, the unfamiliar sound causing him to nearly spill his drink. Setting the cup on the coffee table, he picked up the receiver. "Grant here."

"Callen? It's Angie."

He froze. For a moment his lungs refused to function. He inhaled through his nose, trying to keep his voice calm. "Hey. I didn't expect to hear from you so soon." He leaned forward, his gut knotted with curiosity. "What can I do for you?"

"I wanted to apologize for being so abrupt this afternoon. I was distracted. I thought maybe we could meet for dinner tomorrow night. My treat. Trapper's has the best seafood in town."

Callen didn't want to wait that long. He had too many questions. "Why not lunch? My schedule is flexible."

"Well, I suppose we could eat here at my house. It would save me a babysitting fee, too." She chuckled softly. "How about noon? Edna will give you directions. It's not hard to find."

"Great. Will your husband be there?"

"No. Just the three of us."

The odd tone in her voice raised more questions. "I'll see you then." He hung up the phone, staring at his cup of cocoa. Angie was a mother. He shouldn't be surprised. But he was. He'd always thought her career was her first love. She'd been passionate, even obsessive about her goal.

Is that why she'd dropped out of the music business? Had she gotten married and started a family? But why no explanation? Why no announcement, or a farewell tour to thank her fans? She'd vanished overnight. It had been the lead article in the tabloids for months until a new celebrity crisis had taken over the headlines and Silky Blaine was forgotten.

His gaze drifted to the clock on the bedside table. Eight thirty. He had a lot of hours to fill before lunch tomorrow. And a lot of questions and a lot of memories to keep him awake.

Chapter 2

O h, no, Lily, please don't pull out the toys right now. Mommy wants to keep the house clean for company." The little girl smiled at her, holding up a large pink Lego. "But I want to build a tower. Like 'Punzel."

Angie sighed and shook her head. What did she care if Callen saw a clean house or not? She wasn't trying to impress him. She was trying to distract him. What better way than with her precocious little Lily? "All right. You build the tower, but Mommy has to fix lunch, so you'll have to play by yourself."

Two dark pigtails above little ears bobbed as Lily nodded. " 'Kay, Mommy."

Angie returned to the kitchen, grateful for the open wall to the living room that allowed her to keep a watchful eye on her daughter. Quickly, she ran down her to-do list. The food was prepared, and she would heat the rolls when Callen arrived. She hoped he liked seafood casserole. If not, she'd throw a sandwich together. She knew he liked ham and cheese. But he was a world traveler now and had written about dozens of exotic locales. His taste was probably broader than it used to be.

He was broader, too. In all the right places. Even beneath his thick winter jacket she'd noticed how muscular and solid he'd become. The warm brown hair was worn short now, trimmed to keep the strands from curling. His face was more angular—a man's face, with planes and angles that told of maturity. His mouth had a small scar on one side. She didn't remember that. But the cleft in his chin was still there, giving him additional character.

Angie buried her face in her hands, exhaling a heavy sigh. Callen had always been the most handsome man she'd ever known. He was even more so now. Not that she had any business noticing. He might be handsome, an old love, but he could destroy the new life she cherished. That's what she should be remembering. Not the way his smile tingled down to her toes.

She jumped at the sudden chime of the doorbell. Was he here already? She slid the rolls into the oven then scanned the kitchen. Everything was ready. Except her. Walking briskly through the house, she entered the foyer and stopped to take a deep breath. Lily skidded to a halt behind her. Forcing a smile she didn't feel, she opened the door. "Callen. Come in. I see you found the house okay."

Callen stomped the snow from his feet before entering. "You were right. It's not hard to find." He handed her a small gift bag. "Edna told me you liked these."

"Thank you, but you didn't have to bring anything." She peered inside to find a box of her favorite tea and small bag of chocolate.

"I know. I wanted to." He shrugged off his coat and handed it to her. His gaze drifted downward and a smile lit his eyes. "Hello."

Lily ducked behind Angie's leg. Angie hung the coat on the hall tree then placed her hand on Lily's head, drawing her forward. "Callen, this is my daughter. Lily, this is an old friend of Mommy's, Mr. Grant. We went to school together."

Lily studied him a moment before breaking into a smile. "Did you and Mommy color? I'm a good colorer."

Callen laughed, and hunkered down to speak to Lily face to face. "I'm sure you are."

Angie's heart twisted inside her chest. She'd forgotten how good Callen was with kids. "I hope you're hungry."

"Always." He followed her through the living room and into the large kitchen at the back of the house. "Nice place. Homey."

"I wanted a family home, someplace to raise Lily with roots and security." Callen stopped beside her at the counter, and she became acutely aware of his nearness, the size of him, the way he added a different tone to the room. "Uh, would you rather eat in the breakfast room or the dining room?"

He shrugged, sending a waft of spicy aftershave into her lungs. "I'm not a dining room kind of guy."

She smiled and tucked her hair behind her ear. "Me either. I only use it at Thanksgiving and Christmas."

"So your husband is a kitchen table kind of man, too?"

Angie froze, the pan of warm rolls poised halfway out of the oven. She swallowed, straightened, and closed the door. She moved to the breakfast area, keeping her back to Callen. "There is no husband. I'm not married." She waited for his comment, but it never came. She turned and looked at him. His head was tilted slightly, as if pondering her situation. He knew her so well. Had he guessed the truth? Impossible. No one knew.

She lifted her chin. "Shocked?"

Callen shrugged and shifted his weight onto one hip. "No. Surprised, but not shocked."

Angie finished preparing the meal then helped Lily onto her booster seat. She said a quick blessing before passing the hot rolls to Callen. "So, other than traveling the world, what else have you been doing? Married?"

"No. Never had the time or the inclination."

"Devoted bachelor, huh?"

He held her gaze a long moment. "No. Just too busy. No time for a relationship. You should understand that."

"I do. So you're here to report on our nativity? Hardly seems worthy of your kind of high-adventure advice."

Callen took a sip of his coffee. "Actually, I'm not doing the books any longer. They ran their course. That kind of information is readily available online now."

Angie stared at him. "So now you're covering Christmas events."

"I am. But I'm between jobs. I'm trying to reinvent my life."

Angie squirmed inwardly. She knew that experience all too well. "Why?"

Callen rested his forearms on the edge of the table. "I

stumbled into the adventure travel writing thing. I always wanted to be a serious reporter, covering world events, politics, things that mattered."

"I remember."

"The parent company of my publisher shifted me over to their lifestyle division temporarily. That's why I'm here. But I have an offer from a news group in Florida as an investigative reporter that I'm considering."

A bitter chill chased through her veins. "That's great. Are you going to take it?"

"Maybe. But I'd be starting over from the bottom. I'm not sure I want to do that."

"Starting over is never easy. Sometimes you have to take a few steps back before you can move forward."

"Mommy, all done." Lily lifted her small plate high in the air, sending the scraps tumbling into her lap and onto the floor.

"Good girl. You ate all your carrots and most of your casserole. I'm so proud." Angie stood and cleaned up the crumbs with her napkin. "Are you ready for your cookies?"

Lily clapped her hands, grinning from ear to ear. Angie heard Callen chuckle softly as she moved to the counter for the sugar cookies.

Choosing a cookie from the plate, Lily offered it to Callen. Angie sat down, unable to look away from the warmth reflected in his blue eyes.

"For me? Thank you." He took the cookie and placed it on the edge of his plate.

"You're welcome." Lily focused her attention on the pink sprinkles on top of her cookie, picking each one off and eating it.

Callen met Angie's gaze, and a rush of heat stung her cheeks. He'd caught her staring. Not good.

"She's a great kid. You're lucky."

"Blessed," Angie corrected. Might as well start dealing with the issues. "She's adopted. Her mother was my best friend."

Callen raised his eyebrows. "What happened?"

"She died of cancer when Lily was three months old." She closed her eyes briefly, remembering the rapid deterioration of her friend. "It happened so fast."

"Is that why you dropped off the map? To raise Lily?"

Angie nodded, avoiding his penetrating stare. She picked up her plate and reached for Callen's, too. "I promised her I'd take care of Lily, and I couldn't do that on a tour bus. Or by exposing her to that world. I even changed my name to protect her. I have apple pie for dessert, or you can have more cookies."

Callen grabbed the cookie off his plate as she lifted it. "Cookie first, then pie."

Angie tried to focus on slicing the warm pie and placing it on the plates along with a dollop of ice cream. But her thoughts kept going back to the next part of her discussion with Callen. She'd told him about Lily. Would he accept that as her only reason for quitting the music business, or would his reporter's sense press for more?

Picking up the plates, she started back to the table, only to see Callen bending over her daughter. Lily had fallen asleep, her little head rolled forward. Callen looked up. "I think we bored her."

Angie set the plates down and moved to lift the little girl, but Callen beat her to it. "Show me where to put her."

Hurrying ahead, Angie led the way to Lily's room at the top of the stairs. Callen placed the sleeping child on the bed with a gentleness that warmed her heart. She covered Lily with a small quilt and kissed her cheek before tiptoeing from the room. Back downstairs, they resumed their seats at the table and tackled the pie.

"This is delicious, Angie. Did you bake it?"

"I did. I've become very domestic over the last three years."

"I've noticed."

"Thank you for helping with Lily. She doesn't usually nap during the day anymore, but we played in the snow this morning. I think it wore her out."

Callen held her gaze. "So, you're in charge of the nativity. Does that mean I can get all the inside scoop for my article?"

Relief surged through Angie so quickly she was grateful for the solid chair beneath her. If she'd been standing, she might have collapsed. Her offensive approach had worked. Callen was satisfied and turning his attention to the nativity. She offered up a grateful prayer.

"Of course. You can follow me around all day if you'd like. I'm not working today, but I have a full schedule tomorrow. You're welcome to tag along."

"I think I'll do that. A behind-the-scenes look will add a lot of human interest to the piece."

Angie smiled, the first genuine one since Callen had walked into her house. "I'll call you."

Callen prepared to leave a short while later, and Angie walked him to the door. "It's been good to see you, Callen."

"Same here." He shrugged on his coat and buttoned it up, pulling leather gloves from his pocket. "We have a lot to catch up on, Angie. I want to know everything that's happened to you since you won that contest." He looked into her eyes, holding her gaze.

His penetrating stare sent a shiver down her spine and a pang of guilt through her heart. She crossed her arms over her chest.

"I have a lot more questions, Angie. Things only you can answer." Callen smiled and walked out, pulling the door shut behind him, leaving renewed tension in her chest.

Questions. He had more questions. Somehow she had to keep him from asking the wrong ones.

Chapter 3

C allen walked briskly down the front sidewalk of the Stoval-Mills house the next morning, one hand resting against his stomach. Edna had overloaded him with pancakes, genuine Maine blueberry syrup, and the fluffiest scrambled eggs he'd ever eaten. He normally didn't indulge in breakfast, but the aroma wafting into the large dining room from the kitchen had been impossible to ignore. Plus, Edna had insisted she'd made the entire meal for him, since her other guests, a Canadian couple on their way to DC, had checked out.

Stopping at the end of the sidewalk, he took a moment to survey the area. The homes along Spruce Street were all charmingly unique. Some Victorian, others Tudor, a Colonial, and a Cape Cod. Last night the old houses had glowed with white Christmas lights outlining their windows and doors, and with candles flickering on sills. Today, the charm was still present, only in snowy drifts along evergreen shrubs, colorful wreaths adorning doors, and green garlands draped across eves and around posts. The sight took him back to his childhood in central Ohio and the small suburb he'd grown up in. Where Angie had grown up, too.

Callen shook off the old memories. He didn't like to look backward. Only forward. No point in mulling over what had been. Pulling his phone from his pocket, he realized he still had an hour before meeting Angie at the green in the center of town.

Time to get a better lay of the land. The weather was warmer today, so all he needed was a heavy sweater. Freedom from winter coats and gloves lightened his steps and his mood. Or was he simply eager to see Angie again?

She'd changed. Her blond hair was now more of a warm honey color. Her hazel eyes were still as beautiful, but with a sadness behind them he'd never seen before. There was also a warmth about her, a peace that he didn't remember. Motherhood had probably added that to her loveliness. He was conflicted about Angie being a mom. It surprised him, because she'd been so fierce in her desire to be a singer. Yet, it seemed perfectly natural for her to be raising a child. Watching her with Lily yesterday had seemed right.

Main Street was full of activity when Callen turned the corner, halting his introspection. The sun shone brightly, bouncing off the brick buildings lining the street, and calling attention to the elaborate garlands and the various Christmas ornaments adorning the storefronts and streetlights.

He strolled along the row of stores, glancing in windows, his appreciation for the town of Bethlehem growing with each step. How did a town that looked like a Thomas Kinkade canvas get the name Bethlehem? The baby Jesus would find nothing familiar here.

His wandering finally brought him to the green at the end of the block. After waiting for a passing vehicle, he jogged across the street and headed toward the sprawling assortment of structures depicting the ancient city of Bethlehem. On one end stood a tan building resembling the inn. On the far end was a small rise with boulders, and in the center, the sloped-roof stable, complete with rustic manger and stalls for the animals.

So what made this nativity so newsworthy that he'd had to drive up from Boston to report on it?

"Callen!"

He turned toward the shout, smiling when he saw Angie jogging toward him. His memory flashed back to a winter day during Christmas vacation, an iced-over pond, and a stolen kiss behind a tree.

Her face was flushed a lovely pink and her hazel eyes sparkled with excitement. She looked like a little girl, with her jeans and long bulky sweater, feet wrapped warmly in winter boots. He tore his eyes from her face and gestured toward the display. "Nice. I wasn't expecting something this elaborate."

She chuckled softly. "It's not the buildings that make it special, Callen. It's who's inside. Immanuel. Remember?"

Callen searched his memory for the meaning of the term, but it eluded him. But then a lot of his church exposure had faded away.

Angie started around the sets, motioning him to follow. "I need to check out some things. You can ask questions as I go."

Only one question came to mind. Why did you vanish? But

he sensed this wasn't the time. She was in a friendly mood. He didn't want to ruin that. "So how did this thing get started?" He pulled out pad and pen.

Angie stepped inside the stable and began inspecting posts, latches on animal pens, making notes on her electronic tablet. "It was Kate Walters, the town manager's idea. She wanted to draw tourists here for the holidays and focus on the true reason for Christmas. What better than a live nativity?" She smiled over her shoulder. "When Hurricane Eleanor came through a few years ago, Bethlehem suffered a lot of damage. The town council canceled the event. But Pastor Mike and Emma Townsend pulled everyone together, and we started reviving the nativity in the middle of the devastation. The news picked up the story, and help and donations started pouring in. People came from everywhere to see the performance. It's grown every year. Though this year attendance is down a bit."

"So you're in charge of the whole thing?"

"Kate still oversees everything. I'm more of a stage manager. Logan Franks wrangles the animals."

"Aren't most live nativities static? I mean, people and animals sit there while everyone walks by. What makes this one special?" He followed Angie as she walked around to the back of the stable, surprised to find a platform large enough for several people to stand on positioned above the stable roof, accessed by a narrow ladder. It looked dangerous, even though there was a safety rail around the edge to prevent falling.

"We don't simply tell the story, we put the visitors inside it."

Angie wound her way through the electrical wires to a storage unit. She opened it to reveal an elaborate electronic system. "We have music, dialogue, scripture readings, and the angel's song."

"The angel sings?"

"Of course, silly. You know, heavenly hosts singing glory to God in the highest."

"Right."

Grabbing his hand, she tugged him along with her as she returned to the front of the stable. "We want our visitors to feel like they've been transported to the Holy Land. I want them to see and hear and experience that night when Christ was born. To be part of the miracle of His birth."

Her enthusiasm made him smile and triggered a need to tease her. "Do the animals have speaking parts, too?"

She punched him in the arm. "No. But we do get them to kneel down at midnight."

"Sure you do. So what about the platform in the back?"

"That's where the angel stands, watching over the baby Jesus. We have a youth choir that sings, and for the finale an angel sings 'Hark the Herald Angels Sing.'" Get it?"

She smiled up at him, and his heart flipped over in his chest. "Got it."

"Good."

"So are the actors townspeople, professionals, or what?"

"Townspeople. Actually, we've had so many wanting to participate that we've got a different cast for each performance. Every Saturday and Sunday in December." She glanced at her watch. "I need to meet with the head of this weekend's volunteers. You can tag along if you'd like." She turned and started across the green.

"And you're responsible for each cast? Sounds like a logistical nightmare. Getting one set of actors prepared would be hard enough."

She smiled and shook her head. "Not really. Everyone is so enthusiastic, it makes my job easy. I'm truly blessed to have found a home here."

Something in her tone, in her expression, set off alarms in Callen's mind. He knew as sure as he breathed that there was more to Angie's story than what she'd shared with him yesterday. He wasn't a reporter for nothing. He was more determined than ever to get to the bottom of her story before his time in Bethlehem was done.

❧

Angie bent and kissed her daughter goodnight then tugged up the Rapunzel comforter. "Sleep tight, Pumpkin. Mommy loves you."

"I love you more."

"I love you most."

Lily giggled and snuggled down with her Rapunzel doll. The good-night ritual was the child's favorite part of the movie, and Angie had to agree. She'd come to cherish the words. Her hand was on the light switch when Lily spoke again.

"Mommy, will we see the big man again?"

Angie's throat tightened. She'd ended up spending the whole day with Callen, and he'd tagged along with her to pick up Lily from preschool. She'd promised her daughter pizza at Gino's, and Lily had invited Callen to join them.

Fortunately, Lily had been very chatty, which left little time for Callen to ask questions. She'd made their escape as soon as possible, but Callen's ease with Lily had elevated him to hero status. "I suppose so."

"He's like Flynn Rider."

"He is, huh?" Angie inhaled slowly. Not even. The animated hero was charming, witty, and verbose. Callen was none of those things. Okay, he was charming, but his was a quiet, understated kind of charm. He was a man of serious temperament, a thinker, who measured his words, who studied people with his probing blue eyes and keen intellect.

"Night, Pumpkin."

Angie made her way to her own room, thoughts of Callen swirling in her mind. Today had been one of the most enjoyable she'd known in a while. She loved her life, she was happy and content, but it had been a long time since she'd shared a day with a man. A man she'd cared about and seriously considered marrying before her career had taken off.

Changing into her sleep pants and tank top, she curled up in the chair in the alcove of her bedroom. Truth was, Callen had been on her mind a good bit over the last year. She'd wondered what he was doing, what exotic locale he was exploring, remembering things they'd done together so long ago. Wondering if he'd married.

Closing her eyes, she rested her head on the back of the chair.

Lord, what are you doing? Why did you bring him to my mind and then bring him here?

She really needed to get a grip. Callen could ruin her whole life if he uncovered her real reason for stepping away from singing. The fallout would be devastating. She'd have to move, uproot Lily—it might take years for the publicity to die down.

The logical thing to do would be to avoid Callen as much as possible, but the truth was, she liked spending time with him. She liked the way he made her feel attractive, and interesting, and she liked the way he treated Lily. She'd never realized how lonely she was until he stepped back into her life. Her feelings for him hadn't died. They were as alive and well as she was.

❧

Callen stared out his window at the street below. A light snow was falling, dusting the sidewalks with powdery flakes. Sometimes he hated being a reporter. It was too easy to conjure up all sorts of bad things people wanted to keep hidden.

Like Angie. She obviously loved her little girl and enjoyed being a mother. There was a peace about her he envied, but then, she'd always had a strong faith. So had he. Once. Somewhere along the road he'd drifted away. But there was something else behind Angie's bright smile and friendly attitude. She'd been almost too helpful, throwing open the doors to the nativity event so he wouldn't think about other things. She was hiding something from him. He just didn't know what it could be.

They'd spent two full days together earlier in the week, meeting the people behind the nativity, learning the ins and outs of managing the large production, and meeting every commit-tee chair, but he hadn't heard from Angie in a couple of days. She wasn't returning his calls or texts. He'd even stopped by the house, but no one had been home. Which only fueled his desire to find her and uncover what she was hiding.

Callen worked his jaw side to side. Tonight was the live nativity. She couldn't avoid him there. And she couldn't evade the truth forever. He'd get to the bottom of her story. Whatever she was afraid of, he'd make sure she was safe and protected. Seeing Angie again had torn the cover from his feelings. He still cared for her, more than any woman he'd ever met.

Chapter 4

Callen leaned one shoulder against the thick trunk of a winter-bare tree, watching Angie walk toward him from the now silent and dark nativity display. The field was still covered in a soft glow from the street lamps and the Christmas lights from the storefronts. None of which were as bright, in his opinion, as the smile on her face.

Her eyes sparkled, and he could sense her anticipation. "What did you think of our pageant?"

"It wasn't what I'd expected."

She blinked. "Oh. What had you expected?"

Callen shrugged. "Cheesy. Preachy. But it was very professional."

Her smile widened, sending a new sparkle into her hazel eyes. "Good. The crowd was bigger tonight. I counted six people who stayed to speak with the pastor afterward."

"Not very many, I guess."

"The first night we only had one. It's an improvement, and if we keep increasing each time, think of the people we could reach for the Lord. Our goal is to bring the Christmas story to life. To show the significance of the event, not just sit there like mannequins, assuming everyone understands the meaning of the moment. Immanuel."

Callen raised an eyebrow. He still didn't remember what it meant.

"God with us."

He should have deduced that from the narrative during the nativity, but he'd been distracted, searching out Angie and watching her every move. He'd only paid passing attention to the actual drama. Except for the angel at the end. A dark-haired woman had stood on the high platform lit from a single spotlight and sang "Hark the Herald Angels Sing." The song had touched something inside him, something long forgotten, but he couldn't put a name to it. Probably a long dead memory of a happy holiday. One of the few he could claim. For most of his life he'd ignored Christmas. Except for the years with Angie.

"Are you hungry?"

Callen pulled his attention back to the woman in front of him. "Always. What do you have in mind? And what about Lily?"

"She's with my babysitter. I usually go out to eat with some of the cast afterward."

"So this will be a big party, then?"

Angie shifted her weight, shoving her hands into her coat pockets. "No. Just you and me."

He tried to ignore the jolt of excitement that raced through his nerves. "Lead the way."

"Do you mind walking? It's not far."

Callen fell into step beside her, only half listening as she told him about the little problems that had popped up during the event and how they'd all scrambled to keep things going. He was content to listen to her. To be at her side. Her voice rose and fell with her excitement, making him smile.

They turned the corner onto Chandler Street and she fell silent. The question he'd been longing to ask slipped out before he could restrain it. "What happened to you, Angie? One minute you were the hottest singer in the country, and then you dropped out of sight."

"I told you. It was because of Lily. Her mother, Nell, was my best friend, my assistant, and sometimes backup singer. She was my rock during the rise of my career. She was also my challenge. She wasn't a believer, and I wanted her to be. I loved her so much, but she'd only laugh at me and call me Church Girl."

"You always were strong in your faith."

"Not back then. I should never have entered that contest."

Angie stopped in front of a charming restaurant called Sally's, tucked invitingly between two other buildings. Christmas lights adorned the front door under the sign.

Inside, the hostess led them to a quiet table in the back corner and took their drink order before walking away. Callen appreciated the quiet, intimate atmosphere. He looked at Angie, determined to get some answers. "Why do you think you shouldn't have entered that *American Star* contest? That was your dream."

"No. My dream was to sing Christian music. But you know that wasn't working. The doors kept closing. I was so frustrated.

I wanted to use my voice for God's glory, but it wasn't happening. So I took matters into my own hands, and I entered that contest, knowing in my heart it was wrong."

The waitress brought their drinks and took their orders. Callen picked up the conversation as soon as she left. "You won that contest."

"I thought so, until I got to Nashville and saw how things worked. I told myself it was worth the price, and I could exist with one foot in the world and one in my faith. At first it was easy. I was high on the fame and the money and the joy. But as the years went on, it got harder and harder."

Callen wanted to take her hand, but he feared she'd stop talking, and he needed to know the whole story.

"Nell, despite her unbelief, refused to let me lose mine. She kept me anchored. She buffered the bad stuff and became my emotional bodyguard."

"So what went wrong?"

"She got pregnant. The baby's father wanted nothing to do with her or the child. Then a few months before she was due, Nell found out she had cancer. A very aggressive form. She asked me to raise her little girl. I couldn't refuse. I knew I couldn't have both a career and a family. It just wouldn't work. One would have to suffer for the other to thrive. I chose Lily. But I wanted to raise her without bringing my past into the mix. So I made arrangements to walk away."

"That must have been complicated, with all the contracts and business dealings."

"It was. I carried a lot of guilt. I had people depending on me, but by that time I'd lost my passion for singing. So I came here and started fresh."

"With a new name. Do these people know who you are, were?"

"Yes, but they don't care, and they don't talk about it either."

Their food arrived and they ate in silence for a while. But Callen sensed there was more to Angie's story. "How did you find this place? It's barely on the map."

"I played a concert in Portland early in my career. I'd had a taste of the fame, the fans, and the crazy lifestyle. I was feeling overwhelmed and wondering what I'd gotten myself into, so I asked my manager to find me a secluded place to stay, and he found a bed and breakfast on the coast. It was wonderful. The owners knew who I was, but they didn't care. They said the people here valued their privacy and assumed everyone else did as well.

"There was a couple staying at the inn with me; they were thinking of starting a B&B in a nearby town. When I was looking for a place to live I remembered them. Edna and Simon. Lily and I stayed with them for several months before I bought the house." She looked up at him. "So, now you know it all. I just want my life to be ordinary. To raise Lily in a good Christian environment, with people who care about her."

"Your parents?"

"They retired to Arizona. My brother and his family are in Charleston, and Ellen and her brood are in Kentucky. We see them as often as possible."

"I always envied you your family."

"I never appreciated them until I got Lily. My sister told me once that having a child was like looking through a telescope and adjusting the lens. Suddenly things are more clear. You understand your parents in a whole new way. And then you get an inkling of what our heavenly Father feels, too, how He wants the best for us, even when we don't understand what He's doing."

"You really believe that? That God makes everything okay?"

"Absolutely. Look at what He's done in my life, Callen. I turned my back on His plan and took things into my own hands. But He placed an unbeliever in my life to keep me on track. He placed me in that B&B where I met Edna, who was there waiting when I needed her. He gave me Lily at a point in my life when I realized I might never—" She stopped and took a deep breath. She couldn't tell him about her voice. "When I'd lost my way. I can look back and see His hand in every aspect of my life, Callen. You could, too, if you'd only look."

"Maybe I will. Someday." He looked at her, his heart filling with affection. She looked so beautiful in the soft light. He knew he should probably leave well enough alone. She'd told him her story, but his reporter instincts suspected there was more. He waited until their dessert arrived before pressing on. "Why didn't you make some kind of statement? Disappearing the way you did only fueled people's curiosity."

"We did. We released a statement that I had adopted a child and wanted to take time with my family."

"I don't remember seeing that anywhere." She looked surprised, and he grinned. "I've kept tabs on you over the years."

"The announcement came out at the same time JoJo had her meltdown at the AMAs and all her dirty linen was being exposed. My life fell off the radar. Believe me, I was grateful. Another one of God's blessings."

Callen remembered the scandal over the pop singer. It had consumed the media with never-ending revelations of sex, drugs, and criminal allegations. He looked at Angie, thanking the Lord for protecting her from those evils.

The street was nearly empty when they left the restaurant. "I guess the streets are rolled up early here? Even on a Saturday night?"

Angie nodded with a chuckle. "If you want to party late, you have to go to Portland."

"Where are you parked? I'll walk you back."

"Behind the church, across the green."

They walked in companionable silence for a while, the soft glow of the Christmas lights along storefronts adding a romantic atmosphere to the night. A few cars passed by on the narrow street. One honked, and Angie waved.

Callen looked at her again, longing to bring her against his side and hold her close. He settled for taking her hand. She looked at him with a surprised expression that quickly changed to a warm smile. "I've missed you, Angeline."

"Me, too. I'm glad the Lord brought you back into my life."

"You think my being here is part of some divine plan?"

"Of course. He always has a plan."

Angie stopped beside a dark SUV and turned to face him. The soft glow of a nearby floodlight lit her smiling face. Callen sucked in a sharp breath. What was happening to him? He'd been here only a week, and all he could think about was Angie.

She patted her car. "Thanks for walking me home." A smirk accompanied her remark.

Callen didn't want to say good-bye. "I could get my car and follow you home." A warm rush of embarrassment warmed his neck. He was behaving like a lovesick schoolboy.

Angie reached up and touched his cheek. "That's sweet, but it's early yet. I'll be fine. But thank you for caring."

He placed his palm over her hand as it rested on his cheek. He gazed into her eyes, dark green in the evening light. His heart raced; his entire body warmed with a long-forgotten affection—no, love—that he'd suppressed for years. He took her hand from his face and pulled her closer. With his other hand he gently tilted her face upward and placed a small, feather-light kiss on her lips. He forgot to breathe.

Neither moved. The white puffs of their breath intermingled in the frosty air.

"I'd better go." Angie stepped back, her remote key clicking the car locks. She pulled her gaze from his and opened the door, sliding behind the wheel. She reached for the door handle and looked up at him again. "Will you come to church with me tomorrow?"

Callen knew in that moment he'd go to the moon with her

if she asked. "Sure. What time?"

"I'll pick you up at Edna's around ten. We dress casual, so no need for a tie."

"Good. I didn't bring one."

He watched Angie drive away, mentally starting the countdown until he'd see her tomorrow. He turned toward the other end of town, grateful for the long walk back to the Stoval-Mills house. He had a lot to think about.

How could he have such intense feelings for Angie after only a week? It was nuts. He zipped up his jacket and shoved his hands into his pockets as he made his way along Main Street.

No. What he was feeling was the effect of letting the genie out of the bottle. He'd stuffed his love for Angie deep inside his heart the day she won the contest. He knew he'd lost her forever. He'd loved her and had wanted her to have her dream, but achieving her dream meant that his had to die.

Tonight had taken the cap off those bottled-up emotions and set them free. Over time, they'd distilled, become richer, sweeter. He hadn't expected that. Like a sacked quarterback, he hadn't been prepared for this sudden, all-consuming love.

Chapter 5

Angie sat beside Callen in the pew the next morning, willing herself to pay attention to the sermon. It was nearly impossible to ignore the tangy scent of his aftershave or the warmth of his shoulder so close to hers. She had intended to invite Callen to eat with the cast last night but when the time came, she'd wanted to be alone with him. She had to be careful, because her feelings were starting to override her common sense.

The choir filed out of the loft, and Angie exhaled a sigh of relief. She needed distance. Later today she'd pull up Pastor Mike's sermon on the church website and listen to it online. He never failed to inspire her, but today she'd be hard-pressed to recall a word he'd said. She sent up a quick prayer for forgiveness as she stepped into the aisle. Callen walked with her to the three-year-olds classroom to pick up Lily.

"So, why aren't you in the choir? I never thought I'd see the day when Angie Silkowsky could listen to music of any kind without belting out some notes."

Angie's heart stopped. Her skin chilled. She'd prayed Callen would never ask that question. She couldn't answer without revealing the truth, and that was too big a risk. She had to remember Callen was a reporter at heart. He'd want to publish her story.

She forced a smile, keeping her gaze on the door to Lily's room. "Oh, you know. I'm so busy with Lily, and I'm going to school. I don't think I told you that."

"No, you didn't."

"I'm taking classes online through the university to get my business degree. I'd like to start my own business here in Bethlehem."

"Mommy." Lily darted from the classroom and wrapped her arms around Angie's leg in a big hug. Angie welcomed the contact and the diversion from Callen's question.

"Hi, Misser Grant." Lily smiled.

"Hey, Lily. Did you have fun in Sunday school today?" Callen touched her lightly on the head.

She held up the papers in her hand. "We colored the wise men. I made mine purple, 'cause it's my favorite color."

Callen dutifully admired the handiwork, falling into step beside Angie as she steered her daughter down the hallway to the exit.

"Mommy, look. It's baby Jesus." Lily pointed to a couple standing nearby, holding an infant. Lily grabbed Callen's hand and tugged him over to see. "It's the baby Jesus. See. He's real."

Callen followed, a confused look on his chiseled features. Angie touched his arm and made hasty introductions. "Callen

Grant, this is Jenny and Ben Horvath, and baby Eli. Eli plays the part of baby Jesus this weekend."

"He's not playing, Mommy," Lily insisted. "He's real. Baby Jesus is real. You said so."

The adults exchanged smiles. "Come on Lily, we need to go. We're having your favorite lunch today, remember? Spaghetti."

Angie pushed open the exit door, holding tight to Lily's hand, keenly aware of Callen right behind her.

"I like spaghetti."

His statement made her heart skip a beat. Before she could respond, her daughter issued an offer no one could refuse.

"Mommy makes good sketty. You can come eat with us."

Angie glanced over at Callen, the amused smirk on his face revealing his not-so-subtle plan. She wasn't sure if she was pleased or upset. Both. Neither. It didn't matter. The damage was done. She smiled. "We'd love to have you. If you're not busy."

"There's no place I'd rather be this afternoon."

The smile he gave her sent her heart skipping again.

∽∾

Callen leaned against the same tree later Sunday night as the live nativity got underway. The positioning of the tree gave him the perfect vantage point to watch the performance and catch glimpses of Angie as she directed the players from the shadows, making sure everyone reacted on cue.

The afternoon had passed quickly, with a delicious spaghetti dinner and a tea party with Lily. He smiled as he thought about balancing his six-foot frame on an eighteen-inch chair, pretending to drink tea and munch wooden cookies. It had made Lily happy, and he'd discovered a side of himself he'd never explored. What would it be like to be a father?

He had no role models. It had only been him and his mother, until she'd died his junior year of college. But little Lily, with her sweet smile and her loving spirit, made him want to be a dad, the best dad he could be.

"Away in a Manger" poured from the speakers, drawing Callen's attention to the nativity where Mary and Joseph looked lovingly at the baby Jesus. Little Eli. Lily had been convinced he was the real Holy Child. But little Eli was human. Fully.

Immanuel. God with us. God, come to earth as a human being. Callen pivoted to rest his back against the trunk of the tree, his mind sorting through that information, lining up what he knew with what he was beginning to understand.

God as a human child, with all the experiences and knowledge of life. Callen rubbed his head. The thought was too big, too fantastic to process all at once. He turned back to the nativity. The lights were coming up to illuminate the angel above the stable, her arms spread wide. The music swelled, the words wafting out over the cold, crisp night air.

Veiled in flesh the Godhead see. A man. Like him. Could it be?

The program came to an end. The pastor walked out front and said a few words, inviting anyone with questions to come speak to him. Callen straightened and started across the green, searching out Angie.

She looked up as he approached, and smiled. "Well, was it as good as last night? My goal is to make each one better than the last."

Callen wasn't sure if the event was better or if he'd just paid closer attention. Either way, he could answer truthfully. "It was moving."

Angie grinned. "Moving. That's good. I want to touch people. I want them to be drawn to the Lord through this event. Christmas is more than Santa and presents and garland draped from every surface."

"I know." He loved her enthusiasm, her devotion. It made him want to be a better man, a better Christian.

"So, are you tired of me yet?"

Her question caught him off guard. "No. Why?"

She shrugged. "I could use some hot cocoa and homemade soup. And Lily wanted to know if you could come back and read her a story before bedtime. But if you'd rather go back to your room. . ."

Callen laughed. She was an ornery minx. "Let's see. Room alone. . .house full of beautiful ladies. . ."

"Come on. You can build a fire while I fix the soup." She took his hand, and he felt as if he'd come home.

❧

The fire crackled and popped, sending sparks shooting upward into the chimney. Angie shifted position beside him on the sofa, bringing her closer to his side. He wanted to believe she'd done it on purpose, but he didn't want to overstep any boundaries.

She took a sip from her mug and glanced at him. "Thank you

for reading to Lily. She loves bedtime stories."

"I think she just likes the attention."

"You're probably right. Especially male attention. I worry that she's missing out on a father figure. My dad was a big influence on me. I want that for her."

Callen set his jaw, searching for the right words. Before he could find them, Angie reached out and touched his arm, sending a current of awareness along his nerves.

"I'm sorry, Callen. I know how much you missed having a father. I didn't mean to bring up bad memories."

He shook his head and placed a finger on her lips. "You're right to want a father for Lily. I've accepted that the only father I'll know is the one in heaven. I'm okay."

She smiled. "At least you picked the best dad ever."

Her smile, the brightness in her eyes, was his undoing. He grasped her shoulders and slowly pulled her closer. He bent his head, unable to take his gaze from her lips. Gently he kissed her, gauging her response. It had been so long. Yet the memory was so fresh, so familiar. He pulled her closer, tasting deeper, aware of her arms sliding around his waist.

All his old feelings and needs surged through him with frightening speed. He pulled away, catching his breath. "I'd better go."

She didn't speak, only nodded and touched her lips with her fingers.

He started to go then turned back. "I had the ring in my pocket."

"What?"

"The night you won the contest. We were supposed to have dinner. You called me with the news. I didn't see you until the next day when you were boarding the plane for Nashville."

Angie gasped, her eyes moist. "Oh, Callen. I didn't know. I'm so sorry. I—"

"I wanted you to have your dream, Angie. That's all that mattered." He touched her cheek lightly then turned and left, grateful for the icy cold wind that greeted him and cleared his mind. He'd just made a big fool of himself. A very big fool.

❧

The utter stillness of the air, signaling a heavy snowfall, greeted Angie when she awoke the next morning. Not that she'd slept much. Thoughts of Callen and the kiss they'd shared had kept her tossing and turning for hours. Being in his arms again had unearthed memories—sharp, vivid ones that had roused every nerve in her body.

She'd loved him. No one else had measured up. But she'd been so focused on her singing career, so obsessed, that she'd never fully acknowledged her feelings. There'd been plenty of time. Once she made a name for herself she'd be free to have a life with Callen. It never occurred to her at the time that her choice was either/or.

"I had the ring in my pocket." His words reverberated in her head, each revolution stinging like an angry wasp. Angie rolled onto her side, staring out the window. Snowflakes as large as dimes drifted down. The beauty did little to lighten her mood.

How different her life would have been if she'd waited for the Lord's plan to unfold instead of taking matters into her own hands.

Reaching for her Bible on the nightstand, she slid her finger to the bookmark and pulled open the pages to Luke. *"Are not five sparrows sold for two pennies? Yet not one of them is forgotten by God."* She loved these verses. They told her that God was involved in all the details of His creations, especially His children.

So, did that mean He'd brought Callen back into her life for a reason? Was the Lord trying to work something out with her old love? What if she had made a different choice? Then she never would have known the truth about her dream, the good and the bad. She'd never have met Nell, or have her precious Lily. She would never have come to appreciate her life, or found Bethlehem.

So what did she do now? Callen would be here for another week. Should she avoid him or enjoy him while he was here? Should she admit she still loved him? No. She couldn't do that without telling him the full truth. And what Pandora's box would that unleash?

Throwing off the covers, Angie padded to the bathroom to get ready for the day. Pouring her prescription mouthwash into a glass, she gargled gently. Lily would be up soon. Dealing with Callen wasn't an option today. She had a list of things to do that would keep her busy this morning and then a couple of online classes this afternoon. She'd deal with Callen tomorrow.

Chapter 6

Callen took a swallow of his hot cocoa and stared at his laptop. The edits had arrived for his last travel book, and he dreaded going over them. He'd started transcribing his notes for the Bethlehem feature. It wasn't going well.

Leaning back in his desk chair, he closed his eyes, searching his heart. What if his only talent was lightweight travel stories? What if he didn't have what it took to be an investigative reporter? Angie had achieved her dream, only to find it was a nightmare instead.

He was standing at a crossroads with no clear signpost to direct his way. What did he want to do with the rest of his life? A vision of a tiny teapot and dark hair in ponytails came to mind. He'd never allowed himself to consider having a family, but since coming to Bethlehem, he'd thought of little else.

His cell tone blared into the quiet and he scooped it up, setting his jaw when he saw his boss's name displayed. "Marty, I'm on vacation. I'll have the piece ready by the deadline."

"I know. This is something different. Are you still considering that Clearwater job?"

"Yes. Why?"

"Well, what if I could give you a better offer?"

"For instance?"

"The chief is looking for someone to fill Harrison's shoes. I thought you might be interested."

Bob Harrison was one of the top journalists with the agency. "Where's Harrison going?"

"He's retiring. His wife has cancer and he wants to be there to care for her."

"So are you offering me his job?" Callen's mind filled with the possibilities. He'd be in Boston. Close to Angie and Lily.

"Well, in a way."

His vision crumbled. He should have known better than to let his imagination run away with him. Especially where Marty Kramer was concerned.

"The chief wants to see some proof of your ability to uncover a story. You know, something other than the best places to zip-line in Belize."

A stab of resentment pierced Callen's chest. He was proud of his work. It might not be hard-hitting investigative journalism, but he'd earned a measure of respect in his field. "Such as?"

"I don't know. Isn't there something going on up there in Maine that's newsworthy?"

Angie's face came into his mind. He chased it away. "No." There was a long silence on the other end of the connection, making Callen's antennae vibrate.

"Are you sure?"

"What are you getting at?"

"We got wind that there might be a celebrity hiding out up there. Someone big."

Callen's heart chilled. Who had given Angie away? She trusted these people. "You're nuts, man. I've been all over this place, talked to dozens of residents, and there's no one here that anyone would be interested in. Oh, wait. The owner of the place I'm staying has a cow pitcher collection. She's pretty famous around here."

"Very funny. Look, word is that singer, Silky, is somewhere up there. Just keep your eyes open, okay? If you could track her down, find out why she dropped out of sight, dig up the dirt on her, this job would be a slam dunk. I'm just sayin'."

"I've got to go. I have real work to do. Trust me, there's nothing worth reporting from this backwater town."

Callen ended the call, resting his head in his hands. He had to talk to Angie. She had to know. He couldn't betray her. But if the truth had to come out, then maybe he should be the one to break the story. That way he could control the information.

And what if he did? Would a career in investigative journalism be everything he'd imagined?

∞

The box of crayons scattered on the kitchen table made Angie think of spring, even though the coloring book was titled *Santa's Christmas Eve*. Reaching for a yellow one, she colored in the star on top of a Christmas tree.

"You color good, Mommy."

Angie smiled at her daughter. "Thank you. I like your picture. Purple ribbon on that box is very nice."

Lily nodded. "I want Santa to put purple bows on all my presents."

"You do? Well, you'll have to ask him when we visit him."

" 'Kay." Lily leaned closer to her coloring book, scribbling furiously.

Angie closed her eyes briefly, offering up a thankful prayer. Her life now was so much richer, more abundant than she'd ever imagined. How could she have thought that fame and fortune could satisfy the longing in her soul? She loved her life here in Bethlehem. She loved the cozy colonial house with its fireplaces and generous yard for Lily. She loved the town and its people. Her church family supported her in so many ways, and next summer, she'd earn her degree and start planning a business of her own.

Her life was perfect.

The image of a pair of sky-blue eyes came to mind and she stopped coloring, staring idly at the outline of the Christmas tree she'd been working on. Callen. Having him back in her life, even briefly, had felt so natural, so right. How could that be after so much time? Yes, she'd loved him. Yes, she'd thought about marrying him, but back then, all she could see was herself on a stage, winning awards for her singing and getting a recording contract.

So why had the Lord brought him back into her life now?

"Mommy, when are we going to put up the tree?"

With a heavy sigh, Angie turned her attention back to

her daughter. "Soon. I promise." It wasn't that she didn't like Christmas. It was her favorite time of year, but tackling all the decorating alone was exhausting. She'd gone as far as pulling the boxes from the attic, but they were still sitting in the upstairs hallway. She'd even bought the tree, but it was still in the garage where Simon had left it after he and Edna had taken her and Lily to the tree farm. "We'll put it up soon, sweetheart."

"Today?"

Angie chose a red crayon for the ornaments on the picture and filled them in. "We'll see." There was no reason not to do it today. Her classes were finished until after the new year. She had her duties for the nativity down to a science. Other than a few church obligations and playing with Lily, she had no real responsibilities to worry about.

"We could ask Misser Grant to help us. He could reach the star, and we wouldn't have to use the ladder."

A rush of warmth charged through Angie at Lily's suggestion. The idea of Callen decorating the tree, being part of their tradition, impacted her like nothing else had in a long time. Mentally she scolded herself for entertaining such an absurd notion. Clearly their old feelings were still there, churning just below the surface, but how much of that was merely memories of old love, and how much was genuine attraction based upon the people they were today?

"Please, Mommy? I like Misser Grant."

"I do, too." Saying the words aloud sealed her fate. "All right. I'll ask him."

She reached for her phone, trying not to think about how disappointed she'd be if he refused.

꘎

Callen pulled his rental car into the driveway of Angie's large white colonial and turned off the engine. His thoughts swirled in his head like the snowflakes outside. What would it be like to park in this space every night, to look forward to going inside and finding his wife and child waiting to greet him?

He rubbed his forehead and opened the car door, bracing against the wind and cold. Why had Angie invited him to participate in such a personal family event as decorating the tree? He knew what he wanted the answer to be, but that was taking a giant leap over logic and landing smack dab in wishful thinking.

He knocked on the door, shifting his weight anxiously, trying to tamp down the hope floating in his chest with a healthy dose of reality. The door opened and he had to shift his gaze downward. A pair of bright brown eyes smiled up at him.

"Mommy, he's here. Misser Grant is here." Lily bounced up and down and clapped her hands together then waved at him with a big smile.

Her excitement squeezed his heart, creating a strange, unfamiliar sensation in his gut. No one had ever been that happy to see him. Ever.

Angie appeared around the door, waving him inside. "Hurry before you freeze to death."

Not a chance. His whole being was warm and tingling. He shrugged off his coat, hanging it on the hall tree.

"Hurry, Misser Grant."

Lily took his hand, tugging him into the large living room. He didn't see a tree. Only an empty spot where it would apparently stand. "Where's your tree?" Had he misunderstood?

Lily pointed toward the far wall. "It's out there."

Angie tucked her hair behind her ears and smiled. "I left out the part where you'll have to carry the tree in from the garage."

The sheepish look on her face made him smile. As if that would have mattered. "I think I can handle that. Lead the way."

Lily darted like a rocket through the kitchen and out into the garage. The tree was sitting near the back. An eight-footer, if he wasn't mistaken. His thoughts traveled back in time to the one year he and his mother had splurged for a live tree. His best Christmas memory.

He glanced at Angie. "You have a blanket or something to wrap around this? It'll leave needles all over the house otherwise."

She smiled and shook her head. "Don't worry about it. I'll clean it up later. Lily will burst if we put this off much longer."

When the tree was securely in the designated spot, Callen stood back to make sure the best side was forward and the tree perfectly straight. Lily hugged his leg.

"Thank you, Misser Grant. Can we hang the bulbs now?"

Angie laughed. "No, Pumpkin. First we have to get the boxes down and put the lights on. Then the garland, then the ornaments."

Lily's long, mournful groan was too adorable. Callen rested a hand on her head. "I'll hurry. I promise."

Angie steered her daughter toward the kitchen. "In the meantime, I have some stars that need tons of glitter. Why don't you work on those while Mr. Grant and I get the boring stuff done?"

Within a few minutes, the boxes were transferred from upstairs to the floor in front of the tree, and Callen was untangling and testing strands of lights.

Angie stopped at Callen's side. "This was always the most frustrating part for me growing up. It seemed like my dad took forever putting the lights on. I could never understand the big deal. Toss them on the branches and let's get to the fun stuff. Now that I'm grown, I can see why he wanted the lights to be evenly spaced, and I'm sure my mom wanted them just so. She was persnickety about her tree. Everything had to be perfectly placed."

Callen plugged in the last string of lights, satisfied that all the bulbs were working. "So does this mean I have to get your approval for each string of lights? I could be here all night."

"Normally, I'd say yes, but I think we'll go for quick and easy before Lily explodes."

Draping the strings of lights didn't take long when he didn't have to worry about the placement. He stepped back and gave Angie the signal to press the switch on the electrical strip holding the plugs. The tree glowed, with not a dead bulb to be found.

Angie inhaled softly. "Oh, Callen, it's beautiful."

She moved closer, slipping her arm through his. A lump formed in his throat.

"Don't you love decorating a tree?"

"Hard to say. We usually had a two-footer. The kind that comes out of a box." The words slipped out without thinking. He wished he could call them back. He didn't want to spoil the evening.

She squeezed his arm more tightly. "Then I'm glad Lily and I will be the ones to introduce you to the joy."

Callen looked down into her hazel eyes. What had she said earlier about perfect placement? Right now, standing near her, in this house, seemed like perfect placement to him.

Angie suggested a quick break for cocoa and cookies, and Callen heartily agreed. He needed a diversion from his thoughts. Lily had completed her glitter stars and was eager to hang them. It was all they could do to hold her back while they hung the garland.

Callen tucked the last strand of gold and red around the lower branches while Angie opened the ornament boxes, reminding her daughter that some were made of glass and to handle them carefully.

The midafternoon sun was starting to fade, increasing the warm glow in the room from the fire on the hearth and the twinkling lights of the tree. Only one thing was missing from this Norman Rockwell portrait. "I think we could use some Christmas music. How about it, Angie? Maybe a little Rudolph or some carols?"

Callen looked over at her. She was helping Lily unwrap one of the ornaments. For a moment he thought he saw fear flash through her eyes. He quickly dismissed the notion as a quirk of the low lights. Of course a singer would want music. The Angie he knew always had music playing.

Quietly she moved to the CD player and pressed a button. Strains of "O Holy Night" filled the air, completing the scene. Callen let himself sink into the moment. He laughed at the way all of Lily's additions to the tree were hung at her eye level, making the decorations decidedly bottom heavy. He and Angie would rearrange them later.

The familiar tune of "Here Comes Santa Claus" began, and Lily sang out happily. He joined in, though more quietly. He had a reasonably good voice, but he'd always felt intimidated by Angie's powerful set of pipes. Her voice could stop your heart with its passion.

Angie's voice. He hung the last ornament and turned to look at her. She was picking up stray pieces of tissue paper that had held the ornaments. The tree was almost done. The music continued to play. But Angie wasn't singing.

Why? There was never a time when she didn't sing. Even when there was no music, she'd had music churning inside her head. Sometimes she would burst into song without warning. He'd asked her once why she did that. She'd smiled, pointed to her head, and explained there was music playing inside her all the time.

So where was the music now? Why wasn't she singing? Come to think of it, he hadn't heard her sing once in the weeks he'd been here. Not even at church.

A knot of fear kicked in his gut.

"Are you hungry?" Angie wiped her hands on her jeans. "I'm starved. Are you up for some homemade beef stew and fresh bread?"

"Sure. Sounds good. I think tree decorating whips up an appetite."

Lily had grown bored with the tree once her part in it had been completed and had gone to her room to watch a movie. Callen was grateful for the time alone, because he needed to ask Angie about her singing. He had a feeling he wasn't going to like the answer.

Chapter 7

Angie stood at the stove stirring the stew, smiling as she thought about how enjoyable the day had been. Having Callen here to help with the tree had completely changed her attitude.

Only one small cloud still hovered in her mind. She'd known the very second when Callen had realized she wasn't singing with the music. He'd want to know why. He'd want to know all of it, and he wouldn't be satisfied with some vague explanation. Besides, she didn't want to lie to him.

She heard him enter the kitchen, her breath catching when he stopped behind her. His nearness never failed to play havoc with her pulse. "This won't take long to heat up. Would you like something to drink? I made a pot of fresh coffee."

"Sounds good." He moved down the counter and filled a cup, lacing it with cream.

An odd silence filled the kitchen. Angie braced for what was coming.

"Angie, why don't you sing anymore?"

Her hands stilled on the wooden spoon, her heart racing.

"What do you mean? Didn't you hear me humming?"

Callen remained at the end of the counter. She was grateful for the distance between them. It made it a little easier.

"Angie. What's going on?"

"Nothing." She prayed Callen would let it go.

He reached out and pulled her around to face him. She averted her eyes. "Tell me."

Her shoulders sagged and she exhaled a tense breath. It was useless. She had to face this. Slowly she met his gaze. The fear in his blue eyes tore at her heart. He would be devastated by what she was going to tell him. "You have to promise not to tell anyone. Ever."

"I promise."

She gripped his shoulders. "I'm serious, Callen. I shouldn't even tell you."

"Angie?"

She straightened her spine and faced him. "I can't sing any-more. I damaged my voice."

Callen searched her face, as if unable to believe what she'd told him.

"How? What happened?"

She leaned against the counter, searching for a starting point. "That last year before Nell got pregnant, before she found out she was sick, I was miserable. My career was soaring, but the higher it went, the worse I felt." She wrapped her arms around her waist in a feeble attempt to protect herself. "I'd drifted away from my faith. I was struggling to stay on a moral path. I was involved with someone I shouldn't have been. My managers were booking me everywhere. I was performing nearly every night."

Callen stood silently in front of her, offering quiet support.

"I wasn't taking care of myself. I was miserable and lost, and I didn't know how to find my way back. I hadn't talked to my family in over a year. And every time I sang, I'd channel all my frustration, all my disillusionment, into my voice."

Callen made a move to embrace her, but she stepped past him. If he touched her she'd fall apart. There was more to tell. "I suffered a severe vocal hemorrhage. I had to cancel the next six concerts and put a recording session on hold."

"Wasn't there anything they could do?"

She nodded, keeping her back to him. The pain in his voice brought an ache to her chest. "My producers scheduled surgery with a doctor they used for all their people. But something went wrong. The surgeon messed up. They told me I'd never sing again. I found out later that this wasn't the first time the doctor had botched a surgery. I threatened to sue, but my manager wouldn't hear of it. When I threatened to go to the press, he offered me a deal. He'd release me from my contracts if I agreed to never press charges and never reveal what really happened."

Callen turned behind her, his breath caressing her neck. "You should have exposed them all, Angie. They destroyed your life. Your career."

She faced him, resting her hand on his arm. "No, they didn't. God worked it for good. I wanted out so I could raise Lily. We reached a financial agreement, and I walked away. I rededicated myself to the Lord and moved here and changed my name as an extra precaution."

Callen searched her face, his blue eyes revealing his shock and sadness. "What about another surgery? Special treatments? Maybe in time, if you take care of your voice. . ."

Angie shook her head. "No. I had to face the truth. My singing career is over. After I moved here I was referred to a specialist in Portland. He examined me and thought he could repair some of the damage. Six weeks ago I had surgery. He thinks I might be able to sing a little. Never like I did, but it's something to hope for. I have to be careful and not strain my voice for the next few weeks."

Callen drew her into his arms. "I'm so sorry, Angie. I know how much singing meant to you."

Angie wrapped her arms around his waist, drawing comfort from his strength. "It's okay. I can still listen and hum a little."

"Oh, Angie."

The deep groan in his throat broke her heart. No one had cared as much about her singing as Callen. He'd always been her champion. "I'm taking piano lessons. If the surgery doesn't work, I can express myself that way." She pulled away, missing the warmth of his embrace.

"Why don't you want anyone to know? It would answer all the questions people have. Put the speculation to rest once and for all."

Angie shook her head. "No. It wouldn't. Don't you remember the horrible media storm that surrounded JoJo and her downfall?"

"Yes, but that doesn't mean it will happen to you. Look, I'm a reporter. I can handle things like this. I can manage the information."

Angie touched his cheek. "I know you think you can. But you're wrong. If I break that agreement, the record company could sue me for everything I have. It'd mean a trial, headlines in the paper, my past will come out, Nell's story and Lily's will be splashed across the Internet. I don't want her exposed to any of that. The paparazzi will make it impossible to stay here. I'll have to start all over again. I'm happy now. I want the past to stay there."

A deep frown creased Callen's forehead. He turned away, the muscle in his jaw flexing rapidly. "My boss called the other night. He'd heard a rumor that you were in New England. He wanted me to see what I could find out."

Angie's heart chilled. "You didn't tell him?"

"Of course not. But someone must have. You're pretty visible around this town. Maybe someone isn't as loyal as you'd like to believe."

Angie paced off a few feet, chewing her thumbnail. "It'll die off. It's happened before."

"You talked about God being in the small things. What if he brought me here to help put this question to rest?"

Angie shook her head. "No. I don't think that's why you're here at all. I think it's for a totally different reason."

"What then?"

Heat warmed her cheeks. What would he say if she told him

she hoped his presence here was for her? "Please, Callen, just let this be. I know in my heart this is where I'm supposed to be, and I know God will take care of the rest. Please?"

Callen held her gaze a long moment, then nodded. "All right. We'll do it your way. For now."

She smiled. "Thank you." Callen opened his arms. She didn't hesitate to step back into his embrace. She felt safe and cherished in his arms. She always had.

"I'd make this all go away if I could."

"I know you would."

He held her for a long moment then pulled away. "How do you stand it?" He searched her face. "I can't think of you without thinking of you singing."

"I miss it. Sometimes I'm so happy, so filled with joy, that I want to lift my arms to God and sing at the top of my lungs. It hurts that I can't. So I pray instead. And then I look around at the life I have in Bethlehem with Lily. I'm so blessed. I'd sacrifice my voice a dozen times over for my daughter. In the grand scheme of things, it's not such a big loss."

Callen took her face between his hands. "It's not right. Your voice was a gift and now it's gone."

Angie wrapped her arms around him. "I'm content, Callen. Don't worry about me."

⌀

Callen strolled briskly down the sidewalk, feeling lighter than he had in days. Things between him and Angie had grown comfortable since the tree trimming and her revelation about her voice. They'd spent as much time together as they could, looking at Christmas lights, visiting Logan Franks's wildlife habitat, and taking a trip into Freeport to visit the L.L. Bean store.

This afternoon he was meeting his girls—when had he started to think of them as his?—at the Bethlehem Community Church. Angie had a meeting with the nativity committee, and afterward they were taking Lily to see Santa at a nearby mall.

Jogging across the street, Callen smiled as he scanned the area. He never grew tired of the scenery in Bethlehem. Today it sparkled like one of Lily's glitter-dusted stars. The sun was bright, the snow thick and powdery around the buildings, but conveniently melted away from streets and sidewalks.

People were drifting out of the church as he approached. Angie stepped from the front door, a huge smile on her face. A tall, dark-haired man walked beside her, carrying Lily and smiling back.

Callen's heart burned with a wave of jealousy and fierce protectiveness. A need to defend his territory rocked him backward a step. He had no claims on Angie or her child. She had a right to see anyone she pleased. She owed him nothing. But the feelings remained so strong he had to clamp his jaw shut to keep from shouting. They looked like a family walking together. That hurt.

Angie smiled at him as she and the man approached. Lily waved. It was all he could do to muster a smile in return.

"Hello." Angie spoke softly and smiled into his eyes.

He couldn't think straight.

"Callen, I'd like you to meet Dave Marshall. He used to be one of our selectmen before becoming the head of the state tourism board. Dave, this is Callen Grant."

Marshall shifted Lily in his grasp and shook Callen's hand. "Grant. As in the Granted travel books?"

"Guilty."

"I love those things. When's the next one coming out?"

"May of next year, but I'm afraid that'll be the last one."

"Oh, man. I hate to hear that. Though my wife won't. She swears your books give me bad ideas for vacation. What will you be doing next?"

A wife. The relief nearly distracted him from the man's comment. "Not sure. I have a few options I'm considering."

Lily reached for Callen and Marshall delivered her over to him. "I wish you the best. Nice to meet you."

"Same here." Marshall walked off and Callen smiled.

Angie smiled back. "Are you ready to brave the long line of hyperactive children waiting to see Santa?"

"Is it too late to change my mind?"

Lily gasped and looked him in the eye. "No, Daddy, you have to come. You promised."

His heart stilled. He glanced at Angie and saw his own surprise reflected in her eyes.

"Lily. His name is Mister Grant." Angie's voice was oddly thick as she spoke.

Lily frowned and tilted her head, studying his face closely. "But he looks like a daddy to me."

Her innocent comment cracked the lock on his heart. He touched her soft cheek with his fingertips. "Lily, that's the best compliment I've ever received."

"What's a compulment?"

"That's when someone says something nice about you," Angie explained softly.

Lily peered at Callen closely, one little finger pointing toward his eyes. "You have blue eyes, the same color as my favorite crayon."

Callen laughed. "I thought your favorite color was purple."

"And blue."

Callen hugged her close. "And you have brown eyes the color of my morning coffee."

"Is that good?"

"Very good. My morning coffee is very important to me."

Together, they started down the sidewalk to the parking lot. Man, woman, and child. A family.

Chapter 8

Snow had fallen during the night, making the roads wet and slippery. Angie steered the car cautiously along the ramp to the interstate on her way home. She'd come to Portland this morning for a checkup with the surgeon. She hadn't anticipated any good news. While the doctor was pleased with her progress so far, he reminded her that even with an optimal outcome from the surgery, she would never sing the way she used to. He wanted to see her again in a week and reminded her to not strain her voice.

But it was the season of miracles. God was certainly capable of restoring her voice and giving back the instrument that had provided pleasure and fulfillment her entire life. But no matter the outcome of her operation, she was content with her situation. She'd been totally honest when she'd told Callen that.

Callen filled her thoughts as she navigated traffic. Lily had called him Daddy. He'd handled it with great tenderness. Neither of them had mentioned it again, but the moment had replayed in her mind all night. What did the future hold where Callen was concerned? She knew the old spark was still there. Their kiss had proved that. Did they want to pursue their relationship further?

She did. She'd known from the moment Lily had called him Daddy. That one name had filled a hole in her heart she didn't know was empty. A hole only Callen could fill.

This weekend marked the final presentation of the live nativity. Monday he'd be leaving. She wanted him to stay and spend Christmas with her and Lily. But he had choices to make for his future. She wanted to be one of his options, but she had no right to ask him to stay and take on a ready-made family. Unless, of course, he wanted that, too. So why were they both afraid to discuss the issue?

She knew she'd broken his heart all those years ago. So many things her drive for fame and success had destroyed. All she wanted now was her quiet life and to raise Lily to know God's love. And maybe the love of an earthly father. She shook off the notion. She shouldn't be dreaming of a life with Callen, even if this was the season of miracles. This time, she'd stay out of God's way, and if He had a future in store for her and Callen, then she'd let Him work it out. But she wouldn't stop praying for that very thing.

Angie turned on her blinker and pulled onto the highway that would take her home to Bethlehem.

❧

Callen closed his laptop and shoved back from the small desk in his room. He'd grown fond of the place. The room was large and comfortable, with a fireplace, a cozy chair, and a flat-screen TV. He had a hot breakfast each morning and an open invitation from Edna for dinner with her and Simon each night. He suspected it wasn't because she liked him that much, but that she knew he was an old friend of Angie's.

It didn't matter. He liked it here at the Stoval-Mills house, and he liked Bethlehem. He liked being close to Angie. Only one thing pinched like a too-tight shoe on his spirit. He had to come to grips with his faith and decide once and for all if he was going to embrace it again with renewed dedication, or turn away for good.

Rededication. Angie had used the word. Callen sat on the side of the large Victorian bed and pulled open the drawer in the nightstand. As he'd expected, a Bible rested inside. He turned to the Christmas story, reading the verses with a new interest. He'd never thought about the humanness of Christ. Living His life like other men, He understood all the struggles of mortal man. But because He was also God, He knew His children and had a plan for each of them.

For so long Callen had believed that God was too busy with more important things to care about him. Angie, on the other hand, believed that every event in a person's life was noticed by God. That He'd take whatever mess or wrong turn she made and bring about something good from it.

Lord. Is it true? Do you love me that much? I don't know which way to turn. I don't even know what I want. No. He knew exactly what he wanted. Angie and Lily in his future.

A profound feeling of humility stole his breath. He shifted off the bed, sinking to his knees. Resting his face in his hands, he prayed for forgiveness and restoration. If he couldn't get that on track, then the rest of his life was pointless.

The kitchen smelled like Santa's cookie shop. The chocolate chip cookies were done and cooling on a rack on the breakfast table. The oatmeal cookies only lacked the raisins.

"Now can I put them in?" Lily held the bag of raisins poised over the glass mixing bowl, her face revealing her anticipation.

"Not yet. First I have to put in the oatmeal and mix it all up."

"Can I do it, please?"

Angie measured out the correct amount and handed her daughter the cup just as the doorbell rang.

Lily dropped the bag on the counter. "Misser Grant is here." She scurried down the small stool she'd been standing on and raced for the front door.

What had gotten into her this morning, to invite him over to make Christmas cookies? As far as she knew, he'd already collected all the information he needed for the nativity article. He could have left town days ago. But he'd stayed, and she was glad.

"Wow. It smells good in here." Callen stopped in the doorway, his hand holding Lily's. "A man can never get enough homemade cookies."

Seeing him in her kitchen, Lily at his side, made Angie realize why she'd invited him. Because Callen made her feel like her family was complete. He made her happy. He was the man she loved. Hot, stinging embarrassment flooded her cheeks and she turned away. "Well, I didn't ask you here to watch, you know. You'll have to pitch in."

"We're going to decorate the sugar cookies later." Lily made her announcement with great seriousness.

Callen chuckled. "I'm honored. I don't know how good I'll be with icing, if that's the kind you're talking about."

Lily climbed back onto her stool. "That's okay. You can put the sprinkles on. Mommy and I will do the hard stuff."

"I'm relieved. Just show me what to do. I can follow orders pretty well."

Angie kept her gaze on the bowl, stirring in the raisins as Lily dumped them into the batter. What would Callen say if she gave him an order to join her life and be a father to Lily? Would he follow that order?

She swallowed the lump in her throat. Absurd. What had come over her? She'd spent too much time in the last three weeks imagining Callen in her life. She shouldn't be creating scenarios for her future based upon a magical Christmas encounter.

Several hours later, Angie walked beside Callen toward the nativity stable. This was the final weekend of the nativity presentation and her turn to play the part of the angel, and she couldn't wait. The white flowing garment she wore hid the winter clothing underneath, along with the hand warmer in her pocket and the heated boots on her feet. The wind had kicked up in the afternoon and a heavy snowstorm was on its way. It would make for a long performance standing on that tall tower platform above the stable scene.

"Are you going to be all right up there? Maybe you should get someone else to do it."

"I'll be fine. Cold, but fine. Really."

Callen smiled and touched her cheek. "Baker. Stage manager. Angel on high. Is there anything you can't do?"

A shadow shifted across his face, and Angie quickly held a finger to his lips. He'd forgotten about her damaged voice. The one thing she couldn't do was sing. "I'm an expert at lip syncing. You watch. You won't be able to tell if it's a CD or me."

"Are you using one of your tracks tonight?"

"No. That might be tempting fate. It's a recording a member of my church did."

Callen pulled her close, placing a kiss on her forehead. "Be careful. I'll be right here when you're done."

The performance went off without a hitch, despite the increasing snowfall, but Angie was disappointed by how few audience members came forward to speak to the minister afterward.

"You all right?" Callen stepped forward and put an arm around her shoulders.

She shivered. "The crowd was really light tonight."

"It's the weather, Angie. They're probably all at home curled up by the fireplace. You're freezing."

She allowed Callen to hold her close as they walked back to the church fellowship hall where the staging area and dressing rooms were located.

After hanging up her angel costume and checking on the last stragglers from the pageant, she locked up. Callen walked with her to her car. She pressed the unlock button on her key fob then turned to him with a teasing smile. "Can I drive you home?"

He shook his head, took hold of her shoulders, and pulled her close to his chest. "You make a beautiful angel."

His voice was husky, thick, melting her bones. She leaned into him, slipping her arms around his waist. He tilted her chin upward, his eyes devouring her lips before taking possession.

All sense left her mind, cold vanished, all she knew was warmth, strength, and belonging. Her last line of resistance was giving way when Callen ended the kiss and stepped back.

"I'll see you in church tomorrow."

Unable to speak, she nodded and climbed into the car. Before shutting the door she caught his gaze. "Please let me drive you home. It's cold."

He smiled. "A blessing I'm most grateful for. Good night."

Chapter 9

The night sky over Bethlehem Sunday evening was clear, sprinkled with brilliant stars piercing the navy blue canopy. A light snow was falling, but the air was calm, and several degrees warmer than the night before. The Christmas lights from the surrounding buildings twinkled with holiday cheer, splashing down on citizens as they scurried about their shopping.

And in the center of town, the majestic Bethlehem display stood waiting. In a short while the stable would come alive with the presence of Mary and Joseph. Shepherds and livestock would seek out the newborn child. Camels carrying wise men robed in splendor would come to honor the King.

"Misser Grant!"

Callen turned to see Lily running toward him. He bent down and opened his arms, catching her to his chest as she propelled herself into his embrace. "Hello, Lily Belle."

"My name's not Lily Belle." She smiled and patted his cheeks with her pink-mittened hands.

"Sure it is. *Belle* means pretty, and you're very pretty."

Callen turned his attention to Edna and Simon, who had brought Lily with them. "Thanks."

Edna smiled. "We came a little early. She was afraid she'd miss her mommy as the angel."

Callen knew how the little girl felt. He couldn't wait either. In fact, he didn't want this day to end. After church, he'd taken Angie and Lily to lunch then they'd gone sledding on the hill behind Angie's house, something he hadn't done in years.

Lily had fallen asleep in the afternoon, and he and Angie had spent the time enjoying each other's company. Now it was time for the last nativity. Tomorrow he was due back in Boston. He needed to make a decision about his future. His failure to dig up information on Angie had lost him the top reporter's job, which had reinforced his decision to leave the Wilcox organization. That left taking the bottom-of-the-rung position in Clearwater. Not his first choice.

He set Lily on the ground, and she danced around happily as she waited for the nativity to start. Watching her brought a sweet ache to his chest. He wanted to stay in Bethlehem, but he had no job. Angie, of course, was convinced whatever happened would work out for his good.

"Look, I see goats." Lily grabbed Callen's hand and tugged him closer to the stable scene.

He'd seen the performance several times now over the last three weekends, but watching Lily's excitement gave him a new perspective. The robed shepherds strolled slowly toward the rustic stable, two goats and a sheep walking beside them. The lights came up, revealing Mary and Joseph and the infant settled around the manger.

The narrator began the story, and carols filled the air as the wise men and their camels entered from behind a large fir tree at the edge of the green. Lily lifted her arms to Callen, and he picked her up for a better view.

Something about tonight's event was different. There was an energy in the air, an anticipation that had been missing before. It might be because Christmas was only three days off, or it might be he was viewing this as the end to his weeks in Bethlehem and with Angie.

The play continued and Callen's anticipation grew as Angie's appearance drew closer. When the moment arrived, he pointed toward the spot above the stable where he knew Angie would be illuminated any moment. Lily stared intently.

He waited, but the light failed to come on. Odd. The tower should be lit by now, Angie should be visible, and the carol playing loudly over the scene below.

Something was wrong. Maybe she'd fallen off the tower. He'd never felt comfortable with that arrangement. Turning to Edna, he handed Lily off to her. "I'll be right back."

He walked quickly across the green toward the back where Angie would be. The narrator spoke again, reading the Christmas story from Luke. That wasn't part of the program. Now he knew something was wrong.

He ducked behind the canvas curtain shielding the tower and found Angie talking to John Roland, the man in charge of the sound system. "What's wrong?"

Angie turned, and the expression on her face sent a rush of alarm through his chest. "The CD player isn't working."

John stepped forward and began clipping a lapel mike to her costume.

Realization of what she was planning to do sliced through Callen like a knife. He held up a hand. "Whoa, what are you doing? Get someone else."

Angie shook her head. "We have to finish the program. I'm going to sing the carol."

"No! Angie you can't. You know what will happen."

A smile brightened her face, and she touched his arm. "I've prayed about this. I know what I have to do, and I know it will be all right."

Callen grasped her shoulder. "Angie think about what you're doing. The doctor warned you to not strain your voice. You could lose your ability to speak. No. I won't let you do this."

"It'll be okay. Trust me."

"How do you know that?"

"I asked the Lord what I was supposed to do, and He told me to sing. I can't explain it to you. I just know I have to do this."

"Angie."

She moved away, allowing John to attach the safety line before starting up to the platform. A sour pool of dread churned in Callen's gut as he watched, helpless to stop her.

The light burst on as Angie topped the platform. She spread her arms; the light evening breeze stirred her white robes. She was the most beautiful woman he'd ever known. But she was risking everything for this event. He didn't know whether to be proud or furious.

She began to sing. Each note flowing from her lovely throat tore another piece from his heart. He turned and left the backstage area, walking off a short distance and willing himself not to watch her destroy her voice. But he found he was unable to keep his eyes from her as she sang.

Then he realized what he was hearing. Angie, the woman with the silken voice. She was singing strong, sweet, and with a passion that reverberated along each nerve. It was as if her vocal chords had been restored, but her voice now held a new, softer, richer tone.

The notes issuing forth from her throat took on a life of their own. They were like a sermon, a divine message from the Almighty Himself. He glanced around the crowd and saw expressions of peace and joy. His own heart swelled with a sensation of love and peace that he'd never known before. He looked back at Angie, the words from the carol seeping deep into his spirit. Tears stung his eyes, and he wiped them away with his thumb and forefinger. "Please, Father, protect her voice. Take care of her, because I can't."

Angie sang the last note. It hung in the air like an amen. Callen opened his eyes, afraid to look upward at Angie for fear he'd see pain in her eyes. Instead he focused on the crowd. Dozens of visitors were making their way toward the minister near the front of the stable. More were coming, striding forward, to speak to the pastor. A sob lodged in his chest. Angie's song, her voice, had drawn these people like nothing else could have.

He turned back and ducked inside the canvas. Angie was coming down the steps. He searched her face and saw tears running down her cheeks. He didn't want to think what that might mean. He opened his arms, and she hurried toward him, sobbing against his chest.

"Angie, are you all right?" She nodded. He set her away from him so he could see her face. He cleared his throat and regained control of his raw emotions. "Can you speak?"

Her hazel eyes looked into his. She shrugged and whispered, "I'm not sure."

His heart cried out, and he pulled her close again. "Angie, I love you."

She looked up at him and whispered, "Me, too."

Chapter 10

The winter sun was shining as Callen and Angie pulled into Angie's driveway late the next morning. He'd volunteered to drive her to the throat specialist in Portland to see what kind of damage her singing had done to her vocal chords. He'd hoped and prayed that her voice had been restored, but the doctor had confirmed that her condition was unchanged, and he couldn't explain how she'd been able to sing.

Callen turned off the engine and gripped the steering wheel. "I don't understand." They had ridden home in silence.

Angie looked at him, a smile on her face. "I do. It was a miracle."

"I know, but I'd hoped. . ."

Angie reached over and took his hand. "I'm just grateful I could complete the nativity. What happens now isn't important."

Callen turned to face her. There was something more serious they had to discuss. "Angie, hundreds of people heard you last night. What if someone recognized your voice? What if your life here is exposed?" He could tell by the look on her face she hadn't thought through the consequences of singing in public.

"I don't know. I didn't think about that last night. I should have." She closed her eyes and rested her head against the seat. Then she straightened. "No. The Lord told me to sing last night, and He gave me the ability to do it. Even if it was only one time. He has something already worked out. I know it."

Callen wished he had her faith. "Angie, I have something to tell you. I had a call this morning from my boss. He's already heard a rumor that the singer at the Bethlehem nativity last night was Silky Blaine."

"What did you tell him?"

"That I was there. That it was a local woman, who sounded nothing like Silky. I'm going to meet with him this week, and I'll make him believe me."

"Do you think you can?"

"I will. Don't worry." He walked Angie to the door, gave her a kiss, and returned to his car. He'd tried to sound confident when he told her he'd protect her anonymity. He only hoped he could.

❧

Angie curled in the corner of the sofa, her gaze focused on the tree, but her thoughts on Callen. She hadn't heard from him since Monday afternoon when he'd left for Boston. Her emotions bounced between confidence that the Lord and Callen would keep her world in Bethlehem protected, and fear that she'd misunderstood the Lord's prompting and destroyed her life by singing the carol.

Today was Christmas Eve. She'd wanted to spend the holiday with Callen. Lily was deeply disappointed that he'd left, and

Angie had found it difficult to explain. His profession of love still floated like a beautiful snowflake in her mind. Had he meant it? She loved him. But her first concern was Lily and keeping their life protected. How could she ask Callen to live here and keep her secret forever? And the thought of leaving Bethlehem, to settle elsewhere with him, was too frightening. She had people here who cared for her and would protect her secret.

Her gaze fell on the article about the nativity Callen had written. He'd done a wonderful job of capturing the essence of the nativity, the performers, and the town of Bethlehem. He'd even praised her efforts as director. He'd made no mention of the last angel song.

Reaching for her cell phone, she selected his number, but hesitated to press the call button. She wanted to hear his voice. She wanted to know if he'd convinced his boss that Silky Blaine wasn't the one who sang that night. But she'd promised herself she'd wait for God's plan to unfold no matter how much her stomach churned with anxiety.

"Mommy, can I have a cookie?" Lily climbed up beside her on the sofa.

"I suppose. It is Christmas Eve. But save some for Santa."

"I will."

Angie stood as a low rumble drifted in from outside. A car had pulled into the driveway. She walked to the wide front window and peered out. Her heart skipped a beat. Callen. Was he here to deliver bad news? If so, at least he'd be with her. She forced her feet to move to the door. When she pulled it open,

347

he stood there with a smile, a bag of gifts in his hand and snow melting on his hair. He set the bag down, and she threw her arms around his neck. "I'm so glad to see you."

"Me, too. I've missed you, Angie. More than I ever thought possible."

She gave herself over to his kiss, but Lily's shout interrupted the moment.

"Daddy! I missed you."

Angie bit her lip when she saw moisture forming in Callen's eyes.

He picked her up and hugged her close. "Hey, my Lily Belle. Merry Christmas."

"Are those presents for me?"

"Maybe."

Lily patted his face and kissed him. "I have some cookies for you." She wiggled out of his embrace and ran to the kitchen.

Angie looked into his eyes, searching for some sign that he'd made everything all right. "Callen?"

Shrugging off his coat, he took her hand and led her to the sofa. "You're safe. I convinced my boss that the singer wasn't Silky. I told him I'd known the woman for years and that we went to school together."

"He believed you?"

"Of course. Especially when I showed him this." Callen pulled out their yearbook and opened it to her picture. Angie looked at her high school self with glasses and curly hair.

"Oh, my. Did I really look like that?"

Callen laughed. "No one would mistake Angeline Silkowsky for Silky Blaine."

"Thank you. I've been questioning myself for days about whether I should have sung that night."

"I found something else when I dug out the yearbook." He pulled a small velvet box from his pocket and opened it.

Angie gasped, her eyes tearing at the lovely engagement ring. A sudden realization brought her gaze up to meet Callen's. "Is this the one you had in your pocket?"

"It is. And if it's not too late, I'd like you to wear this until we can complete the set on our wedding day."

"Oh, yes. I've loved you as long as I can remember."

He held her close. "I have another gift for you. Dave Marshall has offered me a job with the Maine tourism office. I told him I'd take it."

Angie wrapped her arms around him. "See, I told you God would work it all out."

"Then let's go tell our daughter that she's getting a daddy for Christmas."

About the Authors

 **Lorraine Beatty** is a multi-published, bestselling author currently under contract with Heartsong Presents. Born and raised in Columbus, Ohio, she lives in Brandon, Mississippi, with her husband of forty-four years. Lorraine has written for trade books, newspapers, and company newsletters. She has lived in various regions of the country as well as in Germany. She is a member of RWA, PAN, and ACFW and is a charter member and former president of Magnolia State Romance Writers.

Elizabeth Ludwig is an award-winning author who is an accomplished speaker and teacher, and often attends conferences and seminars, where she lectures on editing for fiction writers, crafting effective novel proposals, and conducting successful editor/agent interviews. Along with her husband and two children, Elizabeth makes her home in the great state of Texas. To learn more, visit www.elizabethludwig.com

Sandra Robbins is an award-winning author who lives with her husband in the small college town in Tennessee where she grew up. Until a few years ago she was working as an elementary school principal, but God opened the door for her to become a full-time writer. It is her prayer that God will use her words to plant seeds of hope in the lives of her readers.

Virginia Vaughan was born and raised in Mississippi and has never strayed far beyond those borders. Blessed to come from a large Southern family, her fondest memories include listening to stories recounted by family and friends around the large dinner table. She was a lover of books even from a young age, devouring stories of romance, danger, and love. She soon started writing them herself. After marriage, two kids, and a divorce, Virginia realized her characters needed the same thing she needed—the healing grace and restoration power of Jesus Christ. She devoted her life and her writing to His glory and has watched God swing doors open for her to walk through. You can connect to Virginia through her website, virginiavaughanonline.com.